Lisa Ballantyne is the internationally bestselling author of five novels. Her debut, *The Guilty One*, was a Richard and Judy Book Club bestseller, nominated for an Edgar Award and translated into nearly thirty languages. She lives in Glasgow, Scotland.

The
Innocent One

LISA BALLANTYNE

PIATKUS

PIATKUS

First published in Great Britain in 2022 by Piatkus

1 3 5 7 9 10 8 6 4 2

A CIP catalogue record for this book
is available from the British Library.

ISBN 978-0-349-42925-0

Typeset in Goudy by M Rules
Printed and bound in Great Britain by
Clays Ltd, Elcograf S.p.A.

Papers used by Piatkus are from well-managed forests
and other responsible sources.

Piatkus
An imprint of
Little, Brown Book Group
Carmelite House
50 Victoria Embankment
London EC4Y 0DZ

An Hachette UK Company
www.hachette.co.uk

www.littlebrown.co.uk

'The true hero ... of *The Iliad* is force ...

To define force – it is that x that turns anybody who is subjected to it into a *thing*. Exercised to the limit ... it makes a corpse out of him[/her]. Somebody was here, and the next minute there is nobody here at all; this is a spectacle *The Iliad* never wearies of showing us'

Simone Weil, 'The Iliad, or: The Poem of Force'

PROLOGUE

Frankie walked to work, enjoying the early morning air, unaware that today was the day she was going to die. She often went into work this early, when the throng of gawky students was still asleep, but these past few weeks she'd made a point of it because it was the coolest part of the day. She would let herself into her office in the Classics building and plunge into her book on the Macedonian conquest of the Persian Empire. It was due to be published in November and she hoped to present it before then, a keynote speech at Princeton University.

It was going to be another searing hot day and already it was clammy, a film on her skin. She wore a long, loose skirt and flat sandals. It was just over an hour's walk from the riverside cottage she shared with her husband, Jon, just off Fen Road; the rooms small and dusty, the back garden long and semi-wild, leading right down onto the banks of the Cam. Early afternoon she would walk home again, let Artemis out, and eat lunch at the bottom of the garden, waving away hoverflies and looking at the gnarl of bramble. Artemis was her blonde beagle, named after the Goddess of the Hunt, but, even though she was a pedigree, at twelve years old she no longer showed any interest in hunting. She barely opened her eyes if a squirrel came into the garden, and even a rabbit spied on a walk failed to incite any enthusiasm for a chase. Artemis seemed to have decided that she had run after her last rabbit some time ago; Frankie considered that thought probably came to everyone eventually.

Jon was away with work again – three or four countries in a row this time – Malaysia, Singapore and . . . somewhere else. Frankie couldn't remember the last one. She wasn't inconsiderate, but international travel was a constant thing for Jon and after a while she lost track. She was sure he had been due home last night, but he hadn't appeared, and so she expected he was probably in the air just now, sipping a blended malt from a plastic glass while scanning a journal on quantum electronics.

Jon was Professor of Electrical Engineering, his office just a thirty-minute walk from hers, but he was always away 'doing deals' with one foreign university or another, in the Far East or North America. She was used to him being gone. They had been married for fifteen years and she still loved him, but it was easier to love him while he was away. Jon hadn't always been faithful. He was older than she was, by eleven years, but his energy was expansive. Jon, dark-eyed, dark-haired even in his mid-fifties, burst into any room demanding all attention. He was six-foot two, but seemed to take up an even larger metaphysical space. He had absolutely no insecurities. In that sense, he was quite a good advertisement for the potential of positive self-esteem, or the public school system, whichever way you looked at it. Young women seemed to accept that he was as attractive as he proclaimed; he had risen in the ranks academically – professor by the age of forty-two – and now in the university leadership.

Unless Jon returned, she might have a few friends over later to drink sangria as the sun went down. Sangria from the Latin, *sanguis*, for blood. They could bring their swimsuits and take a dip in the Cam. It was delicious to swim in the river at this time of year. She liked to swim out to the deepest point and then slip her swimsuit off underwater. It was uniquely liberating.

A group of early rowers passed and Frankie paused to watch them, even though she had seen them many times. This group were all women. There was almost no breeze and so the Cam was grey-brown, ripples catching the new pink light in scales, like snakeskin. The boat cut through it, even and straight. The rowers' easy rhythm set her up for the day and Frankie unconsciously found their timing as she continued her walk.

She would get her work done and then sit at the bottom of her garden and call her mother, which she did every Wednesday without fail. Frankie was from Liverpool originally and her mother, Bridget, still lived in Kirkby, Merseyside. She was eighty-three, five-foot three, and still went to bingo under her own steam every Tuesday evening. Frankie was one of eight – four sisters, three brothers – and had been her mother's fifth child. When they spoke, Frankie's Scouse accent unconsciously came back, thick and guttural. When she spoke to Jon, or her students and friends in Cambridge, it was smoothed and rounded, like a piece of glass washed by the ocean. She had been in Cambridge since she left Liverpool at the age of eighteen, and it was hard to keep a grasp on her short vowels. They were all but lost now, to everyone but her mother.

While Frankie had felt an oddity at University of Cambridge for a long time – working class in a sea of quaint academics and awkward public school students – she often attested her wish to study Classics here with her background in Merseyside. The noisy pack of her family meant she had all the grounding she needed in Greek drama before she'd even read *The Iliad*, which she had, on a whim when she was fourteen, while all her friends were drinking in the park.

As Frankie turned onto Turpington Street, the bakers had just opened and the sweet smell of fresh bread stopped her in her tracks. She bought a hot roll wrapped in a paper bag and carried it in two hands, her pace quickening with anticipation, feeling the sweat at the small of her back soaking through the waistband of her skirt.

Frankie used her key to enter the Classics building. It was just after six now and the cleaner would not arrive until six thirty. She took the stairs, fanning herself lightly with her hand. If she could summon the courage later in the morning, she would speak to Dean Winters about the Princeton trip. She was already booked into the conference, but the Dean was begrudging of the funding and it seemed as if Frankie might have to pay for it herself. Jon stayed in five-star hotels wherever he went, and spoke on his return of massages in his room administered by lithe, young women who barely spoke English. Frankie couldn't even persuade her boss to fund her economy flight to Newark and then three nights at a Motel 6.

The arts entertain, but science educates, was one of Jon's proc-lamations that infuriated Frankie. Jon thought it fitting that the bulk of university and government funding went to science and engineering. Frankie had argued with him countless times. The Ancient Greeks had had a dazzling knowledge of the universe, and their intricate theories of physics, astronomy, chemistry and biology were the very foundation of science. The arts *gave birth* to science and engineering but now were cast aside as fluff and nonsense.

At the top of the stairs, she paused and touched her moist brow with the back of her hand. It was a relief to be inside, alone, and soon to be deep into her book. She would break open her roll and watch the steam rise from the pores of the dough.

She took out her key and, as she did so, the bag with the hot roll fell to the floor. It was only when she bent to pick it up that she noticed the door to her office was already ajar. She might have forgotten to lock it, or else Harvie, the janitor, might have been in overnight – worried about squirrels chewing the electric cables in the roof again.

Bringing the warm paper bag to her nose, she smelled the hot bread and saliva flooded her mouth. She shouldered the door open.

Frankie took a sharp intake of breath. Something was wrong, although she couldn't say what. She pinched her lips together, noticing that the large chunk of ornamental agate that sat on the middle of her bookshelf was missing.

It was her focal point when she was working. She would look up and admire it, with its ancient crystalline structures in brown, green and purple. Hand-sized and heavy as a bowling ball, it only moved when she stood on a chair and took it down to wash it. Dust dulled the sparkle and so Frankie would wash it every now and again, careful not to crack the porcelain sink in the bathroom with its heavy, jagged stone.

Frowning at the bare shelf, Frankie stepped inside. The door fell silently closed behind her and she turned quickly, hearing the lock click.

At first she smiled, but it fell from her lips. She felt the emptiness of the building, heard the electric hum of the strip lights. She thought about running or shouting out, but he was standing in front of the door and there was no one to hear her.

Professor Frances Isabel Owen, who was forty-three years old with not a single grey hair; who was a European authority on the Achaemenid Empire; who liked swimming in the river at the bottom of her garden. Frankie, who had size-five feet and had to speak to her mother this afternoon. Frankie, who needed to be home at two to let Artemis out to relieve herself; who had so much more life to live, looked straight into the face of the man who was about to kill her.

It was a terrible thing to know you were going to die and not be able to do anything to prevent it. She tried anyway, raising up her hand to protect herself (still holding the paper bag with her warm breakfast roll, as if it was the magic shield given by Athena to Perseus) but then her finger was smashed and her own blood blinded her.

JUDGEMENT

1

He hadn't been sleeping, but, as soon as the alarm sounded, Daniel got up and put on his running gear. No breakfast – he liked to run empty, with only his wits for fuel. In his battered trainers, he padded down the stone steps and began to jog around the circumference of Victoria Park. It was going to be another hot day and already he felt the humid weight of it wrap around him.

His body felt light and energetic, despite barely sleeping. The slight breeze blew him along like lit paper and he let it, knowing that when he climbed back upstairs and closed the door on that studio shoebox, he would feel like crying. He didn't want to be back here, in his old flat.

When he bought the flat in Bow in the early 2000s, as a young criminal solicitor, this part of the East End had been rougher and he'd liked the edge to it. Since the Olympics, and since he had lived here last, it had become gentrified and the whole landscape had changed, so instead of simply looping around Victoria Park, he headed over the canal towards the Olympic Stadium.

Daniel was a runner. Even though he was in his mid-forties

now, he could still complete a marathon in under three hours ten. He had been running ever since he could remember. *Fight or flight*; he chose flight. Flight was, after all, often the most logical course.

As he ran, he tried to shake off the feeling of being in the flat. It felt as if it didn't belong to him, like wearing someone else's shoes. For nearly ten years now, he had rented it out; it was just luck that the short-term tenancy had come to an end when he needed it again, otherwise he would have been sleeping at the office.

A day ago, he and Rene had had a blazing row. They didn't often fight, but it had come out of nowhere. Daniel tried to avoid confrontation when he could and now he considered this strategy had forced their issues underground. He had been blindsided by the stream of hurt and anger she'd thrown at him.

I can't take it any longer. I can't be with you right now, she had said, putting on her coat.

It had been the action of tugging on her parka – a sweltering evening and she'd grabbed any coat – a winter jacket – to escape him. He had thought she just wanted to walk it out, but she'd said she needed to be away from him for a few days. Her green eyes stark in the hall, zipping the jacket despite the humid night, as if to show her seriousness, saying she would go and get Billy out of bed.

He had relented then, put his hands on her shoulders and said he was sorry, but it was too late. To stop her walking out, he had said that *he* would go. Ten years they had been together, married for eight, parents for seven.

Just the thought of leaving them winded him, and his pace slowed. His dirty training shoes beat into the pavement. It would only be for a few days, he hoped. He would stay in Bow and give her space, but already he missed them and he felt the ever-present intensity of that in the centre of his chest, as if there was a fishbone stuck in his windpipe.

Slowing his pace for the traffic on Roman Road, Daniel thought he could already smell the warming tarmac underfoot.

Beginning a circuit of the public running track at the Olympic Stadium, his breathing evened out, slow and deep in his chest as his pace steadied. His hamstrings were tight, and his right leg felt almost mechanical when it swung forward. Whether it was his hamstring, or the fact that he was so tired and distracted – not lifting his feet enough – he pitched forward suddenly into the red dirt. His forearm and elbow took the weight of his fall.

Sitting up, Daniel saw the graze was bleeding a little and he wiped it on his dark shorts. Normally, he would just get back up and start running, but today, as slashes of light cut across the track leaving half of it in shadow, he put his elbows on his knees and let his head rest on his knuckles. Smelling his own sweat, he felt the pulse of his blood in his hands. He'd been listening to music on his phone and he let it and the headphones fall gently onto the track.

He sniffed, ready to get back on his feet, but just then a call came – lighting up the screen of his phone. It was an unknown number but he took the call anyway.

'Daniel Hunter.'

Silence on the line.

'Hello?'

'Danny ... it's good to hear your voice again. It's Seb Croll.'

Daniel picked himself up. He hadn't heard the name clearly, although it was someone who knew him. The name sounded like *subcrawl*.

'Sorry, I didn't catch your name?'

'It's been a long time, I know. It's Sebastian. Sebastian Croll.'

The name resonated deep inside him and then a sudden prickle ran up the back of his neck and across his scalp, as if all the follicles had suddenly tightened.

Daniel grabbed a fistful of his sweat-dampened hair. 'It ... certainly has been a long time. Are you ... ?' Daniel was about to say, *grown up*, but stopped himself as it sounded inappropriate. Sebastian had been just eleven years old when he'd represented him.

'I'm fine. How're you, Danny? You're still ... a solicitor?'

'I am.'

'I'm afraid I need your help again.'

Noticing that he had a smudge of blood on the back of his hand, Daniel waited for Sebastian to continue.

'I think it's just to give a statement or whatever. The police said they wanted to have a chat with me and I've to go in today or tomorrow ... Perhaps I'm being overly cautious, but I wanted to take someone with me. With my history ...'

'Statement? What about?'

'Well, my tutor—' Sebastian's breathing became audible, as if he too was running, or becoming upset. 'My tutor at Cambridge.

It's unbelievable ... it's—' his voice broke slightly. 'She's been murdered.'

Daniel took a slow intake of breath.

'Obviously I had nothing to do with that. I was ... I mean I still can't believe it, but I think the police are just speaking to everyone who knew her. I was prepared to go alone, but then I thought it might be sensible ... to have representation. Because of my history.'

He pronounced the word *history* very carefully, sounding all three syllables.

'You're in Cambridge then? At the university?'

'Yes. I'm studying Classics.'

'So, it's Cambridgeshire Police then?'

'Yes, I wondered about going to speak to them today. I didn't know if that was convenient ... If you would be able to come?'

Daniel wrinkled his forehead as he mentally ran through his diary for the day. In addition to his normal cases, he'd taken on some Family Court work after a colleague fell ill, which meant he was stretched. He thought he had a couple of appointments that he could shift to meet Sebastian, but he'd need to catch a train and wasn't sure it was worth it for a routine interview. He and Rene shared a car, but he'd left it at Herne Hill.

His reluctance was not only because of the inconvenience. Sebastian was not just any old client. The case had got under his skin. It had been an intense time under the full scrutiny of the media, and Daniel had somehow identified with the little boy from a troubled home. Daniel hadn't represented anyone else so young since; but, of course, Sebastian was no longer a child.

Daniel wiped a hand wet with sweat over his jaw. 'My col-league knows some people up in Cambridge. I could get another name for you – an alternative? To save you time?' He deliber-ately pitched this suggestion as helpful to Sebastian, to disguise his wariness, but even as he offered, Daniel sensed Sebastian would refuse.

'That's very thoughtful, but I would prefer if it were you.'

Daniel looked up at the sky as if asking for guidance and saw a jet drawing a white line across the immaculate blue. 'Is this your number? I need to move a couple of meetings and get up there. I can text you a time later and then you could let the police know?'

'Thank you. Yes, this is my number . . . Thank you so much.'

'I'd need to charge you, of course. If you're not suspected of a crime, it won't be covered under legal aid.'

'Of course, that's fine. You can just let me know your fee.'

Ready to ring off, Daniel almost talked over Sebastian with his goodbye and confirmation of arrangements. 'It'll be great to see you again,' Sebastian gasped.

Daniel hesitated, feeling strangely uneasy at the words. 'Yeah . . . you too.'

Before he jogged back to the flat, Daniel stood for a moment reflecting on the call. He could visualise Sebastian exactly – as he had been then – the little sprinkling of freckles on his nose, his large mint-coloured eyes. The thought of meeting him again was unnerving.

Back in the flat, he emailed his afternoon clients and then showered quickly, the graze on his arm stinging under the hot water as he washed the dirt out of it. As he rinsed, he realised it was ten years since he had seen Sebastian, so he would be twenty-one now. He had been a precocious little boy, bright and articulate, but hearing the deep adult voice on the phone had jarred. Of course he'd thought of Sebastian over the years – Rene had been Sebastian's barrister and she and Daniel had started seeing each other after the trial had finished.

Daniel slipped a clean white shirt from its hanger. He had taken just three work shirts with him to the flat, fresh from the cleaners. In the mirror, he watched his face as he dressed. Three days' worth of clothes. He had three days to fix things between him and Rene.

A memory came to him – sudden, surprising – so that his skin prickled under his clean shirt. He remembered the judgement coming in for Sebastian, and then speaking into the warm flashes of journalists' cameras on the steps of the Old Bailey and looking around for Rene. He had caught up with her before she'd gone down into the Tube. *We won*, he'd said to her, and she had stood on her tiptoes to kiss him.

It had been the first time they'd kissed.

This afternoon, Rene had her interview with the Judicial Appointments Commission. When they'd got together, after Sebastian's trial, she'd been recently made a QC, but now she had her eye on the bench. In the spring, the list of judicial appointments had been advertised and she'd applied. He knew she would be a wonderful judge and hoped the JAC would recognise that. He wanted to do something to wish her luck – contact her, send her something – but didn't know how best to do that because of the way things were. Just that thought – reaching out to her – brought such a flare of pain inside him.

Of course they argued – every couple did – but it felt significant, dangerous perhaps, that they needed this time apart after eight years of marriage and a little boy who needed them. Never before had she wanted to be away from him.

As he buttoned his shirt, he saw Rene's face: thin, arched brows; her soft, naturally blonde hair worn down as it was when she was at home, so that it brushed her shoulders. He had never expected to get to a space in life when he felt as if he had a home. To have found that, and now be on the brink of losing it, made everything else in his life seem unimportant.

He couldn't remember a lot of his childhood, but what he did remember, vividly, was running away. The first eleven years of his life he had been in and out of foster homes. Somehow, back then, he had internalised that he would never have a proper family of his own, that he didn't deserve one.

Making a coffee and eating half a slice of toast, he checked his phone to see if there were any messages. Billy sometimes used Rene's phone to message him, something cheeky. There were emails and voicemails from clients and his senior partner, Veronica, but nothing from his family. Two of his afternoon clients had already agreed to the postponed meetings. He would check the times of the trains and then message Sebastian about when he'd arrive in Cambridge.

Just then, Daniel noticed there was a small, white envelope on the floor inside the door. It was addressed to him and he recognised the handwriting immediately. It had to have been hand-delivered the night before or while he was on his run. Through eagerness or fear, he tore the envelope so roughly that he nearly ripped the letter inside.

Dearest Danny,

Since you left I've been thinking a lot about us and what that argument was about. It came out of nowhere, and I don't know who 'started it' but I do know that what came to the surface were things that I've been thinking about for a long time.

I could have expressed myself better – we both could have. We were angry and upset, but, now that the dust has settled, I have come to see the truth of things.

There is so much darkness in you. In some small way, that is what first attracted me to you. But lately, it seems as if the darkness is there all the time – some deep unhappiness that exists in you – a place we (Billy and I) can't reach. I never expected that I would make you happy, or you would make me happy – it's not like we were kids when we got together – but I think I expected us to be happy some of the time.

And the truth, Danny, is that I don't think we've been happy for a while – years. I love you – you know that, I hope. I know you love me. But over the last few years, I have felt the heaviness of you. For a long time I have wondered how long I'll be able to carry it.

I'm not saying it's your fault, but rather that I am now entering a time in my life where I need more energy for me.

17

I might not make it to be a judge, but I want to try. Billy gets more grown up every day but he is still just a little boy and I want to be there for him in a way that is meaningful.

I've been working so hard for so long – and I know you work hard too – but often it feels as if I am a single parent juggling all of that. I have felt your love, but I haven't felt emotionally supported by you in a long time.

I think it's that I was trying to say the other night. Everyone sometimes needs support and I don't always feel sure of yours. And so, after thinking long and hard, and even after a sleepless night without you, I think it is best if we separate.

Billy adores you, and we will work something out so you get the time with him you both need.

I hope you understand. Call me once you've had a chance to think and we can talk about the details of sharing time with our son.

Love,

R.

Daniel sank onto the couch, his mouth suddenly dry. Knuckles to his forehead, he pressed until the pain came, blinking and standing up when his eyes started to water. He crushed the letter into a tight ball and threw it like a tennis ball hard against the bare, magnolia wall.

2

In the early afternoon, Daniel took the train to Cambridge. The air conditioning in the carriage was a relief and he took off his tie and rolled up the cuffs of his shirt for the journey. He had picked up a paper at the station and now set it on the table. Halfway down the front page, he saw a picture of a smiling woman below the headline, CAMBRIDGE PROFESSOR FOUND MURDERED.

Frowning, Daniel skimmed the short article. There wasn't much more information here than what Sebastian had told him, but he did learn that the woman's name was Professor Frances Isabel Owen. She was forty-three years old, married, and had been a lecturer at Cambridge since her early twenties. The grainy photograph of her had obviously been taken at some social occasion; she was smiling broadly, skin glowing.

Not wanting to read any other stories, Daniel folded the paper over and set it on the seat next to him. He looked out of the window where the concrete sprawl of London loosened into fields and green trees, feeling apprehension build under his ribcage. Perhaps apprehension was the wrong word – he wasn't fearful or nervous – but rather felt an auspicious sense of reckoning at meeting Sebastian again. As a little boy, Sebastian had been tried as an adult in the Old Bailey – a murder trial that had fascinated the nation. It wasn't just that Sebastian's trial had changed the course of Daniel's career and life, but back then, when Sebastian was on trial for murder, Daniel too had been subject to judgement.

Sebastian had been accused of murdering his eight-year-old neighbour, Ben. The tabloids had fed on the story for months. Even though Sebastian had looked young for eleven, he'd not been spared the nation's outrage, but neither had Daniel. Vividly, Daniel remembered jostling his way into court, amid shouts of *'child killer, you're defending a child killer'*.

That year was also the year Daniel's mother, Minnie, had died. Of course, she wasn't his real mother – his biological mother – but now he thought of her that way. When he was eleven years old, she became his last foster mother, and then she'd adopted him. She'd taken him from Newcastle to her farm in Cumbria, where he had grown up in so many ways, with the chickens and her sheepdog, Blitz, and the goats. The goats had had names too, but, as he looked out of the train window at the green fields, he couldn't remember what they were called.

Minnie, who'd smelled of gin and damp wool, had left the farm to him in her will. The farmhouse had been on the market and sold while Sebastian's case was being heard at the Old Bailey. With the verdict just in, Daniel had suddenly, and inexplicably, reconsidered selling. The old place had been a wreck even then – bad damp in the outhouse, the roof needed work and wet rot in the beams under the floorboards. He would have been well shot of it, but somehow, at the last minute, just before keys were exchanged, he'd called the lawyer up North and said he didn't want to go through with the sale. Minnie had been his only family and the farm was proof of his childhood with her, her love for him.

Undoing another button at the collar of his shirt, Daniel sighed deeply. It was no use thinking of such things. He made a mental note to sell Minnie's farm once and for all, as soon as he had sorted out his own appalling mess of a life. A thought came to him, bone cold as the high note on Minnie's piano, that she would be ashamed of him now, for letting Rene and Billy down.

He checked his phone again, but there were no messages from Rene. He wasn't sure of the timing of her interview. He tapped her a message, knowing that it might sound as if he was in denial about the separation.

Hope it went well. Thinking about you. Dx

She might think he had not yet received the letter. So typical of her to handwrite him a real note; she would have considered a text or an email dismissive. Was it the barrister in her – briefs tied in pink ribbons – or her good upbringing?

He bit his lip as the message sent. She would make a wonderful judge. She was the only person he knew now that he could describe as wise. Minnie had also been wise, and had also been fond of handwritten letters. She had written him many over the years when he wasn't speaking to her, including one final one to tell him she was dying. By the time Daniel had received it – the same day Sebastian was arrested for Ben's murder – Minnie was already gone.

There was a hard pebble of guilt deep down inside him because of the way he had treated Minnie towards the end. She had reached out to him when she was dying and he had turned his back on her. The guilt pebble was heavy but smooth from the amount of times he'd picked it up and run his thumb over its contours.

An announcement sounded that the train would shortly be arriving at Cambridge Central Station. Daniel had been lost in his thoughts and quickly got to his feet and started to gather his belongings.

It was a fifteen-minute walk to Cambridge Parkside Police Station, where he had agreed to meet Sebastian, but the humidity slowed his pace.

The police station was a three-storey, grey concrete, brutalist block with a door in police blue. A tall, slim young man was standing outside. Daniel walked towards him, wondering if it was Sebastian, even though, in his mind, Sebastian was still an eleven-year-old boy.

'You look just the same,' Sebastian beamed.

Daniel took a moment to respond. Immediately, he realised that Sebastian was taller than him, by about two inches. It caused him to pull back his shoulders, as if trying to give himself height. In Sebastian's features, he could *just see* the boy that he had once been, those same pale eyes, which seemed blue in this light, the shape of his face.

'You've grown up.' Daniel tweaked his shirt at the collar to release the damp fabric from the small of his back.

'It's good to see you again. Thanks so much for coming so quickly.'

Sebastian had been a sweet-looking little boy, almost girlish, but he had grown into a good-looking young man. There was something open and amenable about his face, and his teeth – straight and white – were large and prominent. His hair was much darker than Daniel remembered, almost black, and closely cropped so that the pale, sparkling eyes and wide smile dominated. He was dressed smart casual, in just a white shirt and jeans, but his clothes were clearly expensive. Daniel was pleasantly surprised by his first impression of the grown-up Sebastian. His manner was confident but warm, and it put Daniel at ease.

'So you said that you've been asked to attend because your tutor was murdered? Do you know what happened to her – did you know her well?'

'Professor Owen. I can't understand why anyone would want to hurt her. Everyone loved her.' Sebastian looked into the distance, his eyes misting as he spoke. 'She was the coolest lecturer by far. She was just—' he pressed his lips together as if searching for the words '—funny . . . warm. Did I know her well? No, not really, but I liked her a lot. About what happened, I only know what I've heard . . . that they found her dead in her office, stabbed or something – but that's just the rumour mill. It's all so awful. To think that someone would hurt her—'

They had moved across the street to the shade of a large tree on the edge of the park opposite. Wiping the sweat quickly from his hairline, Daniel put down his briefcase and rested his jacket on top.

Sebastian was talking quickly, frowning into the distance as he spoke about what had happened to Frances Owen. Suddenly, he turned to focus on Daniel.

'My God, you're bleeding.'

'What do you mean?'

Sebastian reached out, as if to touch him – motioning towards Daniel's shirt sleeve. The graze on his forearm, from his fall that morning, had bled onto the material of his shirt.

'Shit.' Frowning, Daniel rolled his cuff down. He would put his jacket back on when he was inside, but it was far too hot to think about that now. He felt strangely embarrassed or caught out, and suddenly felt less polished than he had – sweat notwithstanding – a moment ago. He deliberately brought the focus back onto the meeting with the police. 'Okay, is there anything else you want me to know? No reason they want to talk to you, specifically, do you think?'

Sebastian's eyes widened. 'The police are talking to all her students, and colleagues, as far as I'm aware ... but I do, obviously, worry that they'll know ... about me – my past?'

'You mean the murder indictment, the trial ... ?'

Sebastian nodded quickly.

'Well, they might do. They've asked to speak to you, so they've probably checked if you are known to the police on the national computer. You were acquitted, so your details *should* have been weeded out of there after five to ten years, but maybe, as it's technically still an unsolved murder, it might have been kept on the system longer. I think it's been just over ten years since—' Daniel took a breath in and out, not finishing his sentence. 'However, so long as this is just a routine statement, it's nothing to worry about. If it's any consolation, even if they *do* still have a record of your indictment and have looked into that, I'm *certain* they won't bring it up or ask you about it . . .'

The press had been vociferous during the trial, invoking other children who had killed, and castigating Sebastian as the defendant, even though, as a minor, he couldn't be named by law. Unable to name Sebastian in their articles, the press had nicknamed him 'The Angel Killer' instead. Ben had been murdered in a well-heeled area of Islington not far from Angel Tube Station. Over time, as the trial reporting became more partisan and simplistic, Ben became the angel and the child accused, the devil. All this before the jury even went to consider their verdict.

His advice to Sebastian was not to worry about his past, but it had occurred to Daniel earlier that Sebastian's 'history' might make the police suspect him if his details were still available. The police were paid to be suspicious, after all, and the fact that the Islington murder was still unsolved might lead them to think that Sebastian had potentially killed before.

Daniel buttoned his bloodied cuff and then slipped on his jacket as they left the shade of the park and walked into the police station. The air conditioning inside was weak or non-existent, and Daniel felt the dark material of his suit jacket heavy on his back, but he didn't want to take it off because of the blood on his shirt.

A memory scratched inside his mind, of going to Islington Police Station in the rain to meet eleven-year-old Sebastian for the first time, his youngest-ever client, and finding him crackling inside a paper suit they'd given him to wear, after taking all his clothes into evidence. The person who stood beside him now seemed entirely different. He was still a very young man at just twenty-one years old, yet Sebastian seemed older than other students his age, polished and more self-assured. Perhaps it was the slight height difference or the fact that Daniel had dirtied his clean shirt with his blood, but he felt a strange sense of inferiority. He hadn't expected Sebastian to be so prepossessing.

A team of detectives from the Major Crime Unit had relocated from nearby Huntingdon to lead the investigation into Frances Owen's murder. Daniel managed to speak to one of the members of the investigation team, a Detective Constable Murphy, who was passing reception.

'Could I have a quick word?' Daniel asked.

He seemed too young to be a detective. Daniel knew that it was normal for detectives to have a few years of experience in uniform before moving to detective rank, but Murphy looked as if he hadn't even started shaving yet. Sebastian took a seat, while Daniel spoke to the detective constable in hushed tones.

'I just wondered if you could give me a heads up? I'm here as Sebastian's solicitor, but I understand ... this is just a chat?'

Murphy nodded slowly. 'Yes, we're speaking to a number of people on campus after the discovery of a woman's body.' His accent was thickly South London.

'Professor Frances Owen. It's headline news. She was killed at work yesterday morning?'

'I'm afraid that's all I can tell you. We're interviewing anyone who came into contact with her in the days leading up to her death.'

Daniel nodded. He hadn't expected that the police would offer disclosure, but it had been worth a try.

'Here's the DCI now,' Murphy said, standing back. 'I believe he and Detective Inspector Burrows are going to take your client's statement.'

DCI Lloyd accepted Daniel's outstretched hand. He had a heavily lined face that seemed to pull all his features downwards.

'Daniel Hunter, Sebastian Croll's solicitor.'

'He doesn't need a solicitor,' Lloyd said in a thick Yorkshire accent that made Daniel feel kindred even though he sensed the detective chief inspector was being combative. 'He's not a suspect.'

'That's good to know.'

The interview room was bare apart from a large table and four chairs, but there was a camera in the top corner of the room. It was probably switched off, but still its red eye scrutinised them. Windowless, apart from a high-up, barred slit looking out onto the carpark, Daniel was grateful that it was at least cool. The interview room was like a cell, even the heatwave outside barred from entering.

Sebastian seemed relaxed, no sign of nerves as they waited for the detectives.

The image of Professor Owen from the newspaper came into Daniel's mind again. From her photograph, she had seemed sociable and Sebastian had described her as warm; not how Daniel imagined a Classics professor to be. He'd managed to escape any kind of education in Latin or Classical studies, although he vaguely remembered it had been an option in his high school in Cumbria. Still, when he thought of Classics lecturers, he imagined gaunt, white-haired old men, thinning on top, with prominent yellowing teeth – not bubbly young women. Professor Owen had been only a few years younger than Daniel, yet in the photo she seemed younger – in her thirties.

Sebastian sat up straight as the two detectives came into the room.

'Thank you for coming down. You know you're not under arrest and can leave at any time.' Lloyd focused his attention on Sebastian. 'We'll tape the interview but that's just for our records. We want to speak to you about the murder of Professor Frances Owen—'

Sebastian nodded. There was another female officer hovering by the door, wearing blue latex gloves, and Daniel knew they were about to ask for DNA.

'Before we begin, we'd like to take a buccal smear – a DNA sample from you – if that's okay?'

'I see,' Sebastian said, seeming uncertain.

'To be clear, we're taking a sample from all of Professor Owen's contacts, so that we can identify DNA found in her office. It means we can eliminate you from the enquiry . . . We'll destroy the DNA when the enquiry's over. You don't need to worry about it being kept on record.'

'Fine.'

The uniformed officer approached, holding a swab and vial. Daniel watched as Sebastian opened his mouth. Within seconds it was done and the officer closed the door behind her.

'So, Sebastian, you're one of Professor Owen's students?' Lloyd continued.

'I am.' Sebastian cleared his throat. 'She was my tutor.' His voice was serious and respectful – not defensive in any way.

'How would you describe your relationship with Professor Owen?'

'Um ...' Sebastian's forehead crinkled as he considered. 'Professional? I looked up to her, I mean she's an authority on the first Persian empire ... the things she knows—' he put a sudden fist to his lips, as if realising his tenses were incorrect. Emotion seemed to ripple through him and Daniel wondered if he was going to lose composure. 'It's just so unbelievable that she's ... dead.'

Detective Inspector Burrows was intermittently scrutinising Sebastian and glancing at pencil notes on a small pad before her. She was about Daniel's age, with short, dark hair.

'So how well did you know Professor Owen? Did you see her outside of class, for example.'

'I suppose I know her best of all my tutors ... I mean I've studied under her for nearly three years now. She's been very patient with me – helping me with my essays and research and has always taken a lot of time to answer my questions. And yes, sometimes I saw her outside class—'

'So you socialised?' Burrows said, speaking for the first time. 'Do you know where she lived?'

Daniel took a slow breath in and held it, tensing his stomach muscles. He had a sense that Burrows was withholding information and he hoped that Sebastian had told him everything he needed to know.

'Well, yes … there was a party. Professor Owen invited some students from her tutorial groups. We went to her cottage on the Fen Road …' Sebastian glanced upwards, towards the red eye of the camera. In the stark light of the interview room, Daniel saw that Sebastian still had a sprinkling of his childhood freckles on his nose, but also the slightest shadow of stubble. 'It must have been towards the end of last year. It was good fun – a nice chance to get to know other students on the course, as well as Professor Owen, of course.'

'And did you … get to know her?' Burrows pressed.

'Well, yes and no. It was nice to see her in that context – outside of class, relaxed, having a few drinks. She always seemed to talk to us as if we were equals, unlike some of the other professors. I suppose, she was …' Sebastian hesitated, fingers to his lips, 'close to being a friend.'

'So she was a friend?' Burrows seemed interested.

'I think—' Sebastian hesitated, 'I *considered* her a friend. My professor first, but possibly a friend second. I can only hope she thought of me that way.'

'As a friend, did she share anything personal with you?' Burrows pressed.

Almost out of a need to justify his presence and his fee, Daniel interjected, 'Where's this going, Detective Inspector?'

Sebastian made a gesture with his hand that suggested he was happy to answer. 'No, nothing very personal. I hoped we were friends, but we certainly weren't close. However, I suppose I did . . .' Sebastian pulled at his lower lip briefly, 'I dunno . . . feel sorry for her in some ways – she shared some of the difficulties in her marriage.'

'Sorry for her?' Detective Inspector Burrows repeated.

'Well, her husband travelled a lot – overseas – and for many months of the year Professor Owen lived alone. I dunno, it just struck me as a shame. I've met him once or twice too – her husband – he's older, an Engineering professor. I thought she deserved better, that's all—'

Deserved better resonated in Daniel's mind. It made him think about Rene again and how he had let her down. However, Sebastian's words also seemed incautious, and, sure enough, Burrows quickly responded:

'Who would you have considered better for her? You, perhaps?'

Shaking his head, Sebastian said, 'You misunderstand me. I was just—' he shrugged '—struck by the fact that they didn't seem to fit. You must know couples like that.'

Burrows did not respond, her face expressionless.

Sebastian broke into a smile. 'She did have a lovely dog, though . . . She was there at the party. Artie, she called her . . . after Artemis, Goddess of the Hunt.'

'You're right about her husband travelling. He flew home on the day of the murder. You say you've met him once or twice – how well do you know him?'

31

'Oh, only in passing. I've literally met him once or twice. But she would talk about him sometimes, and so I knew about him being away a lot.'

'When was the last time you saw Professor Owen?' Detective Chief Inspector Lloyd asked.

Sebastian inhaled as he considered. 'It would have been … my last tutorial with her. I don't think I've even passed her outside or in the faculty since then. So the last time I saw her would have been Tuesday at eleven o'clock.'

Daniel glanced down at his pad, noting that the tutorial was the day before Frances Owen was murdered.

'Are you aware of anyone who might've wanted to harm her?'

'Not at all. She was very well liked.'

'Were you aware of any rumours about her? Affairs or …'

Sebastian shook his head firmly. 'Absolutely not. She was fun and warm and interesting, but she was very much focused on her research. She was writing another book, she had a conference abroad planned—'

'You do seem to know a lot about her—'

'Only what she chose to share.' Sebastian's manner was open, but also assertive.

'Finally, where were you yesterday between the hours of six am and nine am?'

'Like most students, I'm afraid I was in bed asleep.' An apologetic shrug.

'Can anyone confirm that?'

'Well, I'm sure several people on my floor in Magdalene College would confirm I was there, after I got up, that is—'

'Alright, Sebastian ... Mr Hunter ...' Detective Chief Inspector Lloyd said, nodding at them both in turn. 'Thank you for coming in. Please let us know if you have any further information.'

Outside the police station, Sebastian raised both arms in the air, stretching them out and upwards, as if to release tension. 'Do you think it went alright?' He let his arms drop by his sides. 'Probably unnecessary, but I was glad you were there. Just for moral support.'

'Well ... possibly better safe than sorry.' The interview had seemed innocuous; it made sense that they were talking to everyone who knew the victim, and Sebastian had been gracious enough. It was really only Sebastian's history with the police that had warranted Daniel's presence, but, even so, the police records might have been wiped after all this time.

Late afternoon now, but the sun was still relentless. Not a single cloud in the sky to protect them from the heat. Daniel took off his jacket and instantly felt his damp shirt begin to dry. His nerves felt overstimulated, as if he had drunk too much coffee. Any other week he would have been looking forward to going home and discussing it with Rene – get it all out of his system and hear her take on it.

'Even though it's not the best of circumstances, it is so nice to see you again, Danny.'

He seemed utterly genuine and Daniel felt a strange sense of relief to find that Sebastian had grown up so well, despite the difficulties in his childhood. His bullish father had been abusive to his mother, and it had seemed a dark, unhappy home, despite its privilege. There seemed no sign of that trauma now, no twitch or sense of being haunted. Even the trial and the months of incarceration leading up to it seemed to have left few scars.

'Yeah, like I said, it's great to see you ... grown up,' Daniel said, feeling both awkward and interested after all this time. 'Why did you choose Classics?'

'Who knows?' Sebastian put his hands in his pockets. 'I was good at Latin at school, but you didn't even need Latin to get into Classics here. I suppose I like the archaeology, the myths – the real bones and then the stories, the space in between ...' he shrugged, and Daniel nodded.

'Do you—' Sebastian indicated over his shoulder '—want to get a coffee or something? That café over there is usually very quiet.'

Daniel didn't go for coffee with clients, no exceptions.

'I have to run for this next train, but if you need me at all, please call.'

Sebastian put his hands on his hips. 'I know it probably wasn't necessary, but it meant a lot to me that you were here today.'

'Always happy to help, if I can.'

'It's sad ... I remember that party, talking to Frankie and thinking her life was like Mum's – with Dad away all the time – in all these far-flung places. That was how it was for much of my parents' marriage.'

Frankie. Daniel realised he was talking about the professor. It was the first time he had heard her referred to as Frankie, instead of Frances.

'I was going to ask, how are your parents?' Daniel cleared his throat briefly. He had got to know Sebastian's family well during the time he'd defended him: his aggressive father and brittle, cloying mother.

'Well, Dad's fine, but he doesn't travel so much since he got the job with the government.'

'He's working for the government now?' Daniel remembered Kenneth King Croll had been a Hong Kong trader, all expensive suits and aggressive jowls. At the time, Daniel had nicknamed him King Kong.

'Minister for Investment, no less.'

'Right,' Daniel sniffed. He remembered feeling an almost visceral loathing of Sebastian's father and had no desire to meet him again. 'How about your mum?' Sebastian's mother had unsettled Daniel too, but in a different way. She had been painfully thin, well-dressed, with large, sad eyes.

Sebastian plunged his hands into his pockets. 'I'm afraid Mum died,' he said, suddenly desolate.

'God, I'm so sorry, Seb. Was that recently?'

'Yes,' he said quietly. 'It was ... only a couple of years ago.'

'That's awful.' Daniel took a breath and held it, wondering if Sebastian was going to say what had happened – if Charlotte had had an illness.

'If it's alright, I don't want to talk about it.'

'Of course ... I'm so sorry, though. I liked your mum.'

'She liked you.' Sebastian scratched his head, as if wondering how to change the subject. 'What about you now? Are you married, or still working too hard?'

'Married,' Daniel said, keeping his face expressionless, a fist of feeling knuckling under his ribs as he thought of Rene's letter. 'Actually, I married Irene Clarke QC.'

'Irene! My barrister. She was wonderful,' Sebastian beamed. 'So in a way, I was your matchmaker.'

'I suppose you were,' Daniel said flatly.

'Are there a lot of barrister-solicitor romances?'

'I'm sure there are many.'

Sensing now that Daniel wanted to leave, Sebastian said, 'Thank you again for today. I know I shouldn't feel—' pausing, searching for the word '—beholden, to what happened back then, but sometimes I can't help it. My friends here ... no one knows about all that stuff. I wanted *you* here, no one else, because I didn't want to have to explain ... I don't want anyone to find out.'

'I can understand that.' Daniel nodded, feeling the equilibrium between them for the first time. 'Remember, you were found not guilty. You don't have a criminal record. I know that the Old Bailey trial was high profile and that you and your family suffered, partly because of the press, but I think you need to let go of all that now. History is exactly what it is – in the past. You don't need to tie yourself to it.'

Daniel turned away for a moment, watching the leaves of the trees move in a breeze that he could not feel at all on the hot pavement.

'If I don't see you again, shall I send you a note of my fee, or ... your dad?'

'Oh God, no, just send it to me. I'll text you my email address.

I didn't say anything to him about all this business. He would just want to interfere, but I'm sure he'd be pleased that I sought legal advice.'

They shook hands.

'You'll let me know if you need anything else,' Daniel said, hooking his jacket over his shoulder and turning to head down Mill Road.

'Bye, Danny,' Sebastian called.

Knowing he was going to be tight for the train now, Daniel picked up his pace. It had been a long day and the only person Daniel wanted to share it with was Rene. He imagined going home to the house in Herne Hill, putting his loose change and his keys into the dish on the stand in the hall and taking off his tie as he went to find her, then telling her all about his day – what had happened and what he had felt. He would tell her everything, watching the attentive sparkle of her green eyes, and then wait, listen to her thoughts. Daniel realised that, for the longest time, Rene was the only person he felt really able to open up to, and the fear of losing her breached him.

He resolved to call her tonight. He didn't yet know what he was going to say, but he knew he had to convince her that their marriage was worth saving.

He made the next train by the skin of his teeth. As the alarm sounded and the doors closed, Daniel felt a brief moment of relief, not just that he had made the train, but that the police interest in Sebastian was merely for routine questioning, and so he would probably never see him again.

He remembered how small Sebastian had seemed during the trial – his strangely affected, needy gesture of leaning his cheek against his mother's arm. The shock of Charlotte Croll's death sat with Daniel now, as he watched the scene outside the window. Like his own mother, Charlotte had suffered a lot. Ken Croll had been savage with her. He wondered how she had finally died. As a child, Sebastian had had a lot to deal with; the press had seemed unaware or dispassionate towards his family background.

At the time of the Angel murder, when Sebastian was arrested, the investigating officers had referred to him as a psychopath, even though he was only eleven years old. Daniel had never considered Sebastian psychopathic, but as a child he had always had an unsettling intensity, a morbid interest in the death that had seemed pathological. Of course there had been psychologists from the defence and the crown who'd introduced competing theories of Sebastian's capacity for violence. But he'd still been a child and no other European country would have subjected him to an adult trial.

Daniel admitted he was surprised that Sebastian seemed to have grown up alright.

He remembered reading an article a few years ago by an American neuroscientist, who thought he'd discovered a template for the criminal brain – a biological basis for behaviour. Mapping the brains of psychopaths, he discovered low activity in the orbital cortex of the frontal lobes consistent with sociopathy, then found his own brain was an exact match. The scientist found that he *himself* possessed a 'sociopath's brain', but his loving upbringing had somehow suppressed his biological predisposition.

The train drew into a station and Daniel closed his eyes, wondering what kind of brain *he* had, not sure if he really wanted to know.

He remembered sitting in the bowels of the Central Criminal Court, just after Sebastian's murder trial had concluded. He and Sebastian had been in a small room off the central hall, while they'd waited on his parents.

I put the brick on Ben's face, Sebastian had whispered. It had taken several seconds for Daniel to realise just what Sebastian meant, and for hours – days afterwards – he'd wondered if Sebastian had really *meant* to kill Ben or even fully comprehended what he had done. Ben had been three years younger than Sebastian, but they had played together before. It might have been a normal childhood fight that got out of control, or some acting out of the violence Sebastian witnessed at home. Sebastian had tried to explain that Ben had been crying and wanting to go home; he'd done what he'd done to keep him. Sebastian had been at such a tender age when he'd attacked Ben that the majority of European countries wouldn't have considered him criminally responsible. Only the English courts saw fit to try the child Sebastian as an adult.

Of course, the case was still open; Sebastian's childhood confession had been shared with no one else. Apart from Rene, Daniel had told no one. He'd had no obligation to report the confession. Only if Sebastian had revealed that he planned to commit a *future* offence would Daniel, as his lawyer, have a duty to report it. Daniel still remembered the heaviness he'd felt knowing he knew the truth but being unable to share it. It had passed over time, but he had felt the weight of knowing as oppressive.

Every time Ben's parents were on the news asking for 'Justice for Ben', Daniel remembered the confession and felt somehow culpable even though the law hadn't allowed him to act differently. Ben's parents had walked away with nothing – no answers as to who had killed their little boy.

It was Daniel's view then, and it was still his view, that children were different from adults. Children did commit crimes, but, unlike adults, they didn't always realise what they were doing.

Daniel took his phone out of his pocket and started to reply to emails.

3

Billy stood in the centre of the living room in Daniel's flat, holding onto his backpack.

'Where's my room?' he said, wandering into the only bedroom.

'I thought you could just sleep in my bed. I've got a lot of work to do.'

'This sucks.'

'Don't say that.'

'I want to go home.'

Daniel had arranged with Rene that he would collect Billy from the childminder and then keep him over the weekend. She hadn't been home when he'd called in to pack their things, although he had seen her at the magistrates' court this morning.

He had been down in the cells seeing a client who had just been convicted and was awaiting transport to Pentonville. As he'd made his way up, eyes cast down, Daniel had become aware of someone headed down towards the cells: black gown, wig in hand, high heels sounding on the marble stairs.

It wasn't the first time it had happened. Before they would

have made the most of the opportunity: *fancy meeting you here*, and stolen a kiss.

This morning hadn't been like that. Daniel had leaned against the white tiled wall as she'd gravitated to the banister on the other side, her slim hands with the carefully filed nails stretching out on the wood. Even in such a narrow passage-way, they'd arranged themselves on opposite sides – striving to increase the distance between them.

'I'll be round after five,' he'd said, unable to conceal his pain and therefore feeling vulnerable.

'Alright.'

She hadn't specifically said that she wouldn't be there and so he'd taken it that she would be. There were still things to be said. He hadn't given up.

'I'm in court five in a minute. I have to talk to my client,' she'd said, apologetically.

As her hand had travelled down the banister, and her heels sounded again on the marble, Daniel was sure that he'd seen she wasn't wearing her wedding ring. He hoped he was mistaken, but just the thought cleaved him.

After his meeting with Sebastian yesterday evening, Daniel had called Rene, as she'd asked him to in her letter. He'd waited until after Billy's bedtime, but knew by the sound of her voice – worn out – that he'd waited too long. Her interview with the Judicial Appointments Committee had gone well, but it would be a while – several weeks – before she heard if she'd been selected, as they had to interview other candidates.

'I want to come back home,' he had said, plainly, then

held his breath on the line, braving her silence, trying to imagine her face.

'It's like I said, I need space to think.'

Now, seeing the flat through Billy's seven-year-old eyes, Daniel said: 'Look, it's not perfect, but it's what we've got right now. I know you'd prefer to spend the weekend in your own house. I'd prefer to be there too. But this is just for a weekend and we'll try and have some fun together, okay? I've even got some pizza in. I'll put it on and we'll have that in a bit.'

Billy's eyes were like dark marbles, glistening.

'Are you and Mum going to get divorced?'

'No,' Daniel said quickly.

'Well, why do we need to stay here then?'

'Just because.' As a solicitor, Daniel was used to answering difficult questions. But right now he didn't know what to say, so he tore open the pizza box and turned on the oven.

Danny had named Billy after Minnie: Williamina Flynn. Rene had agreed as she knew how much Minnie had meant to Daniel, but also her father's middle name was William and it had made sense. Daniel wondered what Minnie would think if she could see him now. He needed her help. He didn't know how to be a father to this little boy.

Billy dropped his hoodie onto the floor.

'Can you pick that up, please?' Daniel asked, not liking how stern he sounded. He checked his watch to time the pizza. It had taken an age to get from Herne Hill to here and it was seven thirty already.

'*You* pick it up,' said Billy, slouching onto the couch, taking a small toy out of his pocket, a little plastic figure.

Daniel weighed up the value of starting an argument now, when it was so close to bedtime. Just then, his phone rang and, turning it over, he saw that it was Rene. His heart lifted for a minute.

'Hello,' he said, his voice hopeful.

'I wanted to say goodnight to him.'

Daniel passed the phone to Billy, whose scowl was instantaneously replaced with a smile. The phone was on speaker and, as he laid out plates and cutlery, Daniel overheard Billy tell his mother they were having pizza and then Rene telling him to be good.

Before he served up, Daniel put on his jeans and a T-shirt. Rene had been keen for him to take more clothes and personal things, but Daniel was reticent to facilitate the separation. Being back in the flat on Old Ford Road felt like going backwards. It was like nearly being at the finish and then landing on a snake's head and having to go all the way back to the beginning.

As Daniel served up slightly charred pepperoni pizza, Billy climbed onto the stool beside the breakfast bar.

'It's all burnt.'

'No, it's not. I gave you the good bits.'

Grudgingly, Billy ate one piece of pizza and then lost interest. They were both the same about food – it was fuel, nothing more.

'It's boring here.'

'We can go to the park tomorrow.'

'Can Max come over?'

Max was Billy's friend, who lived on their street in Herne Hill. Chewing, admitting to himself that the pizza *was* burnt, Daniel shook his head. 'It's too far away.'

'So why did I have to come here?' Billy had taken one bite out of his second slice and now threw it back down on the plate. 'The only person to play with here is you, and you're no fun.'

'I'm fun,' Daniel said, defensively.

He remembered arriving at Minnie's farm and all the excitement to be found in the animals and the wide open space. In contrast, he realised that most nights when he came home, Billy was either asleep, watching a movie or playing with his mother. Despite her workload, she would spend time with him after dinner, then work into the night. Sometimes Daniel would come home to find sheets thrown over the antique table in the front room and his wife and son underneath it, camping. If it was good weather, Rene would chase him around the garden. Daniel had thought all of this came naturally to her, but now he wondered if she had been doing her best to make up for him.

'You're *not* fun. I want to go home.' Billy started to cry. He went to the door and sat down on the doormat, wiping his cheeks with the back of his hand as he tried to get his shoes back on. His movements were slow as if he realised the distance involved. 'I'm going back. I want to sleep in my own bed.'

'How are you going to do that?' Daniel said, folding his arms and leaning back against the kitchen counter. He was faking nonchalance; his heart thudding in his chest because he didn't know how to resolve the situation.

'I'll just go back and get the Tube, I know where to go. I've got my Oyster card.'

Daniel thought of testing him – he might not know the connections – but then feared a correct answer.

'They don't let little boys on the Tube by themselves,' he said, knowing that wasn't strictly true.

'I'm not a little boy.'

'Come on,' Daniel said, opting for distraction by opening his arms a little. 'Let's get ready for bed.'

Billy ignored Daniel, so he bent to pick up Billy's backpack, and was unzipping it in search of pyjamas when he realised that the door to the flat was wide open and Billy's feet were sounding in the communal stairwell.

'*Jesus*, what the . . .'

At the foot of the stairs, Billy was standing on his tiptoes trying to open the Yale lock on the front door. Daniel leapt down the stairs three at a time and then, without thinking, picked the boy up and carried him back upstairs. The racket that ensued – echoing in the stairwell – of screams and tears, was so loud and dramatic, that Daniel worried one of his neighbours would call the police or social services.

By the time they reached the flat, Billy had wriggled a little out of Daniel's grasp. Daniel held him under the armpits, as Billy kicked him with his heels.

'That hurts,' Daniel shouted, feeling the muscle of the thigh twinge from the kicks. He carried the screaming Billy into the bedroom where he threw him, with force, down onto the big bed.

Billy's cries stopped suddenly as the bed winded him, but then resumed with vigour.

'I hate you,' Daniel could just make out through the sobs as Billy turned his face into the pillow. He still had his shoes on and Daniel saw they were dirtying the bedcover, but he was just too exhausted with everything to care.

'Tough, you're stuck with me,' Daniel snapped, along with his last bit of patience. He went into the other room and slammed the door to the bedroom so hard it made his heart skip a beat.

He picked up the phone to call Rene instead and realised he was shaking. He put the phone down, then put his back against the wall, hitting himself hard against the plaster so he felt the thud in his shoulder blades. He waited for the sound of Billy's crying to stop, feeling like the worst father in the world.

The sun finally set over Victoria Park. With an empty beer bottle resting against his lips, Daniel watched the dark haze of the sky extinguishing the pinky-orange glow on the horizon.

He heard again Rene's words: *There's so much darkness in you.*

What did she mean? Did she mean he was depressed – aggressive – or was it just him, that quintessence of experiences that made him who he was? She said that his darkness had attracted her to him at first. They had always been different, and he felt that more so now. They were from different spheres.

As he took another beer from the fridge and sipped it, watching the glow fade over Victoria Park, Daniel remembered going to meet Rene's parents for the first time in their huge house in Barnes.

That's a nice chair, Daniel had said – meaning it – but also needing something to say.

Oh, that . . . lovely, isn't it? Rene's mother, striking with high cheekbones. *Been in the family for generations. I had it re-upholstered when Rene was small.*

Daniel took a deep breath in and out. He had made his family – found them – but Rene's family was there, stretching back, solid and dependable as a Parker Knoll for generations. Not only because he felt unequal to his wife in this regard, Daniel had been trying to find out more about his own roots. He needed more of an explanation about who he was and what he came from.

Daniel cracked open the bedroom door and peeked inside. Billy was still dressed, half the duvet over him, sound asleep with one hand stuck to the side of his face.

His socked feet soundless on the laminate floors, Daniel put on a side lamp and gently sat on the edge of the bed. With his knuckles, he touched Billy's cheek softly. His skin felt hot. One shoe was still on, the other kicked to the floor. Careful not to wake him, Daniel took the shoe off and folded him under the covers. Daniel kissed his fingertips and touched them to Billy's head.

The first day he'd held Billy came back to him and his breath snagged in his chest. He'd weighed six pounds and six ounces, snug in his white blanket, eyes swollen closed. The same weight as three bags of sugar, but in Daniel's hands he'd felt heavier, as if his small body was already carrying all of his father's appre-hension. Two days later, his son's eyes had opened for longer stretches, still struggling to focus, blue eyes that had later darkened. Now Billy's eyes were dark brown, almost black, just like Daniel's. Nothing made Daniel prouder than to be his father, but, at the same time, being a father still terrified him – even seven years in. He didn't know how to do it. He didn't have the blueprints.

Watching Billy sleep felt like looking at himself in the past. He was forty-six years old but he remembered *exactly* what it had been like to be taken somewhere he didn't want to be, and then fighting to get out of there. He remembered the anger in his belly, wanting to be with his mum but not being allowed to see her. He shouldn't have been so hard on Billy.

Daniel let his hand rest on his son's warm face, his small perfect ear. He'd have been younger than Billy – only about five years old, he reckoned – when his mother overdosed and he'd called an ambulance to save her. She had survived, but they wouldn't let him live with her after that.

'I can be better,' he whispered to Billy – realising he'd said the same thing to Rene a day or so ago. 'I promise I can be fun.'

4

'Danny, the police are here,' Sebastian's voice was still so well-spoken, but his composure from the Thursday before had vanished.

It was Saturday morning and Daniel was trying to live up to his word to be fun, having a go on the roundabout in Victoria Park.

'They have a warrant to search my dorm room and also my family home – my bedroom in Islington. Can you stop them? My father's apoplectic.' There was a tremble in Sebastian's voice.

'They *definitely* have a warrant?' It meant the police must have found something.

Billy was smiling, squatting near the centre of the round-about. Daniel jumped off and pushed it harder, pleased to hear him squeal with delight. As he listened to Sebastian, Daniel noticed that his head was still spinning, the trees seeming to rotate above him.

'Yes, I have the warrant here, and my father was in bed when they arrived at the door. He knew nothing about this – me speaking to the police before—'

Daniel looked over his shoulder, in the direction of Islington. It was only about three miles away. Even though he hadn't seen him for years, Daniel imagined the look on Ken Croll's face, tying his dressing gown over his belly as he found police officers on his doorstep.

'Tell me, Danny. What do I do?'

'Well, if they have a warrant, then you can't do anything. They must've found out something that justifies a search of your property. A magistrate will only approve a warrant if the police have reasonable grounds to believe a crime has been committed.' Frowning, Daniel wondered what they could have found.

'But they can't have. I didn't do anything.'

Even over the phone, Daniel could hear the emotion in Sebastian's voice.

'Stay calm, alright. I'll call the station and see if I can get some more information.' Even as he said that, he knew the detectives would be unlikely to share.

There were sounds of cars in the background and Daniel thought that Sebastian must be calling from the street. 'Are you in Cambridge or Islington?'

'I'm in Cambridge. Dad's in Islington – they're searching my bedroom at home as well as here. I just stepped outside. They're taking my computer and they want this phone too. All my friends know they're searching my room. I just—' the uneven sound of his breathing '—can't you stop them? This is mortifying.'

'I'm afraid if they have a warrant, we both have to stand back and let the police do their work. I'll see if I can find out what they've based the search on. Get yourself a new phone and let me know the number. We'll talk again.'

Daniel was about to ring off, when Sebastian interjected.

'There's one more thing. I heard that Frankie's husband, Professor Thompson, has also been questioned—'

'That's to be expected. Standard—'

'He's not a nice man.'

Daniel sighed. 'Well, nice or not, the police would definitely want to speak to him. Try and relax. We'll speak later.'

'Thanks.'

Just then, in his peripheral vision, Daniel saw Billy leap from the spinning roundabout.

'No!' Daniel was about to call, but it was too late.

Billy hit the ground and rolled.

Chastising himself for not paying attention, Daniel squatted on the ground next to his son, expecting a broken ankle or wrist and a trip to the emergency room. 'Don't do that. What are you – a nutter?' he joked, seeing Billy was unhurt. 'You wait until it stops to get off.'

'M'alright.' Billy ran over to the swings and Daniel followed, standing in front as his son kicked towards him, building momentum.

'I've just got to make this one quick work call, alright?'

'Alright.'

Already, without being pushed, Billy was flying high. Daniel could see the soles of Billy's shoes, and then, when he swung back, the determination on his face to go higher next time.

Searching his contacts for Cambridge Police, Daniel saw an incoming call from Sebastian's father.

'You're like the proverbial bad penny,' Ken Croll began, without even saying hello.

Daniel felt the slight was unjustified, but smiled diffidently as he waited for the man to speak. Over ten years since they had spoken, but the sound of the man's voice still made him cringe.

'Seb's only connection to this woman is that she's his tutor, but they've got a warrant and I'm out on the pavement in my slippers.'

Daniel bit his lip to stop himself grinning at the thought of Kenneth outside in his pyjamas. 'I heard. Unfortunately, we need to let them do their job.'

'I spoke to Seb. I think this is a fit-up. They know what happened when he was a boy and they're determined to get him again—'

Daniel inhaled to reply, but Ken Croll was on a roll. Billy's swing was slowing down and Daniel helped him jump off before he ran towards the climbing frame.

'This is going to get out. You don't realise the position I'm in. After I hang up, I'm going to have to get someone from the media team to sit on this. It doesn't look good at all when a minister's home is searched—'

'Oh, yeah, Seb told me you're in government now. Congratulations,' Daniel said, smiling wryly, watching Billy swing from one bar to another. He was agile for his age and Daniel felt a small swell of pride.

'Not for long if this bunch have anything to do with it. Listen, Hunter, I want you to go to Cambridge and make this go away.'

The public-school address, calling him by his second name, grated on Daniel.

'Mr Croll, Sebastian's not been arrested. He is potentially a suspect, but that's all . . .'

'Well, I want you to make him *not* a suspect.'

For a powerful man, Kenneth King Croll had a very hazy grasp of the law. Daniel suspected that was how he had risen to such heights in the first place.

'I'll do my upmost to make sure his rights are upheld. I was just about to call Cambridge—'

'Make it *go away.*'

Daniel inhaled to respond, but Kenneth had already hung up.

Waving for Billy to come down, Daniel called Cambridgeshire Police and spoke again to Detective Chief Inspector Lloyd.

'Is Sebastian Croll a suspect now?'

'We are exploring a number of avenues.' The Yorkshire lilt of his voice was hesitant.

'What's the basis for the property search?'

'We have electronic evidence linking your client and the victim. That's all I can tell you at this time.'

Daniel exhaled as he hung up. He knew that DCI Lloyd had told him more than he needed to.

The investigation had moved on a stage since Daniel was in Cambridge. The Major Investigation Team had obviously found something to make Sebastian a suspect, but there was also the chance that Sebastian's previous indictment for murder had caused the police to focus on him, although it wouldn't have been the basis for the search warrant, and the police would never admit to that bias.

Daniel wasn't surprised Professor Owen's husband had been called in for questioning. When a woman was murdered, it was automatic to suspect the partner, but Daniel remembered the police saying that Professor Thompson had been out of the country when Frances was murdered, arriving home from an international flight after she was found. He could still have been involved though; some men hired people to kill their wives. Daniel wondered about insurance policies.

He imagined Sebastian would be frightened, but there was nothing to be done except hope that the police didn't find anything at either property – in Cambridge or Islington. Daniel made a mental note to ask his firm's in-house investigator to go up to Cambridge and see what she could uncover. Only two days ago, Daniel had been sure that the police would lose interest in Sebastian; now he was not so sure.

'Was that fun, then?' Daniel asked, holding out his hand for Billy. 'Shall we go to the shop – see if we can find some stuff for a picnic?'

Billy slipped a slightly sticky hand into his. Feeling forgiven, Daniel squeezed the small fingers inside his own.

5

'Thanks for bringing him home,' Rene said, meeting Daniel's eye for the first time. Back in Herne Hill, Billy had run out into the garden and he and Rene were standing in the kitchen. There was something about her face – lips tight or a reflective blankness to her eyes – that said she was still closed to him.

Daniel said nothing, quelling the petty anger he felt rising in him, as if bringing his son home was not to be expected. She looked beautiful. The sunlight from the garden was catching her hair so that it looked soft and almost golden. She was barefoot in a pair of loose slacks and wearing a white shirt unbuttoned over a vest top. The sun had pinked the skin on her cheek, nose and collar bones. Billy's friend, Max, was in the garden and so Billy had wasted no time in getting out there. Daniel had already recognised the voice of Heather, Max's mum, as she called to the boys outside.

'So, how did your interview go?' he asked, swallowing. She had replied to his text about the interview but not with any meaningful information.

'It was pretty intensive, but it went well in the sense that all the questions I had prepared for came up. It was that STAR technique ...'

'Yeah, situation, task ... you'd said.' He was acutely aware that he sounded angry at worst, dismissive at best. He tried to check it, but he just wanted to hold her, and anger was programmed into him as the best way to suppress hurt.

'How did it go with you guys? He seems happy.'

'Alright.'

Things felt strangely transactional between them and, with Heather and Max here, Daniel felt as if he was spoiling the party. There was no way to talk to her right now. One of their ritual arguments over the years was that Daniel didn't communicate. He *shut down*, according to Rene, and delivered one-word unhelpful answers. He was self-aware enough to know that he was doing it now.

'I'm glad it went well,' she said, taking a step towards him.

Just then, Heather slipped guiltily into the kitchen to refill her wine glass and Daniel acknowledged her with the slightest tilt of his chin. He could tell from the exaggerated stealth of her movements that she was both tipsy and aware of the relationship drama ongoing. He didn't know Heather well and felt embarrassed. Another time he might have played host.

Rene rested her fingers on the kitchen table. Glancing down, Daniel could see for sure that she was *not* wearing her ring. He felt his heart squeeze. She was close enough now that he could smell her, a summer-happy smell of salt and skin lotion.

'Billy loves when you actually get some time together. He loves spending time with you,' she said, 'he always has ...'

Even though Rene was mollifying, Daniel found he couldn't say a word, or indeed look at her. He wanted to talk, but not with Heather here. He knew they needed to work out their problems, but didn't know how they were going to do that while they were apart. He turned to go, keeping his hands in his pockets. Rene followed him to the door, but she hung back, one hand on the wall, not drawing close to say goodbye as they might have done only a week or so before. He kept his focus away from her eyes, noticing the sunburnt skin of her chest and resisting the urge to touch it with the back of his knuckles – feel the heat.

'You won't believe who my new client is—' he said, suddenly realising he had the perfect stall.

'Who?' she said, her small mouth pinching.

'Sebastian Croll.'

Both hands on her hips, she mouthed the word, *wow*. He watched her eyes move as if she was remembering the little boy and the trial that had brought them together.

'Didn't expect that, did you?'

'What on earth? What's he done now?'

'Well, maybe nothing. I don't know if you saw the news – about the Cambridge professor?'

'Of course. How sad. Sebastian didn't ...?' Her eyes popped open.

'He says he didn't. Professor Owen was his tutor, so he knew her but—'

'How old is he now? He must be ...'

'Twenty-one.'

Unable to restrain her interest, she leaned against the wall to hear more. 'What's he like?'

'Um, he's surprisingly together actually. Tall – taller than me – very well spoken as you might expect. Seems surprisingly normal. Did you know his father's in the Cabinet now?'

'You mean the government?'

Daniel nodded.

'God, no.'

'And his mother's dead. I don't know what happened there, though—'

Rene rested her head gently against the wall. 'You got so emotionally involved with him before. I mean, I know he was just a kid and it's unnerving having a client so young.' She stood up straight, her eyes finding his. 'And I know it was a tough time for you otherwise back then—'

'I think I saw something of myself in him. I wanted to protect him,' Daniel said, looking back down the hall towards the garden, where Billy and Max were still audible running around on the grass.

'Well—' she folded her arms, as if to signal that it was time for him to leave '—you'll let me know how it goes.'

'I will,' he said, nodding, looking down at the worn hall carpet. He remembered their fight and being asked to leave. Billy *never* woke before seven, but somehow that day he'd sensed the impending departure. He had come downstairs, barefoot, one leg of his pyjamas rolled up to the knee. *Don't go, Daddy.* This time Billy was too busy playing in the garden to care.

His home. If she'd touched him at all, he would have pressed her into his arms. He opened the door, unable to look at her, even to say goodbye. Avoiding her eye wasn't meant to rebuke her, but rather to protect himself. There was such intensity in her unflinching green eyes and he didn't want to confront the truth they might hold: to see her love for him gone. She didn't make the slightest move to touch him at all, not even a hand on his forearm to say goodbye, and so he didn't press her into his arms.

Emerging from Mile End Tube Station, the warm city streets smelled dirty, oily. Walking back, Daniel felt spent, hands still in his pockets but his belly alive, writhing at the centre of him, as if all the feelings he had swallowed were turning over and over inside him.

The sun was just beginning to relent. He passed The Crown and decided to go in for a pint and something to eat, mostly because he didn't feel able to be alone right now.

It was busy on the terrace, so Daniel stood at the bar and ordered a drink. The TV was on and he half-watched it as he waited to be served. The Crown used to show all the big rugby and football games, but just now it was news.

As Daniel paid for his pint and raised the cool beer to his lips, he saw a face he recognised on the TV screen. It was Detective Chief Inspector Lloyd chairing a police press conference. A tag-line running along the bottom of the screen read: *police appeal for more information after Cambridge professor's murder.*

There was a small table available near the television and Daniel took a seat so he could hear better. Sebastian's room at

Cambridge and at the family home had been searched yesterday morning, but today the police were appealing for more information. This suggested that Sebastian was not the focus of the investigation, or at least indicated that they hadn't found the information they needed yet, after searching the two properties.

A man to the right of Detective Chief Inspector Lloyd sat with his head bowed and hands clasped, as if in prayer. Daniel wondered if it was Frances Owen's father, but as the camera panned to focus on him and he began to speak, it became clear that it was Professor Owen's husband. The banner along the bottom of the screen changed to read: *Professor Jonathan Thompson appeals to public for information on wife's murder.*

'I arrived back in the country to find my wife of fifteen years had been brutally murdered in broad daylight, in her office ... Cambridge isn't the sort of place where you expect that kind of thing.

'Someone must have seen *something*. It was her habit to walk to work along the banks of the Cam and, even though it was early morning, I'm sure *someone* must have seen her, or seen something untoward that would help the investigation. I *urge* you; if you saw something that day, please come forward.'

Daniel took a sip of beer as he watched the man speak. Reluctantly, he found himself agreeing with Sebastian that Jon Thompson and his wife did not seem a good match. There was obviously a large age difference. Even though Frances Owen looked younger than her years in photographs, it was clear that Jonathan Thompson was well into his fifties, if not older. The man was heavily built, well-spoken with a deep, authoritative voice. His hair was dark and curly and long enough to brush the collar of his brown corduroy jacket. Every so often, he raised large eyes, heavy with emotion, up towards the camera.

'My Frankie was a beautiful, bright young woman and she didn't deserve this senseless, violent death . . .'

Daniel still didn't know how she had died, but the newspapers had stated that the murder had been brutal and that identification had been by dental records, which tended to mean that family had been spared any mutilation of the body.

The picture of Frances that Daniel had seen in the newspaper flashed up on the screen: smiling, slightly out of focus. Another picture was shown of her wearing academic robes at a university ceremony.

Jon Thompson pinched the bridge of his nose with finger and thumb as if to quell tears. 'I implore anyone who thinks they saw Frankie that day – even if the information seems trivial or inconsequential – to come forward and speak to the police.'

There was something about Jon Thompson's manner that jarred with Daniel. The man seemed on the verge of tears, pleading for information on his wife's killer, but at the same time he appeared swelled up, self-important. It was as if on some strange level he was enjoying the drama.

He's not a nice man; Daniel remembered Sebastian's view of Frankie's husband.

Daniel's upbringing in care and subsequent career in criminal defence meant that he was quick to get the measure of people, particularly men. Daniel was sure that Sebastian had not told him everything: he now had a lingering sense that he was more involved than he had protested, particularly after the police search. Nevertheless, as he watched and drank, he found himself gravitating towards Sebastian's assessment of Professor Thompson.

The news camera suddenly focused on a small, round-faced woman, her skin reddened by tears, seated at the end of the table. Even though she was sitting down, her proportions suggested that she wasn't tall. She began to read from a piece of folded white paper, her hands visibly trembling as a tagline ran along the bottom of the screen identifying her as Margaret Owen. Unlike Jon Thompson, Margaret kept her eyes down, seldom looking up into the camera. Daniel immediately felt her distress. He put his drink down to listen to her:

'Frankie was my big sister.' That simple phrase choked her and she fought for composure. 'We're a big family, five sisters, three brothers in all, but there was just over a year between Frankie and me. Our lives were always very different – I live in London, she lived in Cambridge – but we remained very close.'

Margaret's accent was thickly Liverpool. Daniel was gradually building up an image of Professor Frances Owen, from the newspaper photograph, Sebastian, the faculty office where she was murdered, and now her sister. Discovering she was a Scouser made her seem more vivid and real. She might have been a – what was it Sebastian called it? – *an authority on the first Persian empire* – but she was also a *Northerner*. Daniel remained a little bit of an inverted snob. Classics and Cambridge and a cottage on the Cam had not especially endeared Frankie to Daniel, but the fact that she hailed from Liverpool did. Now he was able to see her in the round; someone like him, from working-class roots, finding their way in the ivory towers of Oxbridge. Rene had gone to Oxford. Of course.

'Frankie was a very intelligent, warm, kind, loving sister, daughter and wife. Whoever hurt her in this way has robbed me of my best friend, and the person I loved most in this world. She was a good, good person and she didn't deserve to die in this way. She gave everything of herself, so generously, to the people in her life. I would echo Jon in saying that someone out there must know *something* about what happened to her. *Help us.* Come forward.'

With that, Margaret raised her eyes to look into the lens. Her face was magnified on the enormous HD flat screen on the barroom wall; Daniel saw that her eyelashes were wet and separated. There seemed to be not a touch of make-up on her face. He could see every blotch and pore, but there was something in the shape of her face and eyes that showed a likeness to Professor Owen – the glowing, smiling woman in the photograph.

The detective chief inspector addressed the press conference, describing in detail the clothes that Frankie had been wearing on the morning of her murder: a cream-coloured, full-length loose skirt and white sandals, a pale-blue sleeveless top. She had worn her long, naturally curly, and distinctly red, hair down as depicted in the photograph. Her walk to work would have taken her nearly an hour, and so even though her route along the Cam was taken very early in the morning, she could potentially have been spotted by numerous witnesses.

'We urge you to come forward if you saw Frances Owen that

day, even if you think your information will be too insignificant to help the investigation.'

Contact details for Cambridge Police flashed on the screen with a reminder of the date in question and another close-up of Professor Owen's photograph.

Daniel ran a hand through his hair and finished his pint. He knew that the police would automatically source CCTV footage from the morning of the murder, but assumed that the riverside route Frances had taken would have been only partially covered by cameras, necessitating the public appeal. Had someone followed her to work? More than anything, the press conference seemed to advertise how little the police seemed to know.

First thing in the morning, Daniel resolved to speak to his firm's in-house investigator, Leila, to see if any more could be gleaned about what had happened to Professor Owen and what had prompted the search of Sebastian's property.

The only benefit of staying in the old flat was that Daniel got to work much quicker. On Monday morning, he was on the Central Line by seven thirty and at his desk before eight. He would have happily exchanged his forty-five-minute commute from Herne Hill to be back home with his family, but knew he had to bide his time, still hoping that Rene only needed space, and that he was not going to be served divorce papers.

In the lift, he checked his phone – disclosure emails from the Crown Prosecution Service for his other cases; a reminder about a leaving-do for a work colleague. There was one voicemail from Sebastian that seemed to have come in when he was on the Tube.

Before he went to his desk, Daniel put a note on the computer Leila often used, asking if she had time to speak to him later. He knew she would be in the office today, but Leila rarely arrived before ten. Daniel wanted to know what had been uncovered about Professor Owen's murder from the post-mortem and crime scene, and what evidence, if any, had been taken in the search of Sebastian's dorm room and family home. (Sebastian had already mentioned that his electronics had been seized but Daniel knew it would take time for the police to analyse these.) The police were unlikely to give Daniel disclosure at this stage, so Leila was his only hope. Her time spent in the police force meant she had a knack for getting detectives to share. A private detective attached to the firm, her official role was as a pre-cognition agent, mostly working from home, but she also had a hot-desk station that she used two or three days a week.

Back at his desk, the family photo of him and Rene with Billy reproached him, and he angled it slightly away from him, so that he wouldn't feel Rene's eyes on him as he cleared his inbox. He had a number of legal aid forms to complete and register online – a daily feature of his work but one of his most loathed tasks.

'I'm free now, if you are?' Just after eleven, Leila leaned against the door frame.

He smiled, sitting back in his seat. He often kept his office door open unless he was in a meeting. 'Now's good.'

'Here, or in the boardroom?'

'Here's fine.' Daniel got up and made his way to the small meeting table by the window. Since he had become senior partner, he'd moved to the corner office with its view towards Shoreditch.

Leila swept her long, dark hair to one side as she took a seat, slapping a blank legal pad on the table. She was always immaculately dressed – business attire with a nod to urban fashion. Today she was wearing a sleek skirt-suit paired with combat boots. It made Daniel wonder about her time in Afghanistan. He often wished to talk to her about her experiences there.

'I don't want you to take too much time over this, but I have a client that's been questioned over the Cambridge murder and now had his property searched. I'd like to know what's going on – what the police have—'

'The professor?'

'Yes, Professor Frances Owen. My client's given a statement only to the police but then had his home searched and electronics taken all before the press conference at the weekend. I'm keen to know what the police have so far, in terms of suspects, motive et cetera and also what they have on him to justify the search. It's impossible to get disclosure at this stage.'

Deliberately, Daniel said nothing about Sebastian's *history*.

'Of course. I can make a start on that this afternoon.' Leila crossed her legs, which were well-muscled. Daniel had wondered, but never asked her, if she ran. 'Who's your client?'

Leila had gone to the best schools and her voice was crisp, upper-class English. She was in her late-thirties, but her CV read like that of a much older person. She was British-Iranian, spoke five languages fluently – English, Farsi, Urdu, Pashto and Arabic – as well as conversational French. She had been in the British Army and had spent two years with the Royal Military Police in Afghanistan, returning to work for the Metropolitan Police for a few years before becoming a private investigator.

'Sebastian Croll. He's a third year.'

There was no flicker of recognition at Sebastian's name and Daniel would not have expected it. Sebastian's name and his past indictment had long been part of an injunction for his own protection. Even though it was just over a decade since, the trial was still resonant in the public consciousness. If his identity was ever linked with the child accused from the previous trial, Sebastian's life as he knew it would be over.

Daniel met Leila's eye. 'I need you to be gentle with this one. I figured you would be more unobtrusive asking questions on a university campus than I would.'

'Absolutely,' she said, smiling.

'I don't even know the cause of death. I know nothing apart from the basics that are in the public domain.'

She picked up her notebook, on which she had made not a single note, and told him she would be in touch. Daniel and his partner, Veronica, had interviewed and hired Leila. Almost everyone they interviewed for the post was ex-police, but the candidates had also overwhelmingly been older men. Even though it was unusual – possibly unique – for a pre-cognition agent to be woman, and a young woman at that, Daniel was grateful that they had found her and was convinced she was the best out there.

'Oh ... that personal matter you asked me to look into ...' Leila said as she stood to go, 'I have a couple of solid leads.'

'Really?' Daniel attempted to disguise a vulnerability that washed over him. 'That's good.' It had been a few months since Daniel had tasked Leila with this private request. She was different to the other investigators the firm had worked with; Daniel wasn't sure he would have entrusted anyone else with his quest to try and find out more about his family and his past. His difficult childhood, and the fact that he had so few memories of that time had left him obsessively interested in the gaps. He remembered being with his mother, Samantha Hunter, and loving her desperately before he was taken away from her. But he needed to know more about who he was other than the child of a drug addict, and where he had come from – other than the care system. He'd done what he could to uncover more about his background over the years, but his amateur enquiries had run dry.

Daniel had no idea who his father had been. His mother had left him unnamed on the birth certificate. *Father unknown.* Daniel assumed that his mother had been doing him a favour there, although there was no way to tell. He had gone to Newcastle Registry Office, when he was a student, to pick up his birth certificate; and that had been the source of his fight with Minnie. He'd found out then that she'd lied to him about the timing of his real mother's death. *Real mother.* Samantha Geraldine Hunter – the person she had been – had been little more real to him than *father unknown*. Yet how he had loved her, or the idea of her, before he knew what love was.

'They're only leads at the moment. Don't get your hopes up. It was just in case you thought I'd forgotten about it.'

He hadn't heard anything from her on it since he'd asked her to look into it and had assumed that she too had encountered difficulties. It was a long time ago; people had died and his paperwork was scattered. Although he was paying Leila for this extra work, the fact that he'd asked her to investigate such a private area of his life felt as if he'd taken her into confidence.

'It's great you've got leads.'

'I'll just keep on it – give you a full report when I have something more substantial.'

Daniel thought of that Falkner quote – from his novel about the nun: *'The past is never dead. It's not even past.'*

Daniel had spent a lot of his life believing that his past was dead, but now he was paying someone to pick over the bones.

'Thanks, Leila.'

As Leila was leaving his office, Veronica Steele, Daniel's senior partner, and the founding partner of Harvey, Hunter and Steele, pretended to knock on his open door.

'Have you got a moment?'

She was close to retirement age now, but no less glamorous. Every day she was dressed in something expensive and designer. She looked like she worked for a firm of corporate lawyers in Mayfair instead of the more relaxed criminal lawyer set.

'Sure.' Daniel spun in his chair to face her.

'I put another of Polly's family law clients into your diary. Child custody this one, I think.'

Polly was one of their junior associates who regularly worked in family law. She had been ill with glandular fever for months and Daniel had already taken on a couple of her clients.

'That's fine,' he said, even though he was close to having too much work to do, particularly after accepting Sebastian's case. 'Good to get more experience there.'

He hadn't practised a lot of family law. His main experience had been on the receiving end. He had a strong memory of being in court when he was formally adopted by Minnie. Part of him had always wondered if that empowering experience had led him to the law itself.

Later, Daniel sighed as he glanced over the custody case prepared by his colleague. The file read like a typical family court case – parents squabbling over their children, pawns in their bitter, vengeful dispute. Instead of getting divorced as quickly and cheaply as possible, parents often asked their children to pay the price.

Resolved that this bitterness was not where he and Rene were headed – he was going to do everything he could to win her back – Daniel added the client meeting to his diary.

6

By the end of the week, Sebastian had not had any further contact with the police but Leila had texted Daniel to say that she had information to share about the case. She was already in the boardroom when Daniel went there to meet her, sitting by the window, her long, dark hair swept over one shoulder, a leather file and a pile of neat papers in front of her.

'Sorry,' he said, apologising for his lateness, 'I was on the phone to the CPS. Do you want a coffee?'

'Sure.'

There was a machine at the side of the room and Daniel made drinks for them both.

'How did you get on in Cambridge?' he asked, setting her coffee on the table before her.

'Well, I did make some interesting discoveries . . .' She smiled, as if she knew a secret. 'I expect you saw the press conference?'

Daniel nodded. 'The husband and the sister. It made me think that the police really don't have anything to go on . . .'

'Well, I found out what prompted the search. They got a warrant to search Sebastian's dorm because they have evidence that he and the professor were having an affair.'

'An affair? He told the police that he and the professor were only friends.'

'Well, it sounds as if they were very friendly indeed. Several staff members and students in the faculty seemed to know about the affair and mentioned it to the police as part of that initial gathering of statements. But this rumour was backed up by Professor Owen's emails, which revealed substantial correspondence between her and Sebastian. Significantly, they have evidence that the affair ended several months before she was murdered.' Leila ran her fingernails through her hair. 'I didn't see any of it, but I gather that towards the end of the relationship, the correspondence becomes more aggressive in tone—'

'Okay—' Daniel frowned, trying to guess where Leila was going with this.

'It wouldn't surprise me if they want to speak to Sebastian again soon, but under caution. They might be waiting to see what else they can find on his technology, from the search, but they certainly don't have any physical evidence against him.'

'Are you saying you think he's the key suspect?'

'I think he's *a* suspect, but they are also looking at Frances Owen's husband—'

'He's got an ironclad alibi, though,' Daniel continued. 'He was out of the country at the time of the murder. I think he arrived back the day Frances was found dead . . .'

'It's true.' Leila shifted the papers in front of her. 'I managed to get a copy of the crime scene photographs and the pathology report.'

Daniel wasn't surprised by this. She was incredibly

well-connected, but also had a manner that encouraged people to share things with her.

'Cause of death was blunt force trauma to the head and skull fracture. Frances Owen was hit full in the face with a blunt object; there was extensive damage to the right frontal bone, parietal bone and eye socket. Basically, the left side of her face was completely gone. She would have died instantly.'

As he listened, Daniel touched his lip.

Opening her fingers, Leila indicated the left side of her own face. 'The fact that she was struck here, suggests that the attacker was right-handed. There is also evidence that she was hit *more than once*, although the first strike would have been sufficient to cause death. There were significant defensive wounds. The fingers of her hand were shattered, probably when she tried to protect her face. The report concludes that Frances Owen would have fallen to the ground after that first strike. There is evidence from the crime scene – blood spatter et cetera – that she fell on her side after the first strike, with her face downwards, but the attacker chose to continue a facial attack, striking again almost the same position as he had the first time.' Again, Leila opened up the fingers of her hand over her face to demonstrate the area struck.

'Frenzied . . .' Daniel said, almost to himself.

'Well, no—' Leila sat back in her chair '—the opposite. A frenzied attack would have been much more disparate; when she fell face down, you might imagine that the assault would have continued, but on the back of the head, the crown taking the force . . . but the pathology indicates that the killer actually turned her over to make a continued assault to her face. I wouldn't say frenzied at all; I would say brutal – yes – but also targeted, methodical ...' Leila inhaled sharply before adding, 'and *very* personal.'

Nodding, Daniel felt his stomach muscles tightening.

'Staff from the Faculty of Classics also reported to police that a large chunk of agate—' Leila steepled her hands, bringing her fingertips to touch '—essentially a large rock ... was missing from her office. She kept it on a shelf, had found it herself on a dig in Sicily, apparently. It was an object that staff and students were used to seeing, and is the only thing reported missing. There are no pictures of it, but the size and shape described by several Faculty of Classics staff suggest that this could well have been the murder weapon.'

'And so was any agate found in the wound?'

Leila shook her head vigorously. 'There wouldn't be. That's why it was a good choice of weapon. Agate is hardstone, volcanic, similar to quartz – it's unlikely to disintegrate.'

'But there would likely be prints on it? Whoever killed her took it with them?'

'Most probably. It's missing. The thing is, there would have been a lot of blood and, apart from the blood spatter in the office and significant haemorrhaging on the carpet after she fell, there were no significant blood traces outside the room ...'

'No bloody footprints down the hall ...'

'Or handprints on doors. Nothing. And again that suggests extreme care and attention to detail. There are cameras at the entrance and exit of the faculty building. The way that Professor

Owen was killed suggests that the murderer would have been *covered* in blood. Not only do the police not know who killed her, but they have no idea how the killer managed to get out of the building.'

Daniel clicked his teeth and sat up. 'Almost as if a ghost did it . . .'

'The police have nothing strong to go on. The blood spatter is neat and contained in the office, with sections missing where they would have expected it to be.'

'Missing?' Daniel struggled to understand.

'One theory is that the killer was wearing personal protective clothing, or even laid out sheeting to catch blood spatter.' Leila opened her brown eyes wide. 'If that's true, that's a significant amount of pre-meditation.'

Daniel wiped a hand across his lips. 'So you say there is no physical evidence against Sebastian; do you know if there were prints or DNA recovered from the crime scene at all?'

'Forensics are still at work. Apart from the blood – Frances Owen's blood – it was meticulously clean. Not *a single* print was found, not even belonging to Frances. The office must have been cleaned before and after the murder. But forensics are still at work, and I think they might have gathered other, smaller pieces of evidence. You know as well as I do that now they can get partial profiles from very small amounts of DNA, even deposited by touch . . . so they might yet find something.'

Leila glanced at her notes. 'Oh yeah, one more thing, another anomaly. The pathology report showed that Frances Owen had one strange injury, if we can call it that—'

'What was that?'

'Well, she was missing a few strands of hair.' Leila made a small circle with her thumb and forefinger. 'Not a lot, about the size of a five-pence piece, but it had been torn out by the roots. It was in a strange spot, on the back of her head. You might not have noticed from the photograph, but Frances Owen had a *big head of hair*, and curly, so it could *easily* have been missed, but the pathologist spotted it—'

'So ... what ... the murderer tore her hair out during the assault? You said there were defensive wounds—'

Leila shook her head briskly. 'No, it was a much smaller amount of hair, and very meticulously removed, all of the roots, no breaking. And the place it was pulled would be unlikely to be accessed during an attack. It was such a small section of hair – several strands – that it could very easily have been missed by the post-mortem – perhaps the killer was betting on it being missed. To be honest, I'm surprised the pathologist discovered it.'

'What about—' Daniel looked up, thinking '—y'know that syndrome, where people do that to themselves – tear their hair out—'

'No, it was a single instance, and carried out either just before death or shortly afterwards. The pathologist thought that it might be some kind of trophy. I agree with her that it is a possibility—'

'Jeez—' Daniel breathed.

The boardroom had floor-to-ceiling windows along one side of the room that looked out over Finsbury Circus. As he thought over what Leila had said, Daniel focused on the circular patch of green in the distance.

'So, a brutal yet meticulous murder, but the police have only circumstantial evidence so far and two weak suspects?'

'Yeah, and it's unfortunate that her husband has such a good alibi, because in a lot of ways he fits the bill,' she said, clicking her teeth.

'How so?' His reaction to Professor Owen's husband at the press conference had been instinctive, emotional. He had no reason to suspect him other than the fact that – statistically – women are more likely to be killed by a spouse or male family member.

'Well, everyone seems to think their marriage was unhappy. He cheated while he was overseas, possibly while he was home as well. If he knew about Frances Owen's affair with Sebastian, he would have had motive ... but I think he's a fit because he would have been less likely to be detected entering the building—'

'How do you mean?'

'Well, just like you said.' Leila tiled her head to one side, smoothing her long sweep of hair. 'It's as if a ghost committed the murder. But if someone had to go unnoticed entering and exiting the building, even at strange hours, who better than another academic?'

'He's not a classicist though ...'

'But still, an academic and his wife worked there. I'm sure he was familiar with the building.'

'Big guy. Distinctive. He would be obvious on the CCTV.'

'And we don't have that yet.' Leila pressed her lips together.

'Did the post-mortem say whether or not Professor Owen was sexually assaulted?' This information was crucial to motive but also potential suspects.

'No evidence of sexual assault.'

Daniel clasped his hands and leaned across the boardroom table, knuckles pointing at her as she took a careful sip of her coffee. 'And you managed to speak to a few people on campus?'

'You know me.' Leila smiled, dark eyes twinkling. 'I got talking to several students in the faculty and also over at Magdalene College. Sebastian is well-known and well-liked. Even after the attention he received when his dorm was searched, his friends are sticking with him and no one believes he could have been capable of hurting Frances or anyone else. He's involved in the Amateur Dramatic Club and I think he's had a few small parts in local productions. Most of his close friends that I spoke to were actors. It is pretty well-known that Sebastian was having an affair with one of his professors, and I think there was quite a lot of approval of that. But it was only in the Faculty of Classics that students knew that Sebastian had been seeing Professor Owen specifically.'

Leila's face resumed a serious expression.

'Did they actually use that word – affair?' ·

Leila nodded. 'All of the classics students I spoke to, and among them were a couple of postgraduate research fellows – so essentially staff in the faculty – all were aware that Professor Owen and Sebastian had been having a relationship for several months. One undergraduate – a girl in Sebastian's tutorial group – thought the relationship had continued for as long as a year and then ended abruptly.'

'Any cause given?'

'Most of them seem to think it was on account of Frances being married. The students seemed to know that her husband travelled a lot, and they assume it ended when he became aware of what was going on.'

Daniel wiped a hand over his face. It was near lunchtime and he felt his stomach begin to rumble. 'Sebastian didn't mention this relationship to the police. He must've known it would be uncovered . . .'

Leila raised an eyebrow. 'Maybe he didn't say anything for fear it would put him in the frame. The students said there were several parties at Professor Owen's house while her husband was away. Something definitely happened between her and Sebastian at one of those parties and it probably continued—'

'You could be right.' Glancing at his watch, Daniel gathered up the reports that Leila had prepared for him. 'Is that us? Anything else?'

'Something else about Sebastian.' Leila smiled wistfully, twisting her lips to one side.

'What do you mean?'

'I sensed there was something about Sebastian Croll the detective constable was holding back from me.'

Daniel raised an eyebrow.

'It might be something sensitive, or a piece of crucial evidence – the SIO might have insisted it not be shared with the general team. I just got the feeling they have something else on him—'

Daniel cleared his throat. He wondered if the 'something else' was Sebastian's record on the police computer, if it still existed and had not been wiped. The DCI could well have noted the record – Sebastian's previous indictment – but asked that it be kept confidential from the general team. It was irrelevant, after all.

'Thanks, Leila. This is so much more than I could've hoped for.' He cleared his throat, unsure whether to prompt again about her progress on his personal matter. As if sensing what he was thinking, she said:

'I've been up in Newcastle speaking to some people—'

'Right …' He felt the breath pause in his lungs.

The fact that Leila had been to Newcastle on his behalf felt portentous.

'I spoke to your mother's sister Jacqueline—'

'Aunt Jacqueline, yes—'

'She put me in touch with a close friend of your mother who she'd known since childhood. She knew a Robert Cobain who'd been your mother's boyfriend before you were born—'

The name was familiar to Daniel. Aunt Jacqueline had suggested to him that Cobain might be his father, but Daniel had been unable to trace him.

'This close friend of your mum's told me that Robert Cobain left your mother when she was heavily pregnant.' Leila smiled affectionately. 'I assumed pregnant with you—'

'Nice guy.' Daniel raised an eyebrow, trying to disguise his fascination with humour.

'Let me work on it a while longer. I'm sure I can get to the root of it.'

Roots. Daniel blinked, reflecting on what she had said.

Leila stood up as Daniel gathered his things. They both reached for the door handle at the same time, the skin of their wrists touching briefly. It might have been static from the thick carpet, but the touch brought a spark that made both of them jolt.

Leila startled. 'Did you feel that?'

'Is that another of your superpowers?' Daniel joked, opening the door for her.

Leila laughed lightly. In the hall, he could smell a light perfume from her long, thick hair.

'Whoever killed Professor Owen was fully prepared, methodical, but also very cold. Do you think your client is capable of that?'

Daniel pressed his lips together. 'I don't know.'

As he turned back to his office, he thought about Leila's question. Meeting Sebastian again after all this time, he had kept an open mind. Sebastian's violent actions in an Islington park one afternoon all those years ago were horrific, but they had been the actions of a young child who didn't know what he was doing.

But now it was clear that Sebastian had lied to him and the police once again, as he had all those years ago, instead of being honest about his relationship with Frances. It wouldn't make things easy the next time he was questioned. Of course, children always lie to protect themselves. The impulse to self-protection was natural even in adults, and Sebastian may well just have kept quiet about his relationship with Frances in case he was suspected of her murder.

Even though Frances and Ben had been killed in similar ways, the little boy's murder had been impulsive – a childhood fight that got out of hand – while Frances's had been killed in a much more clinical manner.

He tossed the papers Leila had given him onto his desk, about to check emails before grabbing lunch.

A photograph of Frances Owen's crushed face slid out from the brown paper file onto the keyboard. Daniel inhaled sharply as he glanced at it: the horror worsened because one side of her face was still intact. A bruised but still visible eye, the tip of her nose with its scattering of freckles.

Daniel had seen many photographs from crime scenes and post-mortems. Like a lot of things in his life, he had a knack of keeping them contained so that they didn't affect him. He didn't cross-associate and he didn't absorb them emotionally. Nevertheless, the photograph of Frances's battered face shocked him. Quickly, he tucked it back into the file.

7

In an interview room inside Cambridge Police Station, Sebastian lifted his ashen face and met Daniel's eyes. 'I didn't do this.'

Almost imperceptibly, Daniel nodded. 'You'll be interviewed under caution now. You've lied about your relationship with Frances Owen, so the police will want to know why.'

It wasn't unusual for Daniel to be in this position. So many of his clients lied out of self-protection, lies that would later implicate them. It happened all the time – omissions under questioning that the police would seize upon as evidence of culpability later.

Elbows on the table, Sebastian ran his fingers through his hair. His hands were large with prominent knuckles. Daniel could just remember how small Sebastian's hand had been before, when he had held it to comfort him in court. It was still hard to fit that child with the young man before him now.

'We broke up *months ago*. I didn't think it was relevant . . . or maybe I didn't think the truth would sound good.'

'Lying sounds worse.'

'We got together at that party I told the police about. She was . . . just so wonderful. We kept it secret, of course. I mean, she was married, but I think I might have ... that I—' Sebastian blinked, his pale eyes reddening slightly '—*loved her*. Knowing that this happened to her – you've no idea what it does to me. I thought if I told the police we were together, they would think it was me. Me with my history – they'd think I actually killed her.'

Sitting across the table, Daniel was aware that Sebastian's broad shoulders were shaking slightly. The self-assurance that had been obvious at the last meeting was gone and he seemed truly distressed. Daniel was concerned that Sebastian was now the main suspect.

He went to find the detectives. Waiting in the corridor, he squinted through a dirty window at the hot afternoon outside. The media were camped outside the entrance to the police station: one or two TV vans and a straggle of reporters. The violent nature of Frances Owen's death had been widely reported, and the supposition that the murderer was a Cambridge resident known to the victim appealed to both local and national news. There was speculation about suspects. Daniel was aware that he'd been photographed entering the police station and felt sure the press would know that he was representing the young student who was one of the police's key lines of enquiry. Luckily, there was no way the media could reveal Sebastian's past, as the boy tried for the Angel killing. Sebastian had been a minor at the time of his trial and so his identity had been subject to an injunction. Although he was an adult now, there was still a media embargo on publishing *any* details that could identify him as the child-accused from the Angel murder trial.

As he watched the gaggle of waiting reporters, Daniel

thought how they would *love* to know what the police probably already knew about Sebastian's past.

'Mr Hunter.'

Daniel turned to find Detective Chief Inspector Lloyd standing before him with his hands in his pockets.

'DCI Lloyd. I'm expecting that you'll interview Mr Croll under caution today?'

'That's correct—'

'So he's a suspect now. Can you give me disclosure?'

'Let's say we're keen to talk to him again.' Lloyd's face was forbidding.

Daniel pushed back his shoulders. 'Okay, we can do it like that,' he said, consciously relaxing his vowels, 'but if you tell me nothing now then I'll make sure that Mr Croll says nothing in there. It's your choice.'

DCI Lloyd sighed, a smile or a snarl emerging on his face. He wore a cheap, dark suit and smelled of cigarettes. Daniel knew that detectives didn't have a budget for work clothes and plain-clothed officers suffered in this regard. 'Very well. He's a suspect because we have evidence that he had a sexual relationship with the victim, despite what he told us in his last statement—'

'That's it, I see. Thank you.'

'You're a Geordie?'

Scrunching up the corners of his eyes, Daniel nodded once.

'I didn't hear it in your voice last time.'

'Been down here too long, I guess.'

'We'll talk to Mr Croll in interview room three.'

*

When Daniel entered the interview room, Sebastian sat up and straightened the collar of his polo shirt, seeming anxious. Daniel took a seat beside him, ready for the detectives.

'My father said they'd try to fit me up,' Sebastian whispered. 'I'm still so worried they've got it in for me, because of my past.'

'I told you, they won't bring it up. You won't have to answer any questions about it.'

'Maybe not, but they're thinking it. I was innocent, but they won't let it go.'

Just then the door opened.

As the two detectives took a seat and began formalities – naming everyone present and noting date and time for the recording – Daniel considered Sebastian's turn of phrase strange.

Had he meant to say 'found not guilty'? Had Sebastian forgotten his childhood confession to Daniel just after the verdict came in all those years ago?

Detective Inspector Burrows began the interview: 'You do not have to say anything. But it may harm your defence if you do not mention when questioned something which you later rely on in court. Anything you do say may be given in evidence.'

Burrows had a brown paper file in front of her.

Waiting for questioning to begin, eyes down, Sebastian picked at the cuticle of one thumb with the nail of the other.

'Sebastian, I'd like you to tell us about the nature of your relationship with Frances Owen.'

'She was my tutor . . .'

'Let's not play games. We have correspondence in evidence that proves you were having a sexual relationship with her.'

Keeping his chin down, Sebastian raised his eyes to look directly across the table at Inspector Burrows. '. . . *and my lover.* She was my tutor and my lover.'

Daniel glanced at Sebastian. From this angle, the dark lashes rimming his pale eyes seemed so long. He was staring straight at the detective.

'How did your relationship come about?'

'That party I mentioned when we last spoke . . . I'd been drinking – we all had. I spilled some red wine on my shirt and she took me upstairs to—' Sebastian cleared his throat '—choose one of her husband's to wear instead. It was in the bedroom there . . . I remember I took my shirt off and . . . she kissed me.'

'Are you saying she came on to you?'

'I am, and it took me by surprise.'

'Can you describe your relationship?'

Burrows had a very small mouth, Daniel noticed this time. Her lips were pulled tight, making her seem fierce.

'Well, after that party, we started seeing each other. It was just some fun at first, but then, I suppose things got a little more serious—'

'Serious? How so?'

'Well, I started seeing her regularly, staying over at hers when her husband was away. I'd go over to her house and she'd make supper—'

'And why didn't you mention this when we spoke to you last time?'

Briefly, Sebastian rubbed his eyes with the fingers of one

hand. 'I know I should've spoken about it before. It was just that she was married and we tried to keep it to ourselves as far as we could. And we broke it off some months ago . . . I mean it was *over*. I didn't see the point in bringing it up again—'

Burrows slid a piece of paper in front of Sebastian – an email that Daniel could see was from Sebastian to Professor Owen on their Cambridge University accounts.

Sebastian touched the corner of the piece of paper and it shook slightly in his grasp. Daniel could read it easily over Sebastian's shoulder.

'A love letter,' Sebastian said, setting the piece of paper down on the table. 'A little naïve perhaps . . .'

With an arch tilt to her brow, Burrows sat back in her chair and read: '*You are the most beautiful, intelligent woman I have ever met. I love you deeply*—' she read derisively, with exaggeration. 'Sounds fairly significant to me.'

'I did,' Sebastian stumbled over his words, 'have strong feelings for her—'

With the tip of her pen, Burrows indicated the date on the email – autumn of the previous year. 'That was then. Tell us what happened six months later—'

He looked up at the low ceiling as if for inspiration. 'Well, it finished. I suppose it had just run its course. There was, of course, a large age difference between us.'

'Twenty-two years?'

'Yes, I enjoyed her company, but I didn't think we had a future together.'

'How did it finish?'

'Like I said, I think it had just run its course. She was married, she was much older than me—'

'So it was mutual?'

'I think so.'

'I don't.' Burrows slid another email transcript across the table in front of Sebastian, dated late January this year.

Sebastian lifted the page off the table and Daniel was also able to read it.

To: s.j.croll@stu.cam.ac.uk

From: f.i.owen@cam.ac.uk

Subject: re

Please leave me alone. Just accept that it's over between us. I have asked a colleague to take over the supervision of your dissertation. It is no longer appropriate for us to spend time alone together. You may still come to tutorials, but please stop contacting me. Thank you.

Frankie.

Sebastian was silent, but Burrows prompted, 'that doesn't sound very mutual to me, Sebastian. Tell us honestly now, were you *dumped?*' Burrows had the slightest hint of a smile on her lips.

'Like I said, the relationship had run its course. Both of us realised it had no future.'

'It sounds to me like *she* ended it and *you* couldn't accept it.'

'All endings are hurtful,' Sebastian said, very quietly.

Daniel turned to look at him, but he was just staring down into his hands.

'Very well,' Detective Inspector Burrows flicked her folder shut and clasped her hands on the table, so her knuckles were pointing at Sebastian. 'Three months ago – conveniently not long after Professor Owen wrote this email to you, asking you to "leave her alone" – she reported to the police that she was being *stalked*. She sensed she was being followed and watched, both at home and at work—'

Daniel wondered if the stalking allegation was the thing which Leila had felt her police contact was keeping back. Daniel now felt his purpose as solicitor was clear. He didn't want Sebastian to say much more about this stalking allegation. It seemed like speculation on the police's part. Presumably, no one had been charged with the crime of stalking Frances Owen at the time, and she was no longer here to substantiate it.

'I wasn't aware of that,' Sebastian said slowly, his energy dissipating and turning to confusion, 'that she had been stalked—'

'Frances Owen reported receiving anonymous letters and drawings, and said she felt she was being followed to social events and to her home. *On more than one occasion* she felt as if someone had been *inside her house.*'

'Someone perhaps, but not me ... if that's what you're suggesting—'

'She reported receiving several calls, some of which were sinister, from her own office number, often late at night—'

'Someone called her from her own number? Surely that would mean the person stalking her was a colleague, or—'

Burrows tapped the table with her forefinger. 'The words Professor Owen used in her email suggested she felt *you* to be a threat. "*Leave me alone*", she wrote—'

Daniel interrupted. 'I think you're fishing, Detective. My client wasn't approached about this stalking allegation at the time. Was anyone? I'm assuming either the evidence was insubstantial, or the investigating officers didn't follow it up.' Daniel put one hand on the table, fingers down.

This was a good card to play. It put the onus on the police. Daniel knew that, particularly with stalking, the police found it difficult to substantiate charges. Stalking was a crime of persistence. It was an incremental series of small intrusions: hard to investigate and even harder to prosecute. Actions that might seem innocuous to an outsider could have profound meaning to a victim of stalking, and there was a strong correlation between stalking and further violent crime, but there was no evidence that the police had investigated Frances Owen's allegations at the time or identified a suspect. It seemed as if Sebastian was being fitted up for the stalking because of the affair.

'The stalking could have been a warning about what was going to happen to Frances Owen, but you're telling me the police took no action at the time. It's not appropriate to retrospectively fit my client.'

There was the slightest flicker of anger in Burrows' eyes as she met Daniel's gaze. He found the anger made her seem more human somehow.

Burrows flipped open her brown paper folder. So quickly that Sebastian started back in his chair, she placed photographs of Professor Owen's face from the scene of the crime on the table. Sebastian froze.

Even though he had already seen the photograph, Daniel flinched. 'Detective Sergeant, that's gratuitous. What's the purpose of showing these?'

Burrows kept the photographs on the table for several seconds more. 'Just four months after Frances Owen asked you to leave her alone, someone did this to her—'

Sebastian hung his head in his hands, silent, eyes closed to the photograph until Burrows put it away. 'Someone but not me,' he whispered, almost inaudible.

'Detectives, I have to say that this line of questioning doesn't seem relevant to the murder of Professor Owen. Perhaps it's pertinent to her historical complaint of *stalking*, but the police didn't see fit to charge, or even arrest anyone at the time – certainly not my client—'

'Your client, who lied about being in a relationship with the deceased, was asked by the victim to be "left alone"—'

Daniel pressed his pen into his pad, leaving a small black dot on the page. 'It seems to me that your questions are in response to the victim's stalking complaint. I hope we're not trying to make up for lazy police work at the time?' Daniel realised that his question would nettle the detectives. In synchrony, both Burrows and Lloyd shifted in their seats. 'So, do you have any questions pertaining to the actual murder, or are we finished here?'

Burrows focused her attention on Sebastian.

'Do you have an alibi for the morning of Wednesday the eleventh?'

'I told you before I was asleep in my room.'

'You don't have a roommate do you?'

Sebastian shook his head.

'I need you to answer yes or no, for the recording.'

'No.'

'So, can you name *one person* who will confirm you were asleep in your room between the hours of six and nine on Wednesday the eleventh?'

Daniel watched Sebastian's Adam's apple bob in his throat. Just before Burrows prompted him again, Sebastian replied.

'I can't.'

Tension began to build at the back of Daniel's neck. It was late and he was tired; it was apparent that the detectives had nothing else. As if reading his mind, Lloyd leaned forward and spoke into the recording that the interview was finished.

Sebastian was released again without charge.

The humid air felt thick as Daniel and Sebastian walked out into it together. There were no stars visible in the sky. It was after eleven and the last train back to London was at midnight. The reporters were still there and their long lenses flashed in the distance, twinkling against the black of the park like fallen stars.

Bending over, hands on his knees, Sebastian took a few breaths and then stood.

Daniel put one hand on his shoulder. 'It's tough going, I know. It still sounds to me as if they don't have anything solid, but they could call you back in for questioning again. I'm here if you need me.'

'You do believe me?' Sebastian asked, his eyes shining in the darkness. 'You don't think I could have done that, do you? Killed her?'

'If you say you didn't do it, you didn't do it,' Daniel said again. As far as his clients were concerned, he always took that view of it. It was his job to protect their rights and ensure that investigations were conducted properly; that was all.

'But do you believe me?' Sebastian's brow wrinkled as he waited for an answer. 'It's important to me. It feels as if the police have it in for me—'

Daniel remembered again the small room inside the cavernous insides of the Old Bailey where Sebastian had confessed to him. Daniel had felt shocked, mostly because, for a young child, Sebastian had consistently and convincingly lied. He had even testified, albeit broadcasting into the courtroom from an adjacent room, with a responsible adult present. Rene had only decided to let Sebastian testify because they'd been convinced he was telling the truth. But that had all been a long time ago.

'I believe you,' Daniel said. He said it to appease Sebastian, with no real consideration of whether it was the truth or not.

It wasn't his job to seek the truth; it was his job to defend.

Although he wouldn't say so to Sebastian, as it would exacerbate his fears, he thought it likely that the police *did* know about this past and *were* prejudiced against him because of it. The evidence against Sebastian was thin, but the police probably couldn't resist suspecting the only person ever tried for the still-unsolved murder of eight-year-old Ben.

'Where are you going now? Are you staying here in Cambridge or going back to London?'

'I can stay here for a few more days. Dad won't have me home. Too worried about the newspapers and his job.'

'Term's ended so you have to leave the college?'

'I can apply to stay out of term, but I think it depends on why you want to stay. I don't imagine being wanted by the police is an excuse they normally accommodate.'

'Hey ... Seb!'

Sebastian turned and Daniel followed his gaze. There was a small group – two young men and a young woman, obviously students – who appeared from the side of the police station.

Sebastian took a step towards them.

'You took ages. We've been waiting for you all this time. Let's go get a drink.' The two boys were dressed smartly for students, like Sebastian, in red jeans and polo shirts. Daniel noticed that the girl wore a string of pearls over her T-shirt.

'Thanks, guys,' he called.

Sebastian saluted Daniel, but didn't try to introduce him to his friends. Daniel understood.

'All this is a nightmare for me. I'm still trying to process what happened to Frankie. My friends're sticking by me through this, even after my room was searched, but you've no idea how humiliated all this makes me feel. And then...' again Sebastian's eyes shone with emotion, 'y'know, at the same time I'm still trying to ... grieve for her.'

Daniel watched as Sebastian swallowed, controlled himself. 'Go and try to enjoy yourself.'

Waiting on the dark platform for his train, Daniel checked his phone for messages. There was a missed call from home that had come in just before eight – Billy's bedtime. No message. He frowned, wondering what he had missed. A pain in the centre of his chest as he remembered how, not so long ago, at this hour he would go home to find Rene asleep in their bed, the light left on for him in the hall, whatever they'd had for dinner waiting in the fridge, ready to be warmed up.

Even though he took a taxi from the train station, it was after midnight when Daniel got back to Bow. He pulled off his tie as he climbed the stairs, feeling so weary that it seemed an effort to get to his doorstep. Nevertheless, inside that empty little crate of a flat, suddenly he didn't feel tired.

Of course he was spent, but he knew he wouldn't sleep, his mind still sparking from the police station and the building media awareness of the trial. There was nothing here to distract him, no way to come down. At home, Rene helped him to relax.

He'd bought a bottle of gin a week or so ago and now cracked it open, poured himself a glass. He had tonic but no ice and it tasted harsh, bitter, just like his day. He scrolled through radio stations on his work laptop – sport first, but the chatter made him feel even more on edge, so he finally opted for classical music. Swigging the gin – Minnie's tipple – he thought how this would also have been the radio station she would have chosen. This was how Minnie wound down after a hard week – a glass of gin and classical records spinning on her old record player, bare feet up on her foot stool, one hand dangling beside the chair to stroke Blitz's soft black ears.

He sank back against the couch, the mouthful of gin on an empty stomach already hitting him, bringing a mellow calm. He had to be up to go to work in about six hours but he knew trying to sleep right now was pointless. Nestling the glass between his thighs, he looked up at the ceiling. Somehow this forced isolation seemed apt, as if it was a punishment. He wondered where his life was going now, if all along he had been meant to end up like this. On his own.

He had a deep-seated belief that he was a bad person. Of course, he'd been told so as a child. He remembered one of his foster fathers leering, tobacco-breathed into his face and whispering to him that he was an *evil little bastard*. Daniel knew from personal experience that words said to a child are often imprinted exactly, like feet in hard sand. It was part of the reason why he was so wary with Billy.

For the longest time he'd struggled to come to terms with what had been done to him, and what he'd done to others, but mostly he wanted to understand who he really was. Motherless, fatherless, he had been cared for, abused, entrusted, neglected, and then loved.

As a boy he might have been close to ending up like Sebastian – on trial for some unspeakable act while still in primary school. Minnie had knocked that out of him somehow.

She'd had just the right amount of strength and warmth to deal with him. No one else had got close. But as an adult, he'd cast Minnie out of his life.

Out of a desire to protect him, Minnie had lied to him about the timing of his mother's death. When he had been younger, Daniel had thought this lie had robbed him of his mother. It was as if Minnie had taken his mother, out of some selfish wish to keep him for herself. But now he realised it was the drugs that had taken his mother from him and Minnie had only been trying to protect him. Nevertheless, after their argument when he was still in university, Daniel avoided Minnie for the rest of her life. She, the one who had loved him.

As an adult, he'd abandoned her when she'd reached out to him at the very end, sick with cancer. He couldn't come to terms with his actions now. It had been cruel, but he had been so angry.

She'd died alone, and now Daniel considered that *did* make him an evil bastard after all; that *what-was-his-name* foster father had been right after all. He gulped the gin, felt its warmth radiating inside him.

If Minnie were still alive, he would talk to her now. He would drive up to Brampton and pour them both a drink. He would open his heart to her, tell her everything. As she had been for him in his childhood, so she would be his therapy again.

The classical station was playing some orchestral piece. Daniel didn't recognise it, yet it stirred him. He remembered that Minnie used to play her piano late into the night. From his years with her, he knew Beethoven and Ravel: could name their symphonies now only because of her. She had always dressed in those long, dirty skirts, cardigans and men's boots caked with mud, yet she played piano like a maestro, barefoot, with her tiny, size-three feet – a quarter-inch of hard skin on them – pumping the pedals. Every year, on 8 August, she would get drunk after he went to bed and play the piano until she passed out. It was the anniversary of her daughter's death.

When Daniel was older – a teenager, preparing to go to college – he'd go downstairs and find her in the early hours. He'd put her to bed and whisper that he loved her, when she was asleep and couldn't hear him, as he'd done with Billy.

If she were here now, he would talk to her. He would tell her things that would have hurt her to hear when she was alive. He'd tell her about the steps he'd taken to try and find out who he really was. His biological mother was dead, but there was still a chance to know his father.

Daniel reached for a legal pad and found a pen in the front pocket of his briefcase.

Dear Mam,

Just writing *Mam* caused a stone of grief to form at the back of his throat. It was such a complex sorrow, as he felt complicit in causing it.

Often, I think about the farm and the fun we used to have together when I was young. What is harder to remember is the last time that I saw you. I owe you an apology. I

*had a chance to say I was sorry and I turned away from
it. Through the years, even when I have felt happiness,
your face has come into my mind – open and forgiving, not
judging me – yet taking the light from me, like an eclipse.
The fact that I wronged you is always inside me, a darkness.
I can't seem to escape this feeling of loathing for myself,
there because of how I hurt you. I see now it has affected
my marriage and it stops me from being the kind of father I
want to be.*

*You are gone now, but I would give everything I have to
look into your face again, hear your wise words. I would
take you to meet my little boy, my wonderful wife. I lived
with you for less than a decade, yet those years with you I
learned a lifetime's worth. I don't like to think what would
have happened to me if you hadn't been there.*

*I worry what is inside of me, that you saw and helped to
mould into something good. I fear the 'darkness', as my wife
calls it, is still there, despite all you tried to do.*

*You were always so strong and so brave – always
surprising me. Like that very first week in your house,
when you found my switchblade. Instead of confiscating it,
as all the other foster parents and carers had done, you put
it back underneath my pillow. I'm not proud of the fact,
but I was frightening then, at eleven years old (frightened,
yes, but also frightening). You were a woman on her own
in a farmhouse a fair walk from town. The trust you
placed in me was what helped me to change, but I still
remember the risk you took.*

And yet, I think now that the real pain I caused you wasn't holding a knife to your face within hours of meeting you. I know that I hurt you more when I cut you out of my life. When we fought I was eighteen or nineteen years old, I was blind with rage and it terrifies me to think what I might have done to you. I saw it in your eyes, when I picked up that spade in the yard and you fell into the mud.

Daniel stopped writing. He was shaking a little and the muscle in his shoulder and neck ached. He cocked his head to one side to try and release it, looking down at the scrawl of biro, now covering over a page and a half.

The moon had shed its clouds and was now bone bright, nearly full, so that it almost lit the room. He remembered the last time he saw Minnie, in the flesh. It was in London, on the street. He hadn't known then that it would be the last time he saw her. He was a lawyer by then, a man of thirty-three or thirty-four, with his own flat and a life that he liked well enough. She had come all the way down to London to see him, to beg his forgiveness after all those years of letters unanswered, and calling when he wouldn't pick up the phone.

She'd come to his office on Liverpool Street and waited for him outside in the rain. Now, looking up at the moon, he could see her face so clearly: cheeks pinked with the cold, raindrops on her skin like tears. It must have been only a year or two after that when Minnie fell ill. She had been reaching out to him for years and yet he turned his back on her again.

'Danny, it's Mam,' she'd said.

He had looked her straight in the face and said, 'You're not my mother.'

He set the pad on his knees again, and continued writing:

There was no excuse for the way that I treated you. That I have such cruelty inside me makes me think my wife and child are better off without me. You turned and walked away, drenched. For the longest time afterwards, I, too, was drenched, soaked in a guilt that's with me still.

I didn't mean what I said. You are my real mam. No other came close. I wish I had told you that, wish that you hadn't died knowing that I'd forsaken you.

A pain at the back of his throat, Daniel continued.

I wish you could meet my little boy, Billy. You would like him. We named him after you and that is still so important to me, as if some part of your wisdom might be his, your kindness, your big heart. I wish you were here, so I could ask your advice. I'm not good with him. Often, I think back to how you were with me and I try to emulate you. I know you weren't perfect, but you were just what I needed, when I needed you most.

Nudging a tear from his eye, Daniel flicked the page. Now he was getting to the part that really scared him. He had worked through his shame, which he had been acclimatised to for some time, and he was beginning to address his deepest fear. It was just like therapy after all.

After that argument with you at the farm, when I cut you out of my life, I was busy for a few years. I graduated and moved to London. Once I had finished my Legal Practice Course, and bought a flat in Bow, you would think I would have settled down, but that was when I began to feel most troubled.

Our big fight had been about my biological mother, who by then was also dead. After I pushed you out of my life, I felt a terrible lack inside. I had no mother, no father, no siblings that I knew of, the only parent who had ever loved me – you – was gone from my life and I had, I suppose, some kind of crisis.

I don't know now, but maybe it was a mini breakdown. I kept working, but I withdrew. It's a coping mechanism that is hard-wired into me. I know it frustrates my wife; I think it is self-protective – but it also serves to protect others from me.

My crisis of self was about who I really was. Now that you were out of my life, I had no touchstone. I was a criminal lawyer, where so much of my work is about the invisible minutiae of ourselves, our DNA. Just a partial touch on a surface can reveal our sex, even if not a full profile. And just a single strand of hair can reveal our whole identity – our looks, our tendencies, our vulnerabilities, our family. We were apart and I knew for a fact that my biological mother was dead. I had her death certificate and had been to her grave, but I started to wonder what other family I had, that might still be out there. What brothers or sisters, aunts or uncles. A father?

That line had left Daniel breathless. He sat up and took the pad over to the breakfast bar, looking out onto the clear sky with the elliptical, cynical moon.

He remembered all the time he had spent calling Newcastle Children's and Social Care Services to find out if his mother had had family. He knew Tricia Stern, who had been his social worker when he was in care, had left in the late eighties, but he was able to get in touch with another woman in the department, Margaret Bentley, who he'd had contact with when he was researching his mother's death.

In my mother's file, which included my care order, there were notes from the drugs team that named my mother's sister: Jacqueline Hunter.

So I found out, at the age of about thirty, that I had an aunt. Of course it took me some time to track her down. There was no listing of her in Newcastle and I had to check the marriage records, to find that she had changed her name to Jacqueline Burns. She was still alive, and I went to meet her.

Jacqueline told me that she had met me before, when I was a baby, and that my mother and I had actually lived with her from when I was born until I was nearly two. Of course, I then asked her if she knew who my father was — assuming that he would have been around at that time. On my birth certificate, in the box for father's name, my mother had written 'unknown'. My surname as you know is my mother's maiden name.

Jacqueline didn't know who my father was, but just as
I was leaving, she told me that he was probably one of
two people.

Daniel remembered that his Aunt Jacqueline had struggled
to name both of the potential fathers. One was called Steven
something – she didn't have a second name – and the other
was Robert Cobain. She knew that his mother had been seeing
these two men around the time when she fell pregnant. It was
this that Daniel had tasked Leila with investigating.

Even though I didn't find out who my father was, I was
pleased to have found an aunt. My memories of my mother
were too hazy to say if my aunt looked like her, and Aunt
Jacqueline didn't keep well, but it was nice to know that I
had some family after all. After a few months, she sent me
some baby pictures, which was something I had never had.
Rene's family are all big personalities; she is like her father
in some ways, her mother in others. She has two sisters and
a brother, nieces and nephews, cousins, aunts and uncles
and, until three years ago, a grandmother. I married into this
huge family and I brought no one with me. I had not a single
family member at our wedding. Although I know I had only
myself to blame, I missed you then.
I talked to Rene about you a lot, particularly when we
first got together. But by then, you had already passed away.
I told her about my mother, what I could remember. I still
have almost no memories before the age of five or six, which

*people tell me is unusual. My memory is absolutely no help
in finding out who I am.*

*Since Billy was born in particular, I've thought a lot
about who my father might have been. You know better than
most, that I didn't have the best experience of 'father figures'
either in foster care, or that time I nearly got adopted. I
remember my social worker, Tricia, when she was driving
me to your farm for the first time; she said 'you'll be alright
here with her – no men.'*

*Fathers were violent. Fathers put me down. Fathers hit
my mother or gave her drugs. I struggle to be the kind of
father I want to be, and part of that is because of these
experiences.*

*But life is not just experiences. I wonder who I am – who
my DNA comes from. I look at Billy and see myself in his
darkness (he looks just like me) and his bad temper. I see
Rene in his inquisitive mind, his sense of humour.*

*Even though I worry that he might not be worth knowing,
for a long time now I have wondered who my father is.*

*A friend who is good at finding people is now helping me
to try and discover him – if he is even alive.*

Daniel flipped the pad closed. His hand was cramping slightly
from writing so continuously. He was out of practice. Wiping his
forearm over his face, he felt it wet. Tears, although he hadn't
been aware of them.

Getting up and going to the window, he saw the black shape
of the park rimmed by streetlights. The heat had increased in

the flat and, even though the window was open, the air hung outside. Daniel was still hopeful that Leila would find some answers about his history.

Emotion rippled through him. Still unsure if he would be able to sleep, he knew it was time for bed. He put his empty gin glass into the sink and then stretched out onto the sofa. He couldn't face sleeping in that cold double bed alone tonight. Lying on his side, with his knees curled up, he fell quickly and soundly asleep.

8

It was unlike Daniel not to be well-prepared for a meeting with a client. He wasn't hungover, but he'd had too little sleep. He'd been close to nodding off during his short commute. After a morning crammed with meetings, he gathered together the file on Polly's family court client and headed straight to the boardroom for their first meeting. Daniel's work for Sebastian had taken precedence over this adopted client, and he'd only cursorily reviewed her case.

'Pleased to meet you, Michele,' Daniel said. 'Sorry I'm late, and sorry Polly's unavailable.'

'Glandular fever?' Michele nodded. 'That can be bad.'

Smiling as he took a seat opposite her at the large boardroom table, Daniel was struck by how tiny she was. She sat bird-like, poised, as if she might at any moment take flight. She had an empty cup before her, having been waiting on Daniel for more than ten minutes.

Sun streamed through the window behind her, and he closed the blinds a little so that he could talk to her without the glare in his eyes.

His stomach rumbling noisily, he thought about making

himself a coffee to help disguise it, but felt he had wasted enough of Michele's time.

Flipping open his legal pad, Daniel said: 'So your ex-husband, Greg, has applied for a court order to allow him contact with the son you share?'

Michele nodded once, a single jab of her pointed chin. 'Jackson; he's eight.'

'It's a nice age,' Daniel said, rolling his pen between his fingers.

'Do *you* have children?' There was the faintest hint of a Manchester accent. Daniel imagined it would get stronger if she was relaxed, but right now Michele was using her polite voice.

'A boy, seven.'

A twitch of approval from Michele's small mouth. Her whole body still seemed sprung.

'You object to *all* contact?'

Her eyes were a very pale blue, which made them striking but cold at the same time. Daniel thought about how the care system, even Minnie, had tried to prevent him from having contact with his parent. Every home they took him to, he would run back to his mother. When he was taken to live with Minnie in Carlisle, he still ran away – hitching a ride from a lorry driver to take him back to Newcastle.

'Greg's only doing this to get to me. He has no interest in Jackson. He can't hurt me any longer so he's using Jackson to do that.'

Daniel flipped through the notes that Polly had left. 'There were two incidents when you had to call the police—'

'No, there were more than two incidents, but twice the police arrested him and took him down to the station, once overnight. That was before we separated though. I have an injunction against him and Jackson and I have been fine. Greg hasn't dared come near us but now he's applied for this court order. I've been worried sick that he'll get access.'

Again, Daniel referred to his notes. 'So you've already had the First Hearing Dispute Resolution Appointment and now things have moved forward, so that the Directions Hearing has been scheduled. I'll coordinate with social work to get a Cafcass report to present to the magistrate. I can instruct a barrister for you too.'

'Polly told me a barrister isn't covered any more—'

'You mean the changes to legal aid? That's correct. You would have to pay for a barrister yourself, but I strongly advise . . .'

The cuts to the threshold for legal aid had meant that many on low incomes weren't able to access it. The threshold was now so low that only those on the brink of poverty qualified. Even Michele with her income supplemented by benefits did not qualify.

'I can't. It's too much, and I think Greg won't pay either. I heard through the grapevine that he's going to represent himself. I will too.'

'I advise against that.'

'I just can't afford a barrister. I'm nervous about court but I'll have to do my best. You could give me pointers?' Michele half-smiled.

'I can—' Daniel sat back in his chair '—but you should prepare yourself that if you go down that road it will mean Greg could cross-examine you directly. That can be ... difficult ... particularly if, as you say, there's been abuse.'

Michele looked away for a moment, staring into the distance. 'He's a strange man. So many people love him. He has a big smile. But there's another side to him. He can turn. For a while now, I've felt that he could kill me—'

Daniel thought of Sebastian's parents and how the veneer of their sophisticated lifestyle had belied the brutality beneath. Michele turned back to face Daniel.

'You said he has no interest in Jackson – has he been violent to him, too, in the past?'

Michele shook her head. 'He's never hit Jackson, but he doesn't spend any time with him either. He's doing all of this to get to me. I just hope that social work will say that contact with Greg'll be damaging.'

'Well, we'll see what they say. The difficulty is that Greg still has parental rights and if the magistrate rules in his favour, you would need to let him have Jackson according to the specifications. We might be able to ask that contact with Jackson is managed at a contact centre, so that they're not alone together. Or sometimes social work can ask for another family member to be present, possibly a grandparent? The Cafcass officer will prepare what's called a safeguarding letter, outlining background checks on you and Greg and your respective living conditions, advising what would be best for Jackson.'

Michele sighed deeply. The anxiety in her face aged her, otherwise she seemed child-like. 'It's best for Jackson if he doesn't see his father again. That sounds harsh, but it's the truth.'

As he listened, a shaft of sunlight cut through the blinds and Daniel narrowed his eyes. He believed Michele when she said her ex-husband didn't abuse Jackson, but he knew from personal experience that watching your mother beaten to the floor left its own marks.

Father. For a lot of his life, Daniel had been indifferent to the strange weight of that word, and now here he was sitting at the table, a father himself, separated from his wife and child. He considered how he would feel if he had to get a court order to see Billy.

They hadn't had proper contact centres when he was in care, but he had been allowed to meet his mother in the social worker's office. He remembered one of those brief, awkward meetings in the no man's land of Tricia's messy office. He had only wanted to spend time with his mum; every minute felt weighty and precious, but then she'd asked him to be a good lad and go out and get her some fags. One of the painful themes of his life had been loving without having love returned. As a child, he remembered feeling that he didn't have any choice. Other people decided for him where and with whom he should live.

'If you're confident that Jackson feels the same way you do,' Daniel said, 'you can ask that he give evidence about how he feels about seeing his father.'

Again Michele shook her head vigorously. 'Absolutely no way. I can't put him through that. Not at eight years old.'

'The magistrate might ask for his opinion anyway. That's done sensitively – usually in chambers rather than open court.'

No magistrate had asked Daniel if he wanted to stay with his mother. Newcastle Children's and Social Care Services had made the decision for him, and the magistrate had agreed. The System had always seemed so enormous and inhuman, or even superhuman. Daniel had always wondered how he would have fared if he had been allowed to stay with his real family.

'Jackson'd still have to look his father in the eye and say he didn't want to see him again.'

'He would,' Daniel admitted.

'I can't put him in that position.' Michele looked down at her hands.

Daniel knew that a lot of power would rest on the social work report, and also the sympathy of the magistrate. Without a barrister, he feared Michele wouldn't be able to effectively make her case in court.

Years of austerity had meant that the Ministry of Justice had cut the legal aid budget to the bone. It wasn't only family cases that were affected, but Daniel worried that being unable to pay for appropriate defence would hinder Michele's desire to keep her son away from her abusive ex-husband.

'I need to go,' Michele said, standing up and shouldering her bag.

'I'll let you know when I have the documents prepared for court. Let me know if you change your mind about a barrister.'

Michele gave him a resolute smile in goodbye, which Daniel interpreted as a sign that she would not change her mind.

After his meeting with Michele, Daniel checked his emails before heading out to find lunch. There was a message from Sebastian, anxious because he hadn't heard anything more from the police since his interview. Daniel sent him a quick email to put his mind at rest.

> I understand how hard it is, but the fact that you haven't heard from the police is good news. It means they have nothing on you. It can seem frustratingly slow, but try to put it from your mind while the police do their job.

Outside, Daniel was waiting at a crossing when he noticed that he'd missed a call from Rene. Seeking out the shade of a shop doorway, Daniel returned her call, fully expecting that she would now be in a meeting, or else in court.

To his surprise, she answered and a brief lightness filled him.

'Thanks for getting back,' she said.

'Is everything alright? Have you heard about the judgeship?'

Her work-laugh, controlled and business-like, self-conscious. 'No, of course not. It's too early yet ... I was calling about Billy. I don't know what your day's like, but I need your help.'

'Of course.'

A thrum in his abdomen when he heard, *I need you.*

'I'm in court all afternoon, but I just got a call from the school.'

'Right?'

'Billy's been in trouble. The teacher wants to meet us. I wondered if you could go?'

'Um ... yeah. Sure.'

Daniel took a breath and checked his watch. He had a partners' meeting at five, but could skip it.

'Thank you. I'll be home as soon as I can.'

'Bye.' Daniel assumed the plan was for him to take Billy home and wait for her there. The way she rang off sounded hopeful; *home* as the place where they all would meet. It was the place where they all should be; he wondered if this problem at school would help unite them, if he handled it well.

Billy's primary school was only a short walk from home. Arriving, Daniel was given directions to the deputy headteacher's office. Passing a classroom that he remembered to be Billy's, he peered through the glass panel on the door. The children were all gathered in a group, cross-legged on the floor but Daniel couldn't see Billy inside. He felt like Gulliver in Lilliput as he continued along the corridor: the coat pegs and lockers and benches all made for infants. He walked past walls decorated in children's paintings, friezes of wild animals, crepe-paper grass reaching out into the hall; an underwater scene with pasta and glitter and real sea shells. From the end of the corridor came the muffled sound of discordant choir practice.

Daniel didn't really know the deputy head, or the headteacher for that matter, having only met them briefly at the school gates when he took Billy to school. He had only been to parents' evening twice over the years and had met Billy's class teachers then. As Daniel walked towards the office, a memory came to him, surprising, long forgotten, of going to the headteacher's office in his Newcastle primary school to be given the *tawse*.

He'd held out two hands, one underneath the other. It would've been for the usual things – being disruptive or

116

fighting – but he couldn't remember now. How old would he have been? Probably Billy's age or a little older. He remembered the smell of cigar smoke in the headteacher's office, and the strange look of fear that came into the man's eyes when Daniel didn't flinch or cry. That was mostly what was available to him now in the memory – not the pain or humiliation but the con-flicted distress in the man's eyes.

Thinking about it now, it seemed medieval. It must have been banned a year or so later in English comprehensive schools – beating children. Back then he was hit so much, by most of the adults he knew. It wasn't that he didn't feel it, but he'd become used to it. Daniel had learned early in life that you could get used to almost anything, not just the violence but all the other ways he had been hurt.

They had a name for all that stuff now: Adverse Childhood Experiences. He'd even taken the ACE test on a whim one day at work and scored a bleak nine out of ten, as a tally of the different types of abuse and neglect he'd suffered before the age of eighteen.

Now, Daniel took a seat in front of the deputy head's desk, feeling a strange sense that he, not Billy, was in trouble. Mrs Spalding had an ability to frown and smile at the same time and Daniel marvelled at this as she focused on him.

'Thank you for coming today. I'm sorry to say there's been another incident involving Billy.' She pursed her lips and inhaled deeply. She was a big woman and seemed to swell in her chair as she spoke.

'*Another?*' Daniel said, wrinkling his forehead in response.

Mrs Spalding was probably a similar age to him but he felt younger than her. There was something about her head-teacherly manner that aged her.

'Throughout the course of this year, Billy's behaviour has been causing some concern. I've spoken to your wife – Irene – about it before. Initially, he was a very quiet and polite little boy, but his class teacher has reported that Billy is becoming more and more disruptive. He will regularly get up and run out of class whenever he feels frustrated—'

'Where does he go?'

'He runs around the school, typically, and it can be difficult to persuade him back to class.'

He's a runner, Daniel remembered his social worker Tricia warned Minnie of this, when he was brought to her.

'In addition to this, Billy has recently started stealing.'

'Stealing?' Daniel felt himself blanch.

'Nothing of particular value, and usually not even things that it seems Billy values or wants. He's been caught stealing things from the teacher's desk – items of stationery, an earring once . . . But also, you might be aware of Billy's ongoing conflict with Marcus?'

'They're friends, aren't they?'

Mrs Spalding sighed. 'They were . . . Billy's stolen things from Marcus too, and has been heard calling Marcus names of late. We view both of these behaviours as similar or at least related – stealing and bullying are an attempt to gain power and control.'

'I see.' Daniel felt a deep sadness resonating in him.

'On a daily basis, Billy has also refused to do things he's been asked by the teacher, or else he won't communicate. Have you experienced this kind of behaviour at home?'

'Sometimes.' Daniel at once wished Rene was here, but also was glad that she wasn't. She would have been thinking *like father like son*. More than anything, Daniel didn't want Billy to be like him.

'A couple of times the playground monitor has also caught Billy trying to run off – actually climbing the fence to get out of school – so this year has been marked by a number of challenging behaviours. And then today,' Mrs Spalding continued, raising both eyebrows, 'Billy was overheard in the playground threatening to kick Marcus. You understand, we absolutely have to nip this in the bud—'

Daniel swallowed, his mouth dry. 'Yes,' he said weakly. 'I'm sorry.'

'Well, it does worry me that this is a pattern of behaviour. Billy's teacher feels he needs to be noticed, listened to more and we think his tendency to run away is trying to communicate emotional needs that aren't being met. I wondered if there were any problems at home, or if you feel you need support?'

Daniel didn't know what to say, but he felt responsible. 'We're managing fine,' he said, clearing his throat. 'Billy does misbehave a little at home, but we feel able ...' he let his point drift off as Mrs Spalding put her swollen hands on the desk, as if ready to impart advice.

'Bullying, minor stealing, refusal to communicate and then the attempts to run away ... I mentioned that these things are all about control, but they also fall into a pattern of what we call "fight, flight, or freeze".'

Daniel swallowed. This was primary school nowadays: no more corporal punishment, all theories and psychobabble. *Fight, flight or freeze*. As Mrs Spalding spoke, he imagined the wild falcon that visited the farm in Cumbria – he could visualise the dark shape of it in the sky

'So, we do need to hear what you think – about whether additional support is needed, for you as a family or indeed for Billy?'

'Thank you,' Daniel said quietly, feeling the wings of the falcon move in his chest, as if in time with his breath. 'I think we'll be okay.'

Mrs Spalding clasped her hands and smiled, although her frown remained. It made her seem at once exasperated and resigned. 'Well, like I said, his behaviour is a cause for concern and it does make us wonder if something has changed in his life. Have there been changes at home, anything that might have unsettled him?'

'I'll make sure it doesn't happen again,' Daniel said, rebuffing the question, trying to sound confident. 'I'll talk to him, try to get to the bottom of this.' He was aware that he wasn't answering the deputy head's question, but he couldn't admit to her that he had recently had to leave the family home. It felt too raw to share here, even though he knew Mrs Spalding would regard it as significant. He felt ashamed, of himself and his failures as a parent.

'You're a criminal solicitor, is that right?'

'I am,' Daniel said, with a sigh, 'but right now I'm just his dad.'

'He can be very incommunicative with his teacher but he might open up to you. I would recommend talking to him to see if he is upset about anything . . .'

'Of course,' Daniel said, his voice quiet as he remembered the fight with Billy at the weekend. Knowing that he had to deal with this now felt at once intimidating as well as an opportunity.

'We can offer a range of support – both in terms of parenting, or for Billy himself. We have counsellors that come into school on certain days if that might help?'

'We'll manage, but thank you. I'm sorry for the trouble.'

'It's not a trouble. It's our job. You can think about it, talk it over as a family, and let us know.'

Billy had been separated from the other children and was waiting alone in the support room with a classroom assistant. As soon as Daniel entered the room, Billy picked up his bag with a scowl on his face. When they were outside, Daniel offered his hand, but Billy just gave him the schoolbag.

'It was supposed to be Mum that came to get me.'

'Mummy had to be in court.' Daniel tried not to sound defensive. 'Don't you want to take my hand?'

'No.' Billy folded his arms, something he hadn't quite learned to do, so that he walked holding onto both elbows instead. Even though Daniel knew he was in the huff, it looked comical and smiled to himself as he followed him on the short walk back to the house.

Stepping inside, the familiar smell of home surrounded them: the residual vinegar scent from the home-made potion the cleaner used to wash the inside of the windows, and then the whiff of the wilting bouquet of lilies and roses that sat deprived of light on the half-moon table in the hall.

Billy began to make his way upstairs, as if deciding his own punishment.

'Hang on a minute, I need to talk to you.'

Billy slumped on the third stair, pressing his face into the carpet. Hanging his jacket over the banister, Daniel sat down on the bottom step.

'Hey, you going to look at me?'

Still resting a cheek on the stair carpet, Billy turned to look at him. The single dark eye that met Daniel's was shiny, as if on the verge of tears. The memory of the first night at the flat was fresh in Daniel's mind and he didn't want to lose control again or finish with Billy saying that he hated him.

'Do you want to tell me about what's been going on at school? The teacher told me you've been misbehaving.'

Billy sat up with a scowl. He sat slumped with his chin tucked right into his chest. Inwardly, Daniel checked himself, knowing he should have left the question open instead of starting to accuse. He was able to manage open-questioning with clients, so knew that he had to be able to do it with his seven year old.

'I've not been—'

'Well, the teacher said you've been running out of class and taking things that don't belong to you. Why've you been doing that?'

'Because.'

'Well, I'm listening. Why don't you tell me.'

'I said because.'

'Because what?'

'Just because.'

Daniel tried another tactic. 'You know, when I was at school, I used to sometimes run away too.'

Fidgeting with his small fingers that bent backwards as if they were made of plasticine, Billy looked round-eyed into Daniel's face. 'Why did you?'

'I don't know. I wasn't very happy at home and when I was at school it was hard to sit still because I felt ...' Daniel stared at the wilting lilies. 'I guess I was angry about a lot of things that were happening to me and I didn't think I had any choice about them, so I chose to just run away – like running away from the problem—' Turning to look at Billy, Daniel gave him a small encouraging smile. He wasn't sure where all that had come from.

'Why were you not happy at home?'

Daniel sighed and looked at his son. He had talked to Rene about what had happened to him as a boy, but told Billy very little. Billy knew he only had one set of grandparents because Daniel's parents were dead, but that was as far as it went.

'Well, it was just me and my mum a lot of the time, but she had a lot of problems—'

Daniel was conscious of not wanting to say too much, but Billy's eyes were suddenly enormous, watching him. Stiller than Daniel could possibly have imagined him. Rapt.

'And I didn't have a dad. And I suppose it was hard, because I was still little, but I felt like I had to look after my mum, instead of her looking after me.' He almost said more, warming to the subject, to mention his mother's boyfriends or the men that would come to the flat with drugs, or wanting payment for drugs, but checked himself in time. Billy didn't need to know. Even to Daniel, it didn't really feel like his life, but some archaeological find, a story brushed and translated from buried parchment. It really felt that distant to him, as if he himself had created some of it, fibres of his childhood woven into meaning, trying to make sense of it. 'Are *you* happy at home?'

'Yes.' Billy nodded, breaking his stillness. 'Apart from when you and Mummy are fighting.'

Daniel remembered the argument in the hall, and Billy coming downstairs – almost to this very spot – after he had been asked to leave.

'Mummy and I don't like arguing either. That's why I'm sleeping at the flat right now, to give us some time to ourselves. You know, sometimes, when you argue with your friends, and you need some time by yourself, just for a little while?'

Billy nodded, his black eyes moving as if he was thinking it through.

'What's going on with you and Marcus?'

The scowl again. 'I hate Marcus.'

'Why, what's he done to you? I thought he was your best friend before.'

Billy shook his head violently. 'He's mean to me.'

'How?'

A shrug.

'Mrs Spalding told me that you steal things from Marcus and that today you threatened to kick him?'

'He was going to punch me,' Billy said, jumping to his feet. The tears in his eyes that had retreated now reappeared, as if piqued by the injustice of it. 'So I said if he did, I would—' a tilt of his chin '—kick his ass.'

Daniel had to look up at Billy now. He felt like standing up, telling him not to speak that way, but deliberately stayed where he was, as if willing patience and calm to come to him.

'I don't like hearing you talk like that.'

'I don't like hearing *you* talk like that.'

'Don't be cheeky.'

Billy's eyes narrowed and he slumped back down onto the step. There was a thin, shiny trail linking his nose and his lip and he audibly sniffed. Even though the hallway was cool, Daniel felt himself getting hot and thirsty; a trickle of sweat ran between his shoulder blades.

'If this is how you're behaving in class, it's no wonder the teacher sent you home,' Daniel said, his voice measured, even though he could feel his emotion rising in response to Billy's. He still felt in control, even though he heard himself as *telling* rather than *listening* and knew he had to try harder.

Slumping against the wall, Billy tried to fold his arms again, his dark eyes flat and reflective.

Instead of getting caught up in the current behaviour, Daniel tried to return to the point of the exercise, which was to talk about, and try to understand, what had happened at school.

'So ... you're saying both you and Marcus were to blame for the fight. That's often what it's like in arguments. It takes two people to fall out and two to be friends again—'

Daniel watched Billy's eyes growing rounder as he took in what had been said. 'What about the other things the teacher told me – about running away and taking things from your teacher's desk. Why do you do that?'

Billy shrugged, but then attempted an answer, looking away from Daniel, at the shafts of light coming in the door and spilling onto the floorboards of the hall. 'Well, I suppose I took a block ... of ... y'know, like a row of staples ... once,' he said, his words interspaced by breaths, as if to show the effort in articulating, 'but I wasn't stealing them, I was going to give them back. I just wanted to look at them, 'cause I wanted to know what made them stick together like that.'

'So, next time you ask the teacher if you can look at them. It's not right to just take things from her desk, is it?'

'But I ...'

'Is it?'

Billy shook his head once.

Thoughts flickered in Daniel's mind, about what the deputy head had said about power and control and Billy not feeling his needs had been met.

'And I told you why I used to run away when I was your age. Do you want to tell me why you do it?'

'I suppose,' Billy shrugged again, 'because I feel like ... feel like ... I'm lost or something—'

'Lost?' Sitting up, Daniel felt as if he was learning something.

'Or I'm hiding but no one is coming to find me. And if I stand up and go out the room, everyone sees me.' Billy took deep breaths, as if explaining had been effortful.

It made sense to Daniel. He felt a surge of energy at identifying a problem with a solution. He hunched his shoulders to get closer to Billy. 'I understand what you're saying, but maybe there's other things you could do to get attention rather than running off?'

'Play football?' Billy said, eyebrows raised, as if just randomly naming activities to appease Daniel.

'That's not what I mean and you know it.'

Billy hid his face again. Daniel felt a flare of pain inside him, as if feeling all of the little boy's confusion and hurt. At the same time, Daniel was filled with his own frustration. He looked up at the ceiling, wondering if he would be better leaving it just now, and talking again later, but he had imagined Rene coming home to hear that he had fixed everything. The thought that he would appear to have failed, or at least achieved nothing more than the average babysitter, pressed Daniel to continue.

'Billy, look at me, will you?'

One glistening dark eye emerged from the crook of his elbow.

'What could you do instead of running away? Think about it.'

'I don't know,' Billy whined, slumping down so that he was now sprawled over three steps.

Some part of him realised that Billy was too tired now and the interrogation had gone on too long. Nevertheless, anger lapped inside him. In an attempt to douse it, Daniel reached out to tousle Billy's hair, consolatory.

Billy jerked away from his touch. 'Piss off.'

'Hey – you don't speak to me like that, do you understand?' Voice raised, finger pointed, but Billy didn't move, remaining slumped on the stair. His defiance was impressive in some ways. It showed resolve for such a young child.

Just wanting to right him on the stair, not fully thinking it through, Daniel grabbed Billy by the arm. An electric flicker passed between them. He had a sudden, flaring impulse to hit him or shake him and the thought terrified him so much that he sprang to his feet and backed into the table in the hall. He knocked the vase with the lilies and it smashed dramatically onto the floor. Billy jumped to his feet with fright, burst into tears, turned and ran upstairs.

Chest heaving, Daniel stood facing the door with his hands on the back of his head as if he was being arrested. His throat ached as if he, too, was about to cry. The sound of Billy wailing upstairs crushed him.

For about two minutes, Daniel didn't move. He stood in the hall with his arms by his sides, amid the water and the broken china. The stamens of the lilies had left an orange smear of pollen on the white damask wallpaper as they fell. He felt the pulse of his blood in his fingertips.

Fully defeated now, listening to the echo of Billy's tears from upstairs, Daniel cleared up the mess he had made in the hall. He picked up the pieces of the broken vase first. It was an old-fashioned Chinese-style vase that he was sure had been gifted to them by Rene's mother.

There was the hum of the refrigerator and the still perceptible sound of Billy crying. Daniel became aware of a buzzing sound and thought it was the fridge until he turned towards the doors that opened onto the garden and saw a bumble bee battering against the inside of the glass. It was enormous, almost the size of his thumb.

Immediately, Daniel grabbed a glass from the cupboard and took a postcard from the noticeboard – a note from a friend he played squash with, who'd been on holiday in the Maldives. Deftly, gently, Daniel guided the bee into the glass and then opened the door and set him free. As he stood in the garden, watching the bee's dizzy flight to a nearby bush, a memory stroked him tenderly then stung, like walking through nettles.

Minnie opened her palm. It was creased and pink and the deep lifeline that ran up its centre was blackened with dirt. She picked up the bumble bee with her forefinger and Danny marvelled at the pointed sting of its tail wavering, pulsing on her fingertip. He was sure it was going to sting her and if it did, he was going to laugh.

Nevertheless, when she asked him, he took the spoonful of sugary water they had mixed and poured it into the centre of her palm, so that it was like a miniature lake there, amongst all the hills and creases of her rough farmer's hand.

'Just a drop, mind,' she said, the Irish of her voice lilting, still thick and strange to him. 'Don't want to drown the little fella, do we now?'

She coaxed the bee from the tip of her finger to the centre of her palm, towards the tiny lake of sweet water.

Daniel watched up close, his eyes level with her hand, so that the bee seemed even bigger. The fur of its body made him want to pet it, but at the same time he saw the sting nestling near her skin and didn't want to touch it.

'Look now,' she said, leaning down, so their heads were almost bumping together and he could smell the ming of her: last night's gin and a scent of grass and earth coming off her. 'That's him having a wee drink, so he is ... that'll give him the energy he needs to get going again.'

At first he couldn't see it, and then he did, the tongue coming out, hot and sharp and reddish brown – more like a spear than a tongue – plunging it into the sugar water as if lapping it up.

'He'll sting ye when he's done.'

'No, he won't. He won't sting me. He's thankful.'

'I bet he'll sting ye, like.'

The bee stopped drinking. Its stinging tail twitched and throbbed; the whole body heaving as if preparing for something.

Without warning, the bee took flight. Daniel pulled his head back sharply and watched it go, cumbersome, wavering, then flying in a high arc right over the back yard, above the chickens, clucking and fussing, and the peeved-looking goats and the blossom-heavy bushes that had lured the bee here in the first place.

Minnie was watching too, Daniel realised, with her left palm still held out flat holding the drop of sugar water, and her right hand pressed to her forehead to screen against the sun.

When it had finished its arc, the bee returned, buzzing above them for a second, before alighting briefly again on Minnie's open palm.

Daniel flinched, expecting a sting, but Minnie was smiling. The bee touched down for a moment, then took off again without drinking more.

'Well, now, you're very welcome,' she said, looking up at the blue sky.

Daniel looked up at her, confused.

'Just like I told you,' she said, pleased with herself, wiping her sugary palm on the thigh of her skirt, 'he just came back to say "thank you".'

When Daniel had closed the door onto the patio again, there was silence from upstairs. As he prepared to go up to his son, he thought about the farm in Cumbria, where Minnie had taken him in, taught him the right way, as if he was another of her rescue dogs. He tried to remember how she had won him over, how she had tamed him. He remembered one time when he was in a rage, intent on smashing up his bedroom, she had held him, physically pinned him down on the floor and pressed him into her.

The terrifying, claustrophobic safety of that came back to him now. He couldn't fight any more and so he had relented. The weight of her pressing down on him.

It had worked for Minnie, but Daniel didn't dare get that close to Billy now. He didn't trust himself not to lose his temper. And Billy wasn't out of control. Billy hadn't smashed a vase in the hall.

Minnie had always been even-tempered as a parent. Only once, when he'd killed one of her chickens, had she become really angry with him, but even then her tone and her movements were balanced. For a heavy drinker, she'd possessed a lot of self-control.

Just then, Daniel's phone rang, vibrating on the kitchen counter. It was Rene.

'Hi, I'm just leaving court now. How did it go?'

'Um, okay, not great.' He didn't want to build up false expectations, but also didn't want to admit how badly he had handled things when there was still a chance he could turn it around. 'He's been stealing from the teacher, running out of class, and then today he threatened Marcus in the playground – said he would kick him, but he told me when we got home that Marcus had threatened to hit him first—'

He heard Rene click her teeth on the other end of the phone. 'So you talked to him? Good.'

'Yeah,' Daniel said, aware that she would hear the uncertainty in his voice. He put a hand over his eyes, knowing that his son was probably still crying upstairs.

'I'll be home in about an hour.'

Feeling hollowed out, light, Daniel climbed the stairs. It was as if the earlier anger had burnt out, the remnants of it twisting and light inside him, like paper up a chimney.

The step three from the top always creaked and Daniel knew that, if Billy was listening, it would herald his approach. His bedroom door was ajar and Daniel stepped inside.

Billy's room had superhero wallpaper. There was a miniature goal and a sponge football, Lego strewn in a corner, a lamp in the shape of ladybird that he had had since he was a baby. Billy was sitting in the corner of the room by the bed, knees tucked into his chest.

Daniel plunged his hands into his pockets. 'I'm sorry,' he said, wondering if Billy would know what for. 'I'm sorry I grabbed you like that and . . . broke the vase in the hall.'

'W . . . w . . . why did you grab me?' Billy choked, breaths still snagging in his throat.

'Well, I'm sorry, but you told me to piss off and I don't want to hear it again, okay?' Daniel pressed his teeth together, which made his head ache even more.

'Sorry,' Billy said, his lower lip protruding.

Daniel thought of asking if Billy wanted a hug, but was afraid of rejection. Instead, he dared to reach out and touch the soft hair on his head, knuckled his cheek. Billy wiped his face with his forearm and then, almost as if losing balance, fell into Daniel's arms. Daniel curled the little body into his lap. There was no sound, but Daniel felt more tears shuddering as he pressed Billy into him. Daniel kissed the top of his head.

'Maybe we could go up North sometime soon, just the two of us?'

'Where?'

Daniel moved Billy into his lap, leaning against the wall.

'Brampton. I could show you the farm where I grew up.'

'Where your mum lived?'

'That's right.'

Rene knew the truth about Daniel's complicated childhood, but as far as Billy was concerned, Minnie had been Daniel's mother, dying a few years before Billy was born.

'But not your dad,' Billy sniffed, ''cause you didn't have a dad.'

Daniel nodded once.

'Because he died.' Billy wiped his nose with the heel of his hand, leaving a shine on his cheek.

Daniel smiled, not wanting to go into it all again. He had told Billy little bits and pieces of his childhood, always when prompted and trying to be as honest as possible.

Perhaps when he was older, Daniel would try to explain the mixed-up truth of his childhood.

'So do you want to go up to the farm one time, just you and me?'

'Yeah.'

Brushing his lips against Billy's forehead, Daniel whispered, 'I love you.'

He had said it so quietly that Daniel was sure Billy hadn't heard, but then he felt the vibration in his chest.

'Love you too.'

Easy as that, but Daniel felt his heart rate increase, as if there had been risk involved.

Through the open window, there was the sound of Rene's heels on the front path and then the sound of the front door opening and closing.

'Shall we go see Mum?'

9

'There's a mob outside my halls,' Sebastian said, fear thick in his voice. 'They don't even look like students. I think they're here for me.'

Daniel had just arrived in Cambridge to meet Sebastian, but hadn't been anticipating this. They'd agreed the day before to meet to talk through the police procedures. It had been two weeks since Frances's murder, but Daniel was prepared to explain that it might be months before Sebastian's devices were returned, if at all. It was hard to explain to a client that he was a suspect for murder, but there was insufficient evidence to arrest or charge him. Now, Sebastian's obvious panic set Daniel off-kilter.

'What do you mean, "a mob"?' Daniel said, stepping onto the platform at Cambridge Railway Station and moving away from the departing travellers, so that he could hear clearly.

'I think there might be about thirty people. They're going crazy outside, chanting that I'm the Angel Killer. There's stuff online too—' Sebastian broke off, his voice breathless.

'But, how ...?' Frowning, Daniel began to walk quickly towards the taxi rank.

'I just don't know how it got out. The police have just issued me a . . . a threat to life notice—'

'Shit . . . an Osman warning,' Daniel said, almost to himself. 'What's that?'

'What they've just given you, a warning that there's evidence of a real and immediate threat to your life. They do it because they need to protect you, but there isn't enough evidence to arrest the potential—' Daniel was about to say *murderer*, but swallowed it, not wanting to upset Sebastian further. 'Are the police with you now?'

Daniel had no idea *how* Sebastian could have been identified as the Angel Killer. The only people who had the information about his name and indictment as a boy were the police, and even if the press *had* found out – which was more than possible – there was an injunction against them revealing it. It was as if Sebastian's worst fears had come true.

'Yes, the police're here now. They want me to move somewhere else temporarily – somewhere safe.'

'It's probably best. Will you go to your dad's?'

Sebastian made a noise as if he was in pain. 'Do I have a choice?'

'Listen, I just got off the train. I'll be there as soon as I can.' *How the hell did this happen?* Daniel thought but did not voice. He had been reading the news on the train on the way down. He hadn't looked at social media, but had seen nothing – not even a news article – updating information on the Frances Owen investigation.

'How could this have happened? Everything's online. It was

late last night when it started. Twitter, Instagram. I was getting messages and being tagged in posts. I thought it would go away but it's just got worse, and now all these people are here.'

'Don't worry, the police'll look after you. That Osman warning means they take this threat very seriously.'

'I'm just so scared. There's even a picture of me in the lodge – you'll see. Everyone knows now – everyone. It's gone viral.'

'Magdalene Halls,' Daniel said, getting into the front seat of a private hire cab.

The journey took less than ten minutes, a scenic, tourist-worthy route that took in the botanic gardens, Coe Fen, Mathematical Bridge and finally The Bridge of Sighs, so-called because of its Venice namesake.

He'd walked past the college on one of his last visits: sedate quadrangles and unfashionable students, nothing else of note. Today, even though only twenty or thirty people had gathered, there was a nervous energy in the air as if a riot was about to metastasise. There was a police presence already – a patrol car and one or two officers in high-visibility gear doing walkabouts, chins down as they spoke into the radios strapped to their vests. In front of the college, by the lodge, there was a group of protesters with handmade placards.

Making his way into the college, Daniel noticed that not all of the protesters seemed to be students. Just as Sebastian had said, many of the protesters seemed to be older, organised. It wasn't just a few fellow students who'd found out Sebastian's identity, these seemed to be people with a cause.

Entering through the Porter's Lodge, Daniel was able to read one or two of the placards.

CAMBRIDGE SAYS NO TO CHILD KILLERS

Daniel ducked his head down, trying not to attract attention as he made his way through the ornate arched entrance to the college. The crowd jeered. The police were trying to erect a barrier amid the chanting: JAIL THE ANGEL KILLER. Some of the other placards had pictures of Frances Owen, her smiling photograph blown-up above words that read ANOTHER ANGEL MURDERED.

The traditional media had written about Sebastian being a person of interest in the Frances Owen investigation. The online leak of Sebastian as the Angel Killer meant that the mob seemed to have conflated both cases, historic and present. 'STOP HIM KILLING AGAIN' another sign read.

Daniel stopped at the lodge noticeboard, shocked that what Sebastian had described to him on the phone was still in place. He had assumed it would have been taken down by now. Of course, everything was online, that was why all these people were here, but the poster that Sebastian had mentioned was still pinned up, carefully: the angel, and the devil incarnate.

It was a picture of Ben's face, smiling, the grainy year-two school photo that had been used by the police when he was missing. It had always been a heartbreaking photograph – the eager little smile, fringe slightly sticking up – but now a halo had been photoshopped to hover above the crown of Ben's head. Next to Ben's school photograph was a current image of Sebastian – possibly the photograph from his student ID card – with devil's horns superimposed to appear as if they were growing out of his cropped hair. Below the picture, unadulterated text read: CAMBRIDGE STUDENT SEBASTIAN CROLL IS THE ANGEL KILLER.

Without thinking, Daniel reached up and tore the poster down. He swiped at it in one movement as he passed, walking away while crushing it in his left hand. Even as he squeezed the paper small and tight as a golf ball, tossing it into the next bin he passed, Daniel knew that it wasn't the poster that had brought all these people here. It would be on the university noticeboard online, on Twitter; people had been called to assembly on Facebook and WhatsApp. It would be all over the college and university social media, but could also have been spread by vigilante and activist groups who liked to 'catch' criminals like paedophiles; groups that waited for opportunities like this. Sebastian had said it was viral, but there was nothing in the mainstream press, which didn't surprise Daniel. He'd checked the news outlets on the journey here and there wasn't a single small article about Sebastian. He could go to a supermarket now and buy a copy of the *Mail* or the *Express* or even the *Guardian* or *The Times*; he knew there would be no mention because of the injunction.

Online was different. Online was the Wild West, a new frontier. And who bought newspapers? No one bought them for news, that was for sure. As Daniel slipped inside the college dormitory and made his way to Sebastian's room, he looked out of the windows lining the stairwells and thought it looked like a war brewing. The crowd outside were chanting, overlapping threats and demands, a cacophony of jeering, but 'Angel Killer' still distinctly audible.

A uniformed police officer was standing guard outside Sebastian's room and, when Daniel entered, he saw another by the window.

'Thank God, you're here.' Sebastian was drawn and pale, beads of sweat at his hairline. He was wearing a white polo shirt and shouldering a brown leather holdall. 'I have my own car here, but the police don't think it's safe.'

The female police officer who was by the window turned towards them. 'A patrol car's waiting for you at the rear exit. If you're ready, we can go now.'

The police managed to keep the crowd back, but as they ran for the patrol car, several protesters spotted them and began to run towards the police line. The sun was brutal in the sky, a searing heat. Daniel tried to use his own jacket to shroud Sebastian's face and shoulders, but as the younger man was taller, the jacket fell away before they reached the car.

The female police officer guided Sebastian into the back seat first. Before he was able to enter, Daniel felt a thud and ache in the muscle of his shoulder. He slipped inside the car, knowing he'd been struck but not by what. A cool stickiness soaked through his shirt before he pressed it against the seat. He reached over his shoulder and his fingers found a mess of slime. An egg. He didn't have a tissue and so sat with his sticky, yellowed fingers open on his knee. Sebastian dug into the pocket of his jeans.

'It's clean,' he said, passing a white handkerchief with initials embroidered in red: 'S.J.C.'.

'Back to Islington?' he asked Sebastian.

'I don't want to. My car's here. My friends are here—'

Daniel hoped they were still his friends, but said nothing. 'Best if you keep your head down for a few days.'

The truth was Daniel wasn't sure that Sebastian would be any safer in Islington – the same address where he'd lived at the time of Ben's murder and during the trial. The mob had driven him out of Cambridge, but the family home, right next to Angel, was exactly where the campaigners would want him to be. Again, Daniel wondered how on earth Sebastian's history could have been uncovered.

Sebastian looked out of the window, biting his thumbnail. Daniel felt for him. There was so much polish to the adult Sebastian, but now he seemed younger, shaken. 'You think a few days'll do it, staying at Dad's?' There was a distinct snapping sound of Sebastian's nail breaking. 'I think I'm done for. The secret's out. I'll have to leave my course. Probably have to get the fuck out of the country—'

The car had darkened windows, and Daniel was grateful, but it moved slowly until it reached the main road. As they travelled forwards, protesters jostled the car. There was a thud on the side panel that made Daniel jump.

'How do you think this got out?' Daniel asked, keeping his voice low.

'It has to be a journalist, surely?'

Shaking his head, Daniel said, 'I would say almost definitely not. I'm not saying that the press aren't aware of your previous indictment – they've been very interested in the Frances Owen case and know you've been interviewed; they probably have looked into you and might have found this out – but there's severe legal consequences if they reveal your identity. If you see the papers, there's nothing there.'

The police officers up front were intent on the road, the woman speaking into the radio. On the M11, the car picked up speed.

In the back seat, Daniel leaned a little closer to Sebastian. 'I have to ask you – did *you* say anything to anyone? Could it have been someone you took into confidence who revealed it? Maybe one of your friends here?'

'Absolutely not. My friends here are wonderful, and we share a lot, but I kept this ... tight. Since I've been small, it's been ingrained into me. I know that people are prone to judge and I ... just haven't dared to share that information, even with my closest friends. For a long time it's not been relevant anyway. It all happened when I was child, but it's not who I am now.'

'Maybe ... you got pissed one night. Don't remember mentioning it?'

'This absolutely *did not come from me*,' Sebastian looked down into his hands. 'I haven't told a soul.'

Daniel believed him. 'I'll see if our firm's investigator can find out anything ... Officer?' he said, addressing the police woman in the passenger seat. 'The Osman warning, is there any information about how this information about my client was leaked – putting his life in danger—'

'We're just handling the transfer to the safe location, but I believe Detective Chief Inspector Lloyd will call Sebastian once he's in London.'

'Thank you.'

Sebastian was hunched over his phone, one hand pressed over his mouth.

'What is it?' Daniel asked.

Prodding at the screen, it was several moments before Sebastian answered. 'You won't believe this shit. So many notifications. People saying I'm the Angel Killer and that I murdered Frankie, saying I should be hung—' Sebastian offered his phone to Daniel, as if for proof, but he only glanced at it. He could well imagine the vitriol. Gone were the days when death threats were posted through letterboxes, chopped up headlines compiled by scissors and glue. Social media now meant that anyone and everyone could issue personal death threats, even if they didn't know their victim.

'They're saying they want me dead, there's ... so many ... they say they want to *shoot me, burn me alive*. It's like ... a witch-hunt, a lynching ...' Sebastian whispered. 'I mean it was over ten years ago, I was eleven years old for fuck's sake and I was found *not guilty*. Why won't they just let me move on? It's not fair. I'm as upset as everyone else about Frankie, but they decide I'm to blame—'

'Listen,' Daniel placated, 'let's just get you home. You should delete all your social media accounts. There's no point reading all that stuff. London'll be better. Bigger, more perspective.'

'I wouldn't bet on it. If this has reached Dad, he'll be going crazy. He might have to resign ...'

'Let's not get ahead of ourselves.'

The female police officer turned in her seat to speak to them. 'I've confirmed that you've been allocated a protection officer who'll be based outside your Islington address, round the clock. There's a series of other measures we can put in place to make sure you feel safe—'

'Safe,' Sebastian whispered, 'thank you.'

Daniel was pleased that the police's response had been so swift and comprehensive. Most Osman warnings were issued to people within organised crime, and protection wasn't automatic. It was a way for the police to alert people to a threat to their life, but they didn't always act to protect it. Even though he was glad Sebastian was being looked after, Daniel wondered about why Sebastian merited such extensive care.

As they began to exit from the motorway, Daniel texted Leila to inform her about the leak and what they had witnessed in Cambridge, although he felt sure she would have seen what was happening online. He asked her to find out what she could about the source of the leak. He believed Sebastian that he had guarded this information very carefully and doubted that he would have let it slip, even under the pressure of forming new relationships at university. Daniel couldn't think who would have revealed this information, but one thing was certain, it threatened to prejudice the ongoing investigation and risked people taking the law into their own hands.

GUILT

10

The next morning, as Daniel was climbing to his office floor, a text arrived from Leila to say that she had found out who had revealed Sebastian's identity. She was on her way to the office later and so they agreed to meet. Even though he was anxious to hear what she had found out, Leila was keen to tell him the news in person rather than over the phone. This intrigued Daniel even though it meant he had to wait.

'So what, was it an ex-girlfriend?' Daniel asked when they met late morning. He believed that Sebastian hadn't told anyone, but the most obvious explanation was that someone close to Sebastian had been the source of the leak. 'Surely not his father, the Minister for Trade and Industry?'

Sighing and taking a seat in his office, Leila said, 'I don't know if you met him, but my main contact on the Major Investigation Team in Cambridge was Detective Constable Murphy—'

'I *did* meet him,' Daniel said, moving to the meeting table and taking a seat opposite Leila. 'Young guy—'

'Well, he's mid-thirties, but looks younger, admittedly. Anyway, he's been sacked—'

'What the hell—'

'You didn't share with me about Sebastian's past when you sent me to Cambridge to investigate—' an inflection in her voice.

'No, of course not.'

'Well, obviously when I went there the police said *nothing* about Sebastian being tried as a boy ... for that most famous of trials, one of the most enduring unsolved cases. I was in Afghanistan then, but even I remember it—'

Daniel said nothing, waiting for Leila to expand.

'As soon as Frances was murdered and they began to look into all her students and colleagues, the Major Investigation Team checked Sebastian out on the police national computer and found out about his indictment.'

'I thought they would have. There was a chance the record would've been weeded out; *just* enough time has passed—'

'Sebastian's details are still there, but Detective Chief Inspector Lloyd as the Senior Investigating Officer asked for it *not to be shared* with the general team. When I spoke to Murphy, he probably knew about Sebastian but said nothing to me. I had a sense when I spoke to him he was withholding something—'

Frowning, Daniel reached across the table towards Leila. 'So ... why was Murphy sacked?'

'Well, he didn't share it with the general team, or with me obviously, but unfortunately *he did* have a few drinks and then share with his girlfriend, who works in admin at Cambridge University.'

'Jesus,' Daniel said, whistling. 'So Murphy's girlfriend sets the bomb off—'

'Yes – she's not responsible for all this furore, but she certainly set it in motion. There was no way for Murphy to hide. Checks on the national computer are logged, and so Murphy's details were listed as requesting the record on Sebastian, and then his girlfriend of two years – Janelle – posted the information on the Cambridge Student Noticeboard. It went viral from there—'

Daniel cupped his hands over his mouth and nose as he considered. 'I don't believe it. The fucking *police* leaked Sebastian's identity ... no wonder they pulled out all the stops with the protection—'

'I don't think Janelle realised it would get back to Murphy so quickly, but anyway I think he admitted it when questioned.'

'And that's it – he's out.'

'At the very least.' Leila pursed her lips briefly. 'Data protection offences are bad news—'

Daniel stood up and walked to the window. 'So, the police have been suspicious of Sebastian right from the start. They don't have any evidence against him, but now this has been let out of the box and he's being put on trial all over again—'

'Only this time it's trial by social media.' Leila sighed.

'It's not just trolling,' Daniel said, turning to her, 'bad as that is ... there're a lot of nutters who'll take action on that information – campaigners, vigilantes. The police have compromised Sebastian's safety as well as prejudicing the investigation against him.'

'I think they're aware of that.'

*

As soon as Leila left, Daniel returned to his desk to call Detective Chief Inspector Lloyd, planning to confront him over the leak. It was past lunchtime already and Daniel was starving, but he had a meeting with Polly's family court client, and didn't have time to run down and get something.

Just as he was reaching for his phone, it began to ring.

'Daniel Hunter.'

It was Rene. Even though stress had focused his mind completely on work, the sound of her voice filled him with relief.

'Hey.' He waited, captive. It could be another family emergency, but Daniel hoped she had called just to speak to him.

'Took a chance you'd be at your desk.'

'I am. Where are you?'

'I'm at home actually.'

He half-smiled. He could visualise what she was wearing – those expensive track pants that were neat on the hip and a sweater. It was early. If she was still at home, she wouldn't have showered yet. The memory of her smell filled him with a painful combination of desire and longing.

'So . . .' her voice sounded nervous, brittle. 'I'm not supposed to tell anyone, but . . .'

'You've done it.'

'Yes . . . I'm . . . going to be a high court judge,' she whispered.

He could hear the lilt of excitement in her voice. He turned in his chair, a smile, wide and genuine splitting his face. 'That's amazing. When did you hear?'

'Just this morning. I'm *really* not supposed to tell anyone yet, though, so you have to keep it to yourself.'

'Of course. Thanks for telling me.' He pitched forward in his chair. 'Feels good to know I'm not just anyone.'

'I can't even tell chambers until I get the official nod—' she said, ignoring his plea.

'Oh yeah, you'll get the whole personally signed appointment by the Queen, won't you?'

'Well, apparently it'll take a few days and then I can share—'

'I mean it, thanks for telling me. Should we celebrate?' he asked, realising how risky the question was. They were separated, after all, and he feared she wouldn't want to celebrate with him.

'I think I'll hold off celebrations until it's official. But—'

He heard her inhale, sensed her anxiety. He wanted to touch her so badly, it felt as if he had pins and needles in his extremities.

'—that was *kind of* why I was calling, not so much to celebrate, but I thought we could have dinner – to talk things over. I'll get a babysitter – book somewhere so we have the space to discuss—'

Discuss what? Now Daniel held his breath.

'Dinner would be great,' he said quickly, unease spreading through him. No celebration, so why a restaurant unless she wanted a public space to discuss sensitive topics? Was she trying to avoid a scene?

Again, the thought of losing her winded him. It felt like being plunged into cold water.

'Tomorrow? Say seven?'

'Sure.'

'I thought I'd book that place in Farringdon. Handy for your work and mine.'

'Great,' Daniel said, hearing the strain in his voice, even though he tried to sound light-hearted. 'See you then—'

Emotion swirled inside him as he hung up. He knew the place she meant in Farringdon. It was a gastro pub – big open space with large wooden tables. It was near the Thameslink so she could get back to Herne Hill. Not only was she not inviting him home for dinner – she didn't even want him to cross the river.

Daniel's assistant, Jacob, called his extension to say that Polly's client, Michele Atkinson, was waiting in the meeting room. She was here to talk through the reports from social work and Daniel hoped she had also changed her mind about instructing a barrister. She was early, however, so Daniel asked if Jacob could get her a coffee while he called Cambridgeshire Police.

Expecting to be told that the detective wasn't available, Daniel was surprised when Lloyd's rumbling Yorkshire voice came on the line.

'Detective Chief Inspector Lloyd, thanks for taking my call . . . it's Daniel Hunter, I'm representing—'

'S'alright, lad, I remember you.'

Daniel smiled at *lad*. Detective Chief Inspector Lloyd would be late fifties at most, probably only ten years older than Daniel. Perhaps he should have, but he didn't feel patronised. He didn't mind being thought of as younger than he was, but wondered if there was more currency in his shared heritage with Lloyd – both working-class Northerners stranded in the South East. Consciously, Daniel thickened his accent.

'Sebastian's had actual death threats. It seems as if everyone knows who he is and is out to get him—'

There was a trace of genuine contrition in Detective Chief Inspector Lloyd's voice. 'I've called Mr Croll, personally, to apologise and to let him know about the kind of protection we're offering. We have a duty of care and *we will* protect him. He said he would keep us informed of any direct attacks. We have an officer on his Islington address and accompanying him when he goes out, where possible. We've told him to keep a low profile and to stay offline as much as he can—'

'Let's hope that's enough,' Daniel said, glancing at his watch. 'Another concern, obviously, is that the investigation's prejudiced—'

Lloyd cleared his throat. 'Sebastian isn't our main suspect.'

Waiting for the detective to expand, Daniel pressed his lips together. If the Major Investigation Team hadn't been found culpable, Daniel doubted Lloyd would have shared this information with him.

'We've arrested Frances Owen's husband, Jonathan Thompson.'

Remembering that Jonathan Thompson flew into the country *after* Frances had been murdered, Daniel frowned. 'But I thought—'

'Seems that alibi of his wasn't so ironclad after all.'

'How so?'

'We weren't only looking into Sebastian; of course we were looking at the victim's husband. We doubled-checked passenger lists and Jonathan Thompson flew into Heathrow twenty-four hours before he told us he did—'

'That's quite an omission.'

'That's what we thought.'

'Thanks, DCI Lloyd,' Daniel said, hanging up.

Daniel considered that Jon Thompson being the focus of the Cambridge enquiries could help to alleviate the risk to Sebastian's life. If Thompson had been arrested, the media would be aware that he was now a key suspect. There was a chance it would take the heat from Sebastian; even though it wouldn't change his infamy as the Angel Killer who'd escaped justice, it might persuade the activists that he wasn't to blame for Frances's murder. However, justice didn't seem to matter to the swarm focusing on Sebastian.

If it was at all possible, Michele seemed even smaller than she had last time. She was wearing a sleeveless top and her arms resting on the boardroom table were thin as a child's. When Daniel entered, Michele prepared to stand.

'Stay where you are; don't worry.' He smiled at her, as if to give her confidence, finding the social work reports in the file. 'It's good to see you again. A date's been set for court.'

'I saw that.' She chewed the skin around her thumb, quickly but intensely.

'Social work sent me a copy of the Cafcass report and also the safeguarding letter. Both of these are encouraging, in my view.'

Sliding a copy towards Michele, Daniel noticed that she seemed to be shivering.

'I can turn the air con off?'

'I'm not cold. I'm just ... nervous about losing Jackson.'

'Try and stay positive,' Daniel said, 'The Cafcass report says a lot more than the police reports about the kind of violence you've suffered from Greg. I'm sure the magistrate will consider carefully about awarding him custody.' Daniel knew that fewer than one per cent of parents were denied access in custody hearings. It was a long shot, but he hoped that Greg fell into that category.

The Cafcass report had made sobering reading. The police had been called twice to Greg and Michele's home. The first time, Michele had a broken nose but hadn't wanted to report Greg for the injury. The second time neighbours called the police after hearing raised voices. On arrival, the police liberated Michele from a crawl space under the floor. She had been forced down there and locked in, but was physically unharmed. Reading the report had brought Daniel back to his childhood. His mother had had several partners that he remembered, most of whom were violent, all of whom he'd hated.

Of course some had just been wasters, beached on the couch for months amid a cloud of blue smoke, but one or two of them had really hurt his mother. Even though much of his childhood was a blank, he had flashes of brief trauma: standing in terry-towelling pyjamas (how old would that've made him – five, six … three?) squaring up to some loundering bastard, whose face and name Daniel could no longer place.

Don't you do that to my mummy.

Who's gonna stop me? You, y'sackless nowt?

Sackless nowt. Geordie for 'stupid nothing'. How did kids survive? How had he survived?

'What worries me,' Michele said, 'isn't what they say about me and Greg's relationship. You're right they've detailed a lot of it ... But they also note, explicitly, that Greg has never laid a finger on Jackson. I think they'll use that ... *he'll* use that. He's doing all of this to get to me – to punish me. Just you wait, he'll play the perfect father.'

Listening, Daniel pumped the end of his pen. He hadn't met Greg but already he hated him. It occurred to Daniel that he had spent most of his adult life resenting the system that put him into care as a boy. Minnie's death and the realisations that had come from that, coupled with his own search for his biological family, meant that he was beginning to see things differently. Was he dysfunctional as an adult because he'd been taken from his real family; had the system saved him, ruined him, or a bit of both?

'The safeguarding letter gives a good report about *your* home environment: the garden and the neighbour's children that Jackson plays with, the short walk to school. It highlights that Greg is still living with his elderly mother—'

'God bless her. She had no choice.'

'It won't help his case that he doesn't have a place of his own yet but the letter still states that the mother's home is a safe and stable environment.'

'Believe me, there's no safe and stable environment where Greg's concerned. Joyce isn't well. She's pretty much stuck in that living room chair, goes to bed at three thirty in the afternoon. Joyce is Jackson's gran and she loves him but she's in no state to protect him.'

'You think protection's necessary? You said yourself Greg's never hit Jackson.'

Michele folded her thin arms. 'Like I told you before, this isn't about Jackson. It's about getting back at me and it terrifies me to think what lengths Greg would go to to get back at me.' Tears sprang sudden and panicked into Michele's eyes. 'He can't get his hands round my throat any longer. He can't control my movements, who I see or speak to. He can't take away my bank cards, but he can take my son. That's what I'm afraid of—' her chest heaved.

Daniel reached across the table and placed a hand on her forearm. Michele's stories reminded Daniel of Charlotte Croll and the stories Sebastian had told him about watching his father choke his mother.

Michele nodded thanks, once, briefly, then slid her hands under the table.

'Have you had any more thoughts about instructing a barrister?'

'No. It's like I told you, I can't afford it.'

Taking a deep breath, not even having fully considered it, Daniel said, 'Maybe I could help you out in court – be your instructing solicitor? I can't present your case like a barrister can, but I could give you pointers?'

Michele laughed briefly. He hadn't seen her laugh before. It changed her entirely. 'I can't afford you either,' she said, her Manchester accent coming through.

'I do the occasional bit of pro bono work,' Daniel said, feeling magnanimous.

Because he had been inside all day, Daniel decided to go out for a coffee and some fresh air. Michele's plight, the truth about who had leaked Sebastian's identity and the thought of meeting Rene tomorrow all surged in his mind. He needed sunlight to get perspective on it all.

On the ground floor, as he walked past reception, before he even stepped outside, he could see that something was happening on the street. The security guard, who was normally inside, was standing on the pavement.

Wondering if there had been some kind of accident, Daniel slipped outside. Suddenly, the building security guard began to tussle with two or three people, one of whom had a placard. Daniel was able to read the word *justice* painted in red.

'Leave now. I've already called the police,' the security guard shouted, pushing off the people who had breached the entrance to the building.

Before he'd even stepped onto the pavement, a woman pointed straight at Daniel and screamed, *'That's him – that's his lawyer!'*

Slowly, Daniel realised that this commotion was for him. His fingertips traced the rough stone of the building as his heart rate increased. There were more than twenty people all here to protest his defence of the young man they considered to be the Angel Killer.

Two men bearing placards for the 'Justice for Ben' campaign surged forward. The security guard, a big mountain of a man, opened his arms wide to push them back. The woman who had pointed out Daniel now moved forward, screaming into his face, *'How can you live with yourself? How can you defend that filth?'*

He could see all the whites around her eyes, her tonsils. He didn't say a word in response, standing almost rooted to the spot, amazed that all this anger was directed at him.

It all seemed to happen in slow motion. The woman reached inside her jacket. Unsure if she had some kind of weapon, Daniel slipped his fingers around the entrance door handle, ready to retreat back inside. A policeman appeared, dragging the woman down onto the pavement. Just as the officer was getting ready to cuff her, she managed to get one hand free and hurled something straight at Daniel.

Daniel stepped quickly inside the transparent doors just as bright red splashed over the corporate glass.

Gasping, Daniel backed inside. The receptionist had left her desk and came to join him.

'Is that paint or . . . ?'

'I think it's blood,' Daniel whispered.

The woman was being arrested and the rest of the crowd was dispersing, but Daniel realised that if he'd remained outside a moment longer he'd have been covered from head to toe.

11

The police told him later that it had indeed been blood – pig's blood. The cleaner who served the office block had refused to deal with it and so a specialist bio-hazard cleaning team had been brought in to sort out the internal and external mess. It had taken the police several hours to fully disperse all of the protesters and Daniel had stayed later at the office, nervous of another attack.

The next evening, walking to Farringdon to meet Rene, Daniel still felt rattled. He'd left the office at six thirty, but had thought twice before stepping outside in the fresh shirt he'd changed into just for Rene.

The police had now put an officer on their building and a small group who had gathered at lunchtime had now been dispersed. He slipped out onto the hot, dirty streets seemingly unnoticed but still unnerved. It was just the usual crowds and traffic near the station, but Daniel found himself looking over his shoulder as he walked.

His phone vibrated in his pocket. It was Sebastian.

'Are you alright?' Unsettled as he was, Daniel was aware that Sebastian was dealing with much worse.

'I'm okay, thanks. I just feel like I'm in prison. Remember that place they put me when I was a kid – it feels just like that—'

Daniel was sure Sebastian was referring to the secure unit where he'd been placed on remand after he was charged with Ben's murder. He'd spent several months there, awaiting trial, separated from his parents, and Daniel had visited.

'There was a crowd outside the house on the first and second night, but the police cleared them away. I can't say I feel safer now, even though there's a police officer outside round the clock. They change shifts—' Sebastian sighed raggedly. 'It's hard to get out at all, and, when I do, I feel like someone's following me.'

Waiting to cross the road at the Barbican, Daniel glanced over his shoulder. He knew how Sebastian felt.

'I heard DCI Lloyd called to apologise?'

'Yes, personally. And I accepted his apology. To be honest, I was quite taken aback. I didn't think they would take responsibility, but they absolutely have. He said they have a duty of care for me—'

'They *do* have a duty of care.'

'Well, I'm grateful. And they've put me on a special watch list, and given me a panic button, so that, even if I'm out and about, or if, God forbid, someone actually manages to get into the house or whatever ... I can alert them. Beyond my expectation, really—'

'That's all good. But you're okay? Just lying low?'

'Mostly, yes. The thing I can't get over is that my identity's out there now. I don't think I'll ever get my life back. I can't imagine a time when things'll go back to normal. Everything's changed overnight.'

Daniel didn't know what to say to comfort him. 'They've arrested Frances Owen's husband.'

'I heard that; saw it on the news. But unless they charge him, I don't see how it'll take the pressure off me.'

'Let's be positive. Just keep your head down at the moment, and hopefully things'll get better soon.'

'Thanks, Danny.'

'You take care, Sebastian.'

As he approached the bar and restaurant where Rene had asked to meet him, Daniel slowed his pace, trying to shake off his mood. He thought about Sebastian locked inside his terraced house on this beautiful summer evening, with his panic button and the police officer outside. He thought of the woman who'd carried a bag of pig's blood to central London in the hope of dousing a lawyer she'd never even met.

Named and shamed. Societal disapproval was no longer something it was possible to ignore. That disapproval could cost a job, a livelihood, even a life. Sebastian was still a young man, just twenty-one years old, yet he was being asked to atone for the child he had once been. It felt harsh to Daniel. He wouldn't like to be held to account for the child *he* had once been.

There were wooden tables outside the pub and lazy summer wasps grazed on the nectar of dried beer and wine. Inside, the large wooden space was cool and dark, and he blinked, waiting for his eyes to adjust to the changed light as he searched for her. At first he thought she hadn't arrived yet, even though he was about five minutes late, but then he saw her, sitting in the corner, glancing at a menu card.

The sight of her waiting for him lifted him. He tightened his stomach muscles as he walked towards her, wishing that they could put all their problems behind them and go home together. Meeting her like this felt like the early years, before they were married, both young lawyers meeting up in town. She was also still in her work clothes, a cream silk vest top and black linen trousers.

'Sorry I'm late,' he said. Automatically, he bent to kiss her cheek, noticing that she pulled away from him ever so slightly. He was warm after the walk. He took off his cufflinks and set them on the table, folding over his cuffs.

'Well . . . congratulations, my lady.' He watched her eyes crinkling at the corners in response. He reached across the table but paused when his fingers were an inch from hers. 'Let's get a drink and drink to you. Such amazing news.' He knew that they weren't here to celebrate her success, but he wanted to hold off the inevitable seriousness. The thought that the separation should continue filled him with a disorienting confusion and loneliness. He had let her down and now he needed to prove to her that their marriage still had a chance, that he wasn't the man full of darkness that she had described in the letter.

'Thank you. Not long until it's official,' she said, putting one hand over her mouth as if to suppress excitement. At least he had made her smile.

Unable to stop himself now, he took her hand. Her eyes met his and suddenly the excitement was gone and replaced by sadness.

'So, I understand there'll be a party at chambers to celebrate. Will you come?' She was talking quickly, and there was a tension in her face as if she, too, was trying to avoid the inevitable.

'Sure,' he said, even though a party at her chambers sounded awful, especially as things were between them. He didn't like parties at the best of times.

Looking down, just before she tugged her fingers from his, he saw that she was wearing her wedding ring again. Daniel didn't know if that was promising or a token gesture for tonight. He almost mentioned it, but decided against it, as the waiter came. They ordered drinks: wine for Rene, beer for him. She knew what she wanted to eat – a salad since it was so hot – and so he said he would have the same. He knew no matter what he ordered, he wouldn't want to eat it. Since he had been very small, when he was upset his gut shut down.

When their drinks came, Daniel chinked glasses with her.

'How's it going with Sebastian? I saw that case's just blown up.'

Staring into the dark eye of his beer, Daniel told her about the police leak and the threat to Sebastian's life, the fact that Frances's husband had now been arrested. The mainstream media had reported that Sebastian was a suspect but Rene had also seen some of the online content naming Sebastian as the Angel Killer.

'Just yesterday there was a bit of a furore outside our office too. Someone tried to splash me with pig's blood. I've been outed as Sebastian's lawyer.'

'Oh my God.'

'It was some random woman; she got arrested and I think they've got it under control now. You haven't ...' he'd been worried about this, 'had any kind of negative attention?'

'No, I haven't, but God that's awful. Right outside your office.'

'Crazy ...' Even though this subject was stressful for Daniel, he was happier talking about work than the painful subject of their relationship.

'Funnily, I actually referenced Sebastian in my application for the bench, and they asked me to speak about him in the interview,' she said, leaning towards him and lowering her voice.

'Really? What did they ask?'

'Well, they wanted an example of how I'd changed work practices to accommodate somebody. I spoke about how procedures at Sebastian's trial were completely changed ... to accommodate a child accused.'

'It's a good example to use.'

'And here you are, working with him again. I dug all that stuff out for the application.' Wistfully, Rene looked away, as if thinking of the trial that had brought them together. 'I remember that night, after the verdict came in; we went out to blow off some steam and you told me that Sebastian had confessed.'

Daniel blinked, nodded once.

'Such precociousness. Maybe that's not the right word.' She ran a hand through her hair. 'Strange for a child, and he was *such* a child – young for eleven – to be able to deceive so well. I mean, he even testified—'

'I know.' Daniel wasn't sure if it was the air-conditioned bar after his warm, brisk walk, but he felt a shiver on his skin.

'We wouldn't have put him on the stand if we'd known, of course.'

Rene's eyes changed, the green darkening, becoming flat and reflective. She parted her lips to speak and Daniel knew that what he had been apprehensive about all day was about to come. He pushed back his shoulders, as if to withstand what she had to say. Waiting for her words, he thought of standing in the cold sea at Tynemouth, where Minnie had taken him once or twice when he was a boy. He remembered standing thigh-deep in the icy ocean, trying to keep his balance as the surf hit him again and again.

'Anyway . . . I wanted some time on our own – to talk – just you and me, without interruptions – try and sort out where we go from here—'

Daniel felt his balance waver, a cold swell of fear lapping inside him.

'Like I said in my letter – we could both have expressed ourselves better, but that night . . . that conversation, if you could call it that, had been coming a long time.'

He swallowed, listening.

'I had been trying to tell you those things for a while . . . about needing more support, about feeling how heavy you are . . .' she was whispering.

Her eyes shone with tears, yet there was an awful finality there too that stole all the air from his lungs.

'Anyway, I think it's good for us both to have this space just now – see if that helps get some perspective back . . .'

'The space isn't good for me.' Fear of what she would say splashed inside him. He didn't know what to say to persuade her that they were better together, sorting out their problems at home. Apart, everything became even more complicated.

'Well, I was thinking, there are practicalities that might make it all more do-able.' Her manner now seemed pragmatic and cool, less of the emotion that seemed to be pulsing through him. 'It makes no sense you being at the flat in Bow when you're looking after Billy. There's no sense bringing him home and having to travel all the way back there at night.'

He stared at her, trying to comprehend, nursing a flare of hope inside him that she wanted him to move back home after all.

'I wondered if, until we sort things out properly, the person that's looking after Billy stays in Herne Hill. That way he has his own room, his friends, school nearby . . . and the other one of us will be at the flat in Bow. It's a great base for working in the city. It might work better, just sometimes if it suits us—'

Bravely, he replied: 'Surely, what would work best is if I just come home and then we can both look after him together like we used to.' He ran a hand over his face. 'I'm sorry about that night, but we can work it out—' He hoped he didn't sound as if he was pleading.

'This still gives each of us time with him, hopefully more positive time. And it gives us space, to see if things change—'

Had she even heard him? Change? Did she simply want him to be a better husband and father – or did she want a complete change? Divorce? Someone else entirely? As the thoughts pin-balled around his head, he said nothing, shifting in his seat.

'I think it's fair to say that none of the three of us are happy right now. This new arrangement means you and Billy can have more quality time together. It could be really important.' Rene took a bite of food. 'I mean . . . the other day when you went to the school to get him . . . I'd hoped it would go better, but, still, I think it was good for both of you—'

Daniel took a long sip of beer and then looked down at his food. She had come home to the broken vase and Billy fresh from tears, but at least they had made up. It could have been worse, if Daniel hadn't gone back upstairs to try again. He searched her face, trying to read how she was feeling.

'I know I lost my temper, but I think I turned it around at the end.' Daniel realised that he had to try harder to explain to Rene. If he shut down, as was his habit, he feared that all would be lost. Words tumbled from him. 'I tried, but he wouldn't listen, and then the vase got broken . . . I know I frightened him. I'm not proud of that.' He pushed his plate away and leaned towards her, lowering his voice. 'It scares me, sometimes,' he said.

'What does? Being a parent?' She laughed briefly, sadly.

'I get angry so quickly. He brings it out in me. Sometimes it's like looking at myself and that's hard.'

It also made him think about what it was in his make-up that made him so angry. He thought about Leila trying to track down his father.

'He knows how to push your buttons. You need to take a step back – realise that he's only playing up because he's lost his trust in us? He needs our support and love, not our anger.'

'Sometimes I forget he's a little boy—'

'Yes, *you do*—'

'Often it's like there's no line between the two of us. Sometimes it's as if I'm not reacting to him at all, but at some small version of myself. It frustrates me. I see myself in him, but at the same time . . .' Daniel paused, struggling to articulate how he felt, 'I don't know what he needs.'

'He needs a father. He needs *you*.'

'He told me he hated me the other weekend.'

'All kids say that . . .'

'Well—' Daniel picked up his fork and pushed at a piece of potato, a welt of feeling inside him '—I thought about taking him up to Brampton in the summer holidays. I mentioned it to him.'

'Minnie's old house?'

'Yeah, you know I've been meaning to sort it out, get it ready for sale again. I thought I could take him up there – father-son road trip – show him where I grew up—'

His words drifted off. Rene had not understood when he'd pulled out of the initial sale, and then over the years had been frustrated when he dithered with the needed repairs and delayed getting it on the market again. She didn't interfere – she seemed to know it was more than a house to him – but she'd made clear she didn't think he was being rational.

'I just thought it would be a chance for us—' again he began a sentence and let it hang. When he said *us* he didn't just mean Billy, he meant *us*, the *three* of them, his family.

'This is partly why I wanted to talk to you. I had hoped that this—' she met his eyes '—this *separation* – might bring you and

Billy closer. I thought it would give you more time together. You don't see just how much he needs you.'

'I don't want a separation.' Emotion trembled inside him. 'I'm sorry,' he whispered, 'for everything—' He'd felt so deeply lonely since they'd been apart. He cleared his throat, frightened that he was going to lose composure.

There's so much darkness in you, he remembered again from the letter. He could imagine how he'd been that night when she'd asked him to leave: aggressive, depressive. Believing she loved him all these years had helped him grow into a person that he could *almost* suffer to face in the mirror. At the same time he felt such a failure, for letting her down – she and Billy both. She needed him and he had failed her. He tried to imagine what she must have been going through all those years before she finally broke.

'You haven't dealt with what happened to you when you were a child.'

The expression in her eyes was kind but serious. He wondered how long she'd been waiting to tell him that.

'Maybe you should think about talking to someone about it—'

'Therapy?' He was unable to quell the hurt that flared in him. He *had talked to someone* about it: he'd talked to *her.* He almost told her about the other night when he'd sat up drinking gin, writing a letter to Minnie. He wondered if Rene might think that counted as therapy, although he doubted it.

'You have so much going for you – a family that loves you, a career you excel at – there's such richness, brightness in your life and you don't see it. You only see the shadow.'

He pressed his teeth together until his temples began to throb.

'Anyway, let's try this new routine for a while,' she continued, reasoned, calm, while he felt as if an ocean was crashing on the inside of his ribs. 'I'll stay at the flat when it's your time to be with Billy. We'll move around him instead of making him shunt between us. I think that'll do us all good. Does that sound okay?'

It was anything but okay, but Daniel felt he had no recourse to refuse. He lifted up his beer and drank deeply.

12

Daniel and Leila decided to move their meeting to the restaurant across the road from work, as neither of them had had a chance to eat lunch. Daniel was wary as the street outside his office seemed to be a lot busier than normal, but unlike the day before, there were no protesters waiting to harangue him. Daniel hoped that the attention was waning because of Jon Thompson's arrest.

It was delightfully cool inside the sushi restaurant, vigorous air conditioning and sleek metallic surfaces. The other diners were a mixture of workers from the nearby offices. Even though it was a transit hub, this district had a wide range of offices, from lawyers and corporate blocks, to creative arts and design.

They chose their dishes quickly, so they could get down to work. Leila was going to brief Daniel on Jon Thompson. He hoped Cambridgeshire Police were on the brink of charging him with his wife's murder. Leila had a small, hardback notebook that she laid on the counter. Before she began to list off what she had found out, Daniel grasped his chance to ask if she had made any more progress in the search for his father.

'I wondered how things are developing with that personal matter of mine? Any further forward?'

'Yes, and no. I made some progress with Robert Cobain. I told you he was with your mother on and off for a couple of years before you were born?'

'Yeah, and left when she was pregnant. Just the kind of guy I imagined when I started all this. My mum was an addict, so I wasn't imagining that my father was anything great, don't worry.'

Daniel was forty-six years old – he didn't need a father figure now. He'd managed this long without one. What he wanted was some kind of resolution, he wanted to close the circle, to fill the gaps in his history. He wanted to understand himself.

'Well, I managed to track down Robert Cobain.'

Just a little, Daniel held his breath.

'He's still alive, but he moved to New Zealand in the early noughties—'

'Okay,' frowning, exhaling, Daniel nodded. His potential father couldn't get much further away, but it would be easy enough to contact him.

'Apparently – this friend of Aunt Jacqueline's told me this – the reason he gave for abandoning your mother was that he didn't believe the child – *you* – were his. Your mother was alone and penniless, and so she moved in with her sister, your aunt, until after you were born.'

Daniel said nothing, absorbing what she was telling him.

'It doesn't mean you're *not* his, but I want to dig a little deeper. I have a couple of leads into Steven's identity.'

'Steven Something,' Daniel nodded. Quietly, he thanked her. 'How much do I owe you for all this? I haven't given you a penny yet and you've been working on it for ages. I must be due an interim bill—'

'I'm keeping a tab, don't worry,' she winked at him.

'Good, I'm glad.' He put one elbow on the counter. 'What about *your* family? Have you actually been to Iran?' There were so many questions he had always wanted to ask her – about her upbringing, her time in the army and the police.

'Only when I was little. Went with my dad to see my grandma before she died.'

'Whereabouts is your family from?'

'Mazandaran – it's north of Tehran, on the Caspian Sea.'

'What was it like?'

'I was too little. All I remember were the mountains, all covered in snow.'

Leila chose a small saucer of what looked like seaweed from the bar and put it in front of her. She was better with chopsticks than he was. Every now and then as she brought the food to her mouth her bare arm would brush against his. He was startled to be very aware of it, his skin resonating to the touch.

He wanted to ask her more about her life, found himself fascinated by her. Even though her outfit was unremarkable, a loose linen top over black khakis, she was striking with her dark sweep of hair pulled back. Daniel thought that none of the other customers would guess the richness of her experience. They had grown close through working together and there was a sense of energy between them that, at another time in his life, he might have thought was attraction.

Wrestling a piece of cucumber, he wondered if the energy he

sensed between them was real or imagined, conjured from the restless flux of his family situation. He had always been faithful to Rene and had no desire to share his life with anyone else. He hadn't cheated on any of his previous girlfriends, but he hadn't been in a real long-term relationship until Rene. Before Rene he'd rarely been single, but he would date only for a year or two, no longer, living together only briefly if at all. He and Rene had been friends and colleagues before they got together, but right from the beginning it had felt different with her.

'Where's this relationship going?' his friend Simon had asked him about Rene, firing another vicious shot at the squash court wall.

Daniel had never been able to explain how deep and sudden his feelings for Rene had been, but he remembered telling Simon, 'It just feels like a done deal.'

With Rene, but no one else before her, he had felt immediately settled on a course, as if he didn't need to look any further. It had felt portentous, somehow meant. Within months of starting a relationship with Rene his whole life changed, but there had been no doubt in his mind. Moving to South London, getting married, having Billy – that traditional momentum had swept him along and not once had he wanted to challenge it.

He brought the conversation back around to work. Leila had new intelligence about the Frances Owen murder investigation.

'There's still no compelling physical evidence from the scene of the crime: no fingerprints were recovered, not even belonging to Frances Owen—'

Daniel frowned. 'How're you getting this stuff, now that your pal Murphy has been sacked?'

'I thought it would be difficult, but I managed to make a connection with another member of the Major Investigation Team – another DC who I worked with. She and I were posted to the same police station in Brixton just after we qualified.'

'I'm amazed by your connections,' Daniel said, smiling.

'Murphy and I were trainees together. I knew him pretty well, so it was easy. I feel for him through all this—

'Anyway, some more information from forensics – Frances's office had been scrupulously wiped down, with acetone after her murder. Traces of that chemical were found. It suggests what we'd discussed before, that significant preparation went into the murder and that whoever killed Frances had time for a meticulous clean afterwards. There was *some* circumstantial evidence recovered from the office, however. The police have forensic evidence from the office that links to both Sebastian and Frances's husband,' Leila said, dabbing her mouth with a napkin. 'Forensics have found fibres from Sebastian's college carpet, and from Sebastian's clothing in the room. They've also found hair samples belonging to JT.'

'But that's to be expected, no?'

'Of course – Sebastian was in her office attending tutorials, quite legitimately, and JT was there frequently to see his wife. Like I said to you before – he was in and out of that building all the time.'

Daniel shook his head. 'Let's not call him "JT": makes him sound too innocuous.'

'He doesn't sound like a terribly nice man.'

Swallowing a mouthful of rice, Daniel raised an eyebrow. 'Funny, that's what Sebastian said about him.'

'I learned something very significant about Frances's marriage when I spoke to her sister, Margaret—'

'The one from the press conference? The journalist?'

'Correct. She's lovely. Used to work for the Screws of the World before they went under. She does a lot of online stuff just now – but she told me two things that interested me . . . one was that Jon had been violent to Frances in the past.'

Daniel put down his chopsticks.

'Margaret told me about one incident she heard about from her sister. Frances said Jon pushed her when they were in the bedroom. She fell over the bed and broke her wrist in two places, and then lied about it, telling others that she tripped over the dog. I don't have to tell you – you know yourself – the eight-stage homicide timeline . . . a partner who is abusive has a high chance of going on to kill—'

'Yes, that's significant.'

'I found out something else . . . doesn't mean he's a murderer . . . but he took the family pet, a Beagle, to the vet to be euthanised *three days* after Frances was found dead.'

'Artemis,' Daniel said, remembering the dog's name from Sebastian's police interview. It wasn't funny, but he laughed lightly, 'I suppose it does mean he's a dog murderer.'

Leila shrugged. 'Well, it gave me pause for thought. Choosing *that moment* to get the family pet put down is strange. It's just the time when most people struggling with loss would rely on a pet . . . more . . . or at least have had enough of death.'

'So you think he's guilty?'

'Well, one thing about Jon Thompson ... he might have lied about when his plane landed and cruelly had the dog put down a few days after Frances was murdered, but ... he's left-handed. It's not huge evidence, but still, Frances's murderer was most likely right-handed. What about Sebastian – left or right-handed?'

'I'm pretty sure he's right-handed,' Daniel said, visualising Sebastian as a child and an adult. 'How do you know Jon Thompson's a leftie?'

'I saw a photograph of him signing a university agreement.'

'He could have got someone else to kill her. Hired someone.'

'You want it to be him, don't you?'

'Let's just say I'm glad I'm not representing him.' Daniel returned to his sushi.

'How does that work, anyway, I've always wanted to know.'

'How does what work?'

'Well, I'm an ex-cop. We don't get defence lawyers—'

Daniel laughed uncomfortably.

'I mean it. We don't ... do you ever refuse to represent a client, for example if you think they're guilty?'

'Um ... no. I'd starve if I did. And I don't choose clients – mostly they choose me ... It's not my job to judge; it's my job to *defend*, that's how I earn my living.'

'But are there people you just wouldn't defend?'

'Um ... it's about the case really. I mean if I really don't like a client then, yeah, I probably wouldn't work with them, but that happens surprisingly rarely. What is more common, and perhaps more unsettling, is that often people are really nice and you really get on well with them, but they've committed a horrific crime.' Frowning, Daniel looked into Leila's face. Her brown eyes were huge, watching him as if trying to comprehend.

She shrugged and returned to business. 'The police are still working through the electronic evidence. What's interesting is that a number of staff from the Faculty of Classics report that Professor Thompson—' Leila put her hand on Daniel's thigh and leaned into him slightly, 'is that better than JT?'

'Thompson's better,' Daniel said, glad when her hand left his leg. Even though he didn't think he'd encouraged it, and wouldn't act on it, thinking there was an attraction between them filled him with an inky guilt.

'Well, staff report that Professor Thompson stormed into the Classics building just over a week before Frances was murdered and several colleagues heard them arguing in her office.'

'That could have been the last time they spoke. He must have flown overseas not long after that.' Daniel made a mental note. 'Do we know what the argument was about?'

Leila's shoulders rose and fell. 'Well, that's less clear. Witness statements focused on the row – hearing raised voices, Thompson's anger and aggression – but there is speculation that Jonathan Thompson had become aware of his wife's affair with Sebastian, which was well-known in the faculty.'

'According to the correspondence the police found, the affair would have been over months before then. It doesn't really follow that he had just found out.'

'Husbands and wives,' Leila said, sage-like, arching one of

her neat brows, 'they don't always communicate as much as you would think.'

Daniel half-smiled. He was sure Leila wasn't married. She probably had a boyfriend, though; as that thought crawled, unedifying, into his mind, he reproached himself again.

'And wasn't Thompson supposed to be unfaithful too – numerous affairs while he was overseas? Why the outrage if he was at it too?'

'Yes, Professor Thompson is reputed to have had numerous affairs not just while he was overseas, also in Cambridge, with not one, but two of his PhD students. Who knows though. It did make me wonder if Frances hooked up with Sebastian as a way to get back at her husband—'

'Frances reported to the police that she was stalked – this was after she and Sebastian broke up. I wonder if the stalking – flowers and phone calls – made Jon Thompson think that the affair was continuing—' Daniel mused.

'Possibly. I know the police are trying to gather evidence on who might have been stalking Frances, but that's very difficult now she's dead.'

'They missed their chance,' Daniel said, severely. 'Who knows, they might even have saved her life if that had been investigated properly at the time.'

Leila nodded. 'For me – probably for the police as well – what is most damning about Jon Thompson is that he lied about his arrival time into the country. The police did well to catch him out on that, by checking passenger lists.'

'Do you know what Jon Thompson's excuse is for lying to the

police – about when he arrived in the country? Surely that's fairly damning.'

'It's thin,' Leila wiped her fingers on her napkin and twisted it before placing it on her plate. 'He says he went straight to his office from the plane and then fell asleep there. Jet lagged and confused, mixing up his dates—' She rolled her eyes.

'Possible?' Daniel mused.

'No one's convinced. More probable is that he's guilty and lied to get himself out of trouble. But let's say he *was* confused; I'm sure finding out his wife had been murdered while he was (supposedly) asleep in his office would have brought everything into sharp focus. Yet he continued to insist to police that his flight arrived a day later than it did – until they found out the truth for themselves. Ultimately, Thompson is my key suspect.'

'I was surprised that DCI Lloyd *actually told me* they had arrested Thompson, and why, but I think he feels guilty about the leak. Because of what's happened to Sebastian I can see them trying to put pressure on Thompson now, build a case around him—'

'Fit him up?' Leila raised an eyebrow. 'He's a good fit – apart from being a leftie, of course.'

Daniel shrugged.

'It would be good to see if Jon Thompson turns up on the CCTV. The police are working their way through CCTV from campus and that's what I'm most interested in at the moment.'

'No results yet though?'

'Nothing significant. They have Professor Owen as the first to enter her building on the morning of her death. She opened the door with a key and locked it behind her. She is early enough that the killer would have had time to murder her and clean up afterwards. The next entry was by the cleaner, who found her body. There is no record of anyone else entering the building since it was locked up by the janitor the night before. There is no sign of a break-in, although entry through the windows out of sight of the cameras has not been ruled out . . . Some areas of campus have patchy CCTV coverage and then there is duplication in other areas, like shared entrances, so it is taking the police some time to work through it.'

'I wondered about other premises,' Daniel interjected. 'The police often just get the official CCTV, but the area is covered by cameras owned by a number of premises. That was the case with Sebastian's trial actually . . . there was evidence on CCTV that I got from shops that had a view of the park; they weren't included in disclosure from the police, but they revealed more than the official street cameras.'

'Us stupid cops, huh?' Again she raised a teasing eyebrow.

'That's not what I meant. Is there anything near to the Faculty of Classics that you think covers the same area and would have cameras? Get a different angle?'

'No, it's all university buildings. One of the theories is that whoever killed Frances Owen entered the building the *evening before*, and failed to leave when it was locked up for the night, so in going through the CCTV the police are also trying to account for everyone who enters and exits, rather than just spotting a key suspect or intruder.'

Sighing, knowing that they would have to wait, Daniel waved for the bill.

'I forgot to mention,' Leila said, 'because there is so little physical evidence, there's a big push right now on trying to find the murder weapon, and with it the blood and other matter from the office. That forensic material would probably identify the killer.'

'Do they have leads?'

'No. They've been dredging parts of the Cam and looking into whether either of the suspects – both Jon Thompson and Sebastian – has a lock-up or garage where it might be stored.'

'Keep me posted.'

'I'm heading back to Cambridge tomorrow,' Leila said, reaching for her purse. Daniel waved that he would get it. 'Meeting a distant contact of Sebastian's. Someone I wanted to speak to when I first went up there, and now they're willing to talk – a friend of one of Sebastian's ex-girlfriend's—'

'Be careful it's genuine,' Daniel said, as the server took his card. 'They might be coming forward as a result of Sebastian's identity being leaked online—'

'Somehow, I don't think so,' Leila said.

13

The next morning, Daniel emerged from Liverpool Street Station into a gust of smog and heat. It was nearly nine o'clock, later than he normally arrived at work.

The papers on display at the mouth of the station all bore a photograph of Ben, just as they had years ago when Sebastian was on trial. As if in response to Sebastian's identity being revealed, and the chaos unfolding in Cambridge and Islington, there had been a news alert from the 'Justice for Ben' campaign looking for fresh evidence, asking people to come forward with information. Daniel thought it seemed neatly timed. The newspapers could report this piece, but not the underlying story that Sebastian was the little boy who'd been tried for Ben's murder, who'd also been questioned in relation to Frances Owen's brutal killing.

Daniel paused at the newspaper stand to look at the photograph of Ben's mother, Madeline Stokes. She looked a lot different than she had ten years ago, but was still recognisable. As he had then, Daniel felt for her. He remembered Madeline walking to the witness box to testify about discovering her son missing from the pavement outside their house where he had been riding his bike back and forth. She'd walked across the courtroom, shackled by grief, her hair pulled back to show a thin face and sunken eyes.

Years of campaigning after Sebastian's acquittal meant that Madeline now seemed more robust and engaged. She had put on weight and her hair was now almost completely grey. She called for the evidence from the original trial to be re-examined. Since the murder of Stephen Lawrence, double jeopardy – or being tried for the same offence twice – was allowed in murder cases, but having new meaningful evidence was key to launching a retrial.

Daniel knew that there had been no legal wizardry at the first trial and doubted that new evidence would be available now. There had simply been insufficient evidence to convict Sebastian. A lack of forensic evidence and key witness testimony about an unidentified adult seen near the spot where Ben died introduced a special defence of incrimination. This had meant that Rene, as Sebastian's barrister, had been able to create enough reasonable doubt in the jury's mind and they chose to acquit.

'Justice for Ben' was subtle in their new campaign – there was no specific mention of Sebastian.

'I won't rest until Ben's murderer is brought to justice,' Madeline said in her statement. 'Years go by, but someone killed my son. I wouldn't be surprised if he has gone on to kill other innocent ones.'

Daniel had a full day of meetings and mid-afternoon discovered that Sebastian had called him twice. It was almost five before he managed to call him back, standing before the big windows, looking out onto Shoreditch, the awnings of pop-up bars and restaurants already crammed with customers.

'How're things going?'

'I had to press my personal alarm today.'

Daniel frowned as he waited to hear what had happened. One or two campaigners were still showing interest in his office – a young couple who held up a banner that read CRIMINAL DEFENCE IS CRIMINAL, which Daniel found laughable.

'I was just getting lunch in the kitchen. I knew that another big group had gathered outside ... I could see them on the pavement. They shut out the light from the kitchen—'

Daniel remembered that the kitchen in the Crolls' Islington townhouse was in the basement, visible from the pavement via a basement window.

'The police were there, so I tried to ignore it, but then – God ...'

Daniel placed his fingertips on the window pane.

'—It just came out of nowhere. A brick just shattered the kitchen window; I was eating a sandwich and suddenly I was showered with glass—'

'Oh, Sebastian, I'm sorry. I had the feeling that things had eased off since Frances's husband was arrested. We've had smaller numbers near our office since then.'

'Oh, they did ease off, but it seems they're back with a vengeance.'

Daniel wondered if 'Justice for Ben's new campaign was making an impact. 'What happened? Did the police—'

'It was awful. With the window broken, I could hear all the noise from the street. The people on the pavement, they just seemed *right there*. I thought they were going to climb inside, so I pressed my alarm. The brick was lying in the middle of the kitchen floor, wrapped in a piece of paper that said, "murderer".' Sebastian's voice thickened.

'Did the police get the guy?'

'No, he got away; they arrested someone else that had tried to get in the front door. They've taken the brick. They say there might be prints on it—'

'That's good.' Daniel imagined that intrusion would have been more frightening than if a window above street level had been smashed. He remembered the townhouse well, with its flagstones and hallway, and winding staircase. The street where it sat was normally quiet and sedate, but the lack of even a small front garden meant that the groups of campaigners on the pavement outside would seem scarily close.

'Where are you now?'

'Still at home, in my bedroom. I'm going crazy; I spend so much time here. I've cleaned up the kitchen, my father's organised some guys to fix the window and they're doing that now.'

'I know it doesn't seem like it, but this *will* get better.'

'I hope you're right.'

Daniel worked late. Slowly, one by one, all of his colleagues said goodnight. He called home to speak to Billy before he went to bed, feeling an ache inside him as Billy excitedly told him all his news. He'd been the only one in the class to get full marks for his spelling test, so had been allowed to take the class mascot home overnight: a stuffed badger. It was a privilege and Billy felt proud, which Daniel was pleased about as he hoped that it signalled a change in how he was relating to his teachers and the other kids. But Daniel wasn't there, to see the badger and tuck him in with it.

Trying to push it from his mind as he finished up his work, he thought again about what Leila had told him about Jon Thompson: known to have been violent towards his wife, known to have lied about when he arrived in the country, but left-handed, although that didn't rule out him hiring someone else to kill Frances.

The sun went down and the city-scape outside changed to sparkling lights and illuminated buildings. Tired, but dreading going back to the flat in Bow, Daniel began to gather together his things, wondering about calling in on The Crown on the way home.

The office always felt strange with everyone gone. Harvey, Hunter and Steele had a whole floor in the building and the glass office partitions meant that he could see just how empty it was, the only sound the buzz of the lighting.

Daniel switched off the lamp over his desk, picked up his phone and headed for the stairs.

Perhaps it was because he was alone in the building, but he felt strangely unnerved.

The security guard opened the door to let Daniel outside. No welcoming committee at this hour – no angry group with placards. Daniel wished the security guard goodnight.

He didn't have any cash, and, because he was thinking about going to The Crown, he headed down a side street to the ATM. Despite the streetlights, this road – with its cobbled alleyways, overflowing dumpsters and dank, urine-smelling corners – was always in shadow.

Daniel wasn't aware of anyone behind him. He put his card into the machine and took out fifty pounds. As he was sliding the cash into his wallet, he heard someone say:

'D'you have the time?'

About to reply, Daniel spun round just as the person hit him in the face. His wallet fell from his grasp and the cash fanned out onto the pavement. He felt his left eye and cheekbone swell and bent over, in shock, hand to his face. Before he could react, or even call out, the man hit him in the stomach.

Nausea and pain washed through him. Daniel managed to throw a couple of punches back, feeling adolescent, glancing a blow off the man's shoulder. Adrenalin staggered his senses. Everything seemed so close-up: a sharp scent, the blur of the man's build and clothing – he was tall, wearing black casual gear, a hoodie pulled over his head.

Daniel was just aware of the man bending to the pavement. Cash in hand, the hooded figure shoved Daniel, hard, right back into the ATM. As he was being pushed, Daniel was sure that he heard the man say:

'Keep your mouth shut.'

Panting, Daniel felt his knees buckle for a moment. Hips against the wall he bent over, as if he'd just finished a race. 'What the fuck—'

Fingertips to his eyebrow, there was blood. He felt as if he had receded back into his childhood. It had been that long since he'd been hit.

14

Two days later, Daniel was in the Central Criminal Court, where he'd been attending an appeal hearing for one of his clients. He felt self-conscious as, for the first time since he'd lived in Cumbria with Minnie, he had a black eye.

A passer-by who had witnessed his assault had called the police, and they had arrived within five or ten minutes – a special task force that dealt specifically with street robberies. The police had taken Daniel in the patrol car, looping around Liverpool Street, to try and identify his attacker. Even as he was asked to view CCTV, Daniel knew it would be fruitless. He hadn't got a good enough look at the person who had assaulted him.

He was about to leave the cool, marble interior of the Old Bailey when he got a call from Leila, asking to meet about information she had gathered on Sebastian's case. As she wasn't far from St Paul's, Daniel suggested they meet in the Old Bailey, and spoke to a security guard about using one of the small conference rooms off the main hall.

Daniel's firm had received a few online threats because of Sebastian's case. As a defence lawyer, Daniel was accustomed to enmity. In the past, particularly when defending clients that had been members of gangs, he had been threatened and had once received a suspicious package, delivered to the office, which turned out to be just a hoax. The furore over Sebastian seemed relentless and more fatiguing because it was mostly alive online, an unseen threat. The police had managed to shut down many of the accounts that had been particularly threatening to Sebastian, but more seemed to reappear in their place, like electronic weeds, spreading and reseeding despite attempts to eradicate them.

It made Daniel worry about Rene, and he'd texted to make sure she still hadn't been targeted, as Sebastian's one-time barrister.

'No, I haven't had any threats, online or otherwise,' she said. 'Maybe by moving to the bench I've slipped under the radar.'

During the trial, Daniel's role as Sebastian's solicitor had also garnered the most attention. It had been Daniel not Rene who'd sat day after day, holding the little boy's hand in court, and so Daniel had been targeted: *You've got blood on your hands. The little bastard should fry.*

Daniel texted Leila the location of the meeting room and she joined him in there within a few minutes. It was a small, windowless conference room, with only a table and four chairs.

'Oh my God, what happened to you?' she asked as soon as she entered the room.

Feeling himself blush, Daniel said, 'I got . . . mugged the other day, just outside the office.'

'No way. Was it more of those campaigner nutters?'

'Dunno. Probably not. It was at the cash machine. They got fifty quid.'

Does it look that bad? Daniel was about to ask, about his eye, before stopping himself.

'I'm going to put all this in the report for you,' Leila said, taking a seat at the table, 'but I just wanted to keep you up to speed.' She fanned herself briefly with her notebook, still flushed from the heat of the day.

'And this is about Sebastian?'

She nodded. 'When you first sent me to Cambridge, and I spoke to Sebastian's drama friends, I'd heard that Sebastian had an ex-girlfriend called Sarah Doyle and I was keen to speak to her—'

'So you managed to meet her?'

'No, I still haven't managed to speak to Sarah, but I was able to talk to Sarah's close friend, Dania – an Italian student still studying at Cambridge. She told me that Sarah transferred to another university shortly after her relationship with Sebastian ended.'

Sensing there was a story there, Daniel sat back in his chair to listen, crossing an ankle over his knee. Leila spoke quickly, her large eyes seeming almost black in the dimly lit room.

'Sarah and Sebastian dated during first year, so it's been two to three years since they were together. I still want to speak to her in person, but I need to look into which university she transferred to. Her friend wasn't sure. Sarah was looking at a number of options when they lost touch.'

'Why did she transfer?'

'I think it was a combination of the stress of Cambridge, and her thing with Sebastian. She studied at Trinity, not far from Sebastian's Magdalene College, and they were both Classics students together. Dania said Sebastian and Sarah were just friends at first, but Sebastian wanted more. By the sound of things, he pursued her quite heavily and she must've relented because they *were* together, in a relationship, for a short period, no longer than three months. But then Sarah ended it—'

Leila locked eyes with Daniel. 'Sarah told her friend that there was something about Sebastian that frightened her. Dania didn't go into details, but said that Sarah told Sebastian she didn't want to see him any more, even as friends. The thing is that Sebastian wouldn't accept that and he began to stalk Sarah—'

'Did she report it?'

'Not to the police, but to University Services. They did investigate it, but—' her sentence trailed off as she shook her head sadly. 'It was incessant letters, flowers, following her to and from class and turning up when she was out socialising . . .'

'She was sure it was Sebastian—' Daniel said, thinking out loud.

'The way Dania told the story, it was definitely Sebastian. It was just that he wouldn't leave her alone, there like a shadow whenever she turned around.'

'No action was taken?'

Leila sighed. 'That's not entirely surprising. There are examples of worse complacency that I can think of in recent university history. Women have been assaulted, raped and university courts have done nothing. I think in this case the university didn't regard the behaviour as threatening, even though Sarah perceived it to be—'

Daniel frowned.

'Shortly after that, Sarah transferred. I suppose it irritates me that they didn't take her more seriously . . . It was something I came up against in the army.'

Leila's face was expressionless, but Daniel took note. He wondered what she meant and if she was reading something from her own situation into Sarah's harassment. He almost asked her about it, then decided against it. Did she mean that, as a member of the Royal Military Police, she had been involved in investigations where institutions rallied to the detriment of individuals – women – in their command; or did she mean that she'd been sexually harassed?

'What do *you* make of it all?' he asked instead.

Leila shrugged, turning one of her hands upwards on the table. 'I don't know, but I thought it was an interesting story. Dania's a contact I found myself, just from asking around about Sebastian, but I wonder if the police are also aware of the story.'

Daniel said nothing. As far as he knew, the police were still focused on Jon Thompson. He knocked twice on the table to signify that the meeting was over. There was the sound of heels on the marble flagstones outside as lawyers walked back and forth.

'Oh, and this is just random, but you had asked,' Leila said, standing. 'I found out what happened to Sebastian's mother—'

'Right?' Daniel raised his eyebrows. 'Tell me. I didn't feel able to press Sebastian any further. I knew his mother. Sad that she died so young—'

'There was a post-mortem after it was noted as a suspicious death. It was finally ruled suicide, but frankly I was shocked when I read the report.'

'How so?'

'The ruling of suicide surprised me: there was a history of violence in the home—'

'That's correct.' Daniel had read the family case-conference reports, confirming not only that Kenneth had been physically abusive to Charlotte, but had once thrown her down the stairs, causing her to lose a pregnancy. Even in comparison to Daniel's own upbringing, Sebastian's family had been deeply troubled. It had been one of the main reasons why Sebastian's plight had resonated with Daniel.

'So ... there were a number of domestic assaults on record over the years – no charges brought, but police were called to the home.'

'Sounds about right from what I remember.'

'Well, when Charlotte died, both her husband and son were in the house. She died in the bath. The cause of death was drowning. Toxicology showed that she had ingested benzodiazepines—'

Daniel remembered Charlotte popping Valium throughout the trial, but he'd also read in the Case-Conference Reports that Charlotte had forced the infant Sebastian to take benzodiazepines during one of her suicide attempts, in an effort to *take him with her.*

'So that makes sense,' Leila continued. 'Overdose, drowning blah blah – but when you read the post-mortem report, Charlotte had *bruising* on her neck.'

Again, Daniel remembered that Charlotte frequently wore polo necks to hide the bruises on her neck. As a little boy, Sebastian had shown Daniel how his father would hold his mother by the throat. It had been chilling to watch such a young child demonstrate the act.

'Are you saying you think Ken Croll murdered her?'

'Well, I'm just saying, it struck me as odd. I had to investigate a couple of suicides in Afghanistan when I was in the RMP – both of them very complex. Suffice to say that the verdict in this case surprised me. If it had been up to me, I would have put it to an inquest—'

Cracking a smile, Daniel said, 'And you would probably have been right – you're always right.'

Just then Daniel's phone vibrated on the table. It was Billy's school.

Half-turning from Leila, Daniel bit his lip as he waited to hear what had happened – whether Billy had been stealing again or running out of class. Today wasn't his day to have Billy overnight and Rene had to be in court.

'Mr Hunter, Billy's got a fever and the nurse thinks he should go home. I wonder if someone could come and collect him?'

Daniel inhaled sharply and looked at his watch.

'Of course,' he said. 'It'll take me forty-five minutes or so to get there—'

'Problem?' Leila asked, picking up her bag and jacket, opening the door onto the busy central hall.

'My son. He's not well. I've got to pick him up from school.'

'Is he alright?'

'Dunno, they said a fever. Little kids are always getting random things.'

Leila smiled in a sweet way – an expression he had never seen before.

'How old is he now? Billy, right?'

'Seven.'

'My God, how time flies. I just see that picture on your desk from when he was a baby. You forget that they keep growing.'

'Yeah, he's not a baby any longer, that's for sure.'

'And both of you have got big jobs – it's not easy,' Leila said, pursing her lips as if she understood.

'Well, it's not easy, particularly at the moment. Rene and I have separated.' Even as he said it, folding his jacket over his briefcase in preparation for the journey on the Tube, Daniel wasn't sure why he'd shared that information.

There was a flicker of acknowledgement in Leila's eyes. 'I'm so sorry.'

They were both headed to St Paul's but Leila told him to go on ahead, said she had a call to make.

'Just to let you know,' she said before she parted, 'but I'm going to try and track down Sarah Doyle. You know I like finding people. I'd like to hear about Sebastian from her ... better than going through a friend.'

'Great.' Daniel nodded and waved.

The smell of school dinner still lingered in the corridor when Daniel arrived at Billy's school: sweet, overcooked carbohydrate that he identified as institutional. As a child he had smelt it in social work canteens. As an adult, the smell was familiar from secure units, care homes and prisons.

Billy was hunched over and despondent, sitting on a chair in the nurse's office, his feet unable to touch the ground.

'Hey, little man.'

'You took *ages*.'

'I'm sorry, I got here as fast as I could.' Daniel placed his palm on Billy's forehead and immediately felt a raging temperature.

'I've given him Junior Paracetamol,' the nurse said. 'Lots of fluids, early bed.'

Standing up to go, Billy noticed Daniel's eye. 'What's that? Is it a bruise?'

'I bumped into something,' Daniel said, a conspiratorial nod to the nurse as they left.

'Does it hurt, Daddy?'

'No.' Daniel's pride hurt more than anything.

Outside the building, he offered his hand and Billy took it. It felt cold despite his fever.

'How do you feel?'

'Okay.'

As they approached the house, Daniel broached the subject of going back to Bow – he'd left some files there that he needed for work tomorrow.

'Is it okay if we go back to the flat tonight?'

'I suppose so.'

'We'll just pop home and pick up your things, then.'

'Is Mummy at work?'

'Yeah, she's in court.'

By the time they emerged from Mile End Tube Station, nearly an hour later, Billy's face was grey with fatigue. Daniel picked him up and immediately felt him curl into his arms, putting his face in the space between Daniel's neck and shoulder.

'My skin hurts.'

'It's okay, don't worry. You'll feel better soon.'

There was no reply and twice Daniel stopped on the walk to check that Billy was still awake. The burden felt precious; this a chance to be close. As they approached the flat, Daniel became aware of Billy's forehead burning onto the skin of his neck. He really wasn't well, and Daniel regretted taking him on the journey to the flat. He carried him carefully upstairs – even unlocking the door without rousing him.

'Are we here already?'

'I think you slept most of the way. Do you want some dinner?'

Billy shook his head and then, as if the action hurt, put a hand on top of his head. He didn't have a blanket, like they had at home, and instead took out a large clean bath towel and laid it over Billy on the sofa before making toast and tea for them both. He changed out of his work clothes into jeans and a T-shirt and took out Billy's pyjamas.

After just a mouthful of toast, Billy's pale face was starting to turn green. Daniel carried him to the bathroom and then to bed.

'Will you read me a story, Daddy?'

But Daniel didn't have any children's books here – just a dictionary of legal definitions, a *London A-Z* and an old copy of *Runner's World*.

'Sure.'

Daniel lay down beside Billy, kicking his feet up onto the edge of the bed.

'Once upon a time there was a little boy called Billy, and he was seven years old and he . . . lived on a farm with some goats and a sheepdog called Blitz, who could be fierce but liked to have his ears tickled; and a pen full of chickens that smelled funny—'

Billy was already asleep, suddenly unconscious in the crook of Daniel's arm. He wasn't sure where he had been going with that story anyway – at what point Minnie would turn up, or indeed Tricia the social worker, or his mum asking for fags.

'Goodnight.' Daniel kissed the hot brow. 'I love you, Billy. Very much.'

15

Even though he wasn't looking forward to it, Daniel told Rene that he would attend the party in her honour at Heathcote Street Chambers. Billy was being looked after by his grandparents in Barnes, who would pick him up from school and keep him overnight. He was feeling better, thankfully; by the time he'd woken up in Daniel's flat, the fever had broken and he'd had two bowls of cereal for breakfast.

Daniel hated parties, especially lawyer parties, but he wondered if this would be an opportunity for him and Rene to sort things out between them. He could celebrate with her, and maybe go home with her, knowing they would have the house to themselves? Thinking about it, he tried to suppress the flare of hope inside him.

But that was for later this evening. Now, he was headed to the Central Family Court, to assist Michele Atkinson at her custody hearing for Jackson. Michele had persisted in saying that she couldn't afford a barrister, and so would represent herself, as her ex-husband, Greg, intended to do. Michele had accepted Daniel's offer of being her instructing solicitor, on a pro bono basis.

A block away from the family court, he spotted Michele

hiding in a doorway, finishing a cigarette. He reached her just as she crushed the butt under the heel of her shoe. He saw her gaze drift to his bruised eye as soon as she turned around, but then, perhaps out of politeness, she didn't mention it.

'I feel sick to my stomach,' she said, by way of hello. 'I wish I didn't have to face him.'

Daniel let his hand rest on her thin arm. 'Think of it as us facing him together. Like I said in my email, I can pass you suggestions for you to present to the magistrate—' He was here pro bono and had done everything he could in terms of lodging her pre-trial documents, despite the furore over Sebastian's case stealing his attention.

Michele nodded. 'It's just having to see him again that makes me sick – looking him in the eye. I suppose I could look at you instead of looking at Greg.' Even though the nerves made her face seem stiff and severe, she half-smiled. 'Not a bad trade off, I suppose.'

'Come on.' Daniel laughed at the compliment as he steered her towards the entrance. He could feel the bones of her shoulders through her summer jacket.

'You said you have a little boy,' Michele said when they were inside the corridor. 'D'you love his mum?'

'I do,' Daniel said. Despite everything that was going on with him and Rene just now, that fact was immutable.

The courtroom was quiet and the gallery empty when Daniel took his seat. Greg sat at the front of the court, with Michele on the other side of the room. There was the usual ritual

of business and then they all stood and sat as the magistrate entered.

Daniel took a seat at Michele's table, laying out a legal pad
and a pen, ready to advise when things got going. Glancing
across the courtroom, Daniel saw Greg. Even though Michele's
ex-husband was sitting down, Daniel perceived that he was a
short man, with a thick neck and triangular upper body that
suggested he worked out. The seams of his grey suit jacket
strained to contain the muscular body within. Greg was
nervously looking over notes that he had written on a pad
before him.

Beside him, Michele's spine was curved in dread. She kept her
face turned from Greg at all times. Daniel didn't try to reassure
her. He was not here as her representative; she had to do it all
by herself, albeit with the occasional pointers from him.

Judge Janice Palmer convened the session. She acknowledged
that both parents, the applicant and respondent, were representing themselves, as neither could afford a barrister and did
not qualify for legal aid. Rubbing a hand over his mouth, Daniel
leaned forward to hear what would happen. He had done all he
could, by making sure that the police disclosure was there in
time for the hearing. This was now presented to the magistrate
by the clerk of court as part of a number of submissions. The
Cafcass officer had written a report detailing violence in the
home, but noting that it was directed at Michele and not Jackson.
There were witness statements from neighbours who said they
had heard assaults through the thin walls, and Jackson crying
Mummy but no allegations of abuse involving the child directly.

In addition to ensuring that police disclosure was available for the hearing, Daniel had also submitted an advance request that the magistrate implement 'special measures' to protect Michele from cross-examination from her ex-husband. Daniel had expected that the magistrate would ask both parties to submit questions that she would then ask as part of cross-examination, or perhaps implement a screen to hide Michele from the direct confrontation of cross-examination. There was little else Daniel could now do to protect Michele.

Judge Palmer began by introducing the 'Schedule of Allegations' and first addressed Greg.

'It is my understanding that you systematically deny each of the allegations of assault and sexual assault which are listed in the schedule.'

'Yes, your honour,' Greg said.

Daniel noticed that the magistrate did not correct him about the appropriate way to address her. Greg had obviously been watching too many American legal dramas.

'The respondent will now take the witness box to be cross-examined by the applicant,' the clerk announced.

Daniel prompted Michele to remind the magistrate about the request for special measures, but the magistrate replied that, as parties were representing themselves, the screen had not been deemed appropriate. She did add that if special measures were needed, the hearing could be put forward to another date.

Michele didn't wish to delay until another day, and so submitted to questioning by Greg. Daniel felt tense as he watched her walk to the witness box, a trembling shuffle. She needed a barrister who would not only prepare her case properly but ensure that Greg was examined in detail about the schedule of allegations. Before she had even composed herself, and taken a shaky sip of water, Greg was already on his feet, ready to begin questioning.

The energy in the courtroom changed as soon as Greg began questioning and Daniel felt darts of tension running up the back of his neck. The man was probably no taller than five feet five but he held an aggressive energy that seemed to magnify his stature. He was tanned with blue eyes and deep laugh lines that suggested he smiled often yet his impression was menacing. He was smiling now, as he approached the witness box. Daniel was close enough to see that Greg's eyes, although sparkling, had the watery sheen of a heavy drinker.

Finger pointed at Michele and standing so close to her that Daniel thought she might feel the man's spit on her face, Greg began his examination.

'You know for a fact that I never lay a finger on our son. You know I do everything for him – it was me bought him his tablet, what he needed for school—'

The magistrate frowned and leaned down from her bench. 'Mr Atkinson, I have approved your questions for this witness. I ask you to remember that *you* are not in the witness box, and cannot testify. You should measure your tone and ask the witness only your prepared questions and nothing else.'

Greg nodded once then turned back to Michele.

'You tell me then, what have I not provided for our son?'

Her shoulder blades pressed into the back of her chair, as if the millimetres of extra distance it gave her from her previous partner was worth it. Michele replied, 'A safe home – you didn't provide that. An iPad doesn't make up for watching your mother threatened. What kind of example is that?' Her voice was breathless, as if the fear of confronting him was literally winding her.

'You try to turn him against me. When he's with me and we're on our own, me and my little man, he's happy. A boy needs a father.'

The magistrate was tapping her forefinger inaudibly on the table as Greg finished, as if impatient for his speech to end. 'Mr Atkinson, once again you may only *ask your questions*, not make any other remarks, or I will have to ask the questions of the witness for you.'

Daniel pitched forward, clasping his hands over his nose. If Michele had been near him, he could have advised she request that the magistrate ask Greg's questions, but she was in the witness box, out of reach.

Greg resumed questioning.

'Tell me *one instance* when I have been violent towards our son?' Greg's voice was authoritative and clear in the courtroom. Michele did not speak, but shook her head.

'Ms Atkinson, are you able to answer the question?' Judge Palmer pressed.

'You've never hit him but he doesn't like it when—'

'Thank you. No further questions, your honour,' Greg said, cutting Michele off with a flourish, and took his seat.

As Michele left the witness box, Daniel saw that her whole

body was visibly trembling. Daniel reached out and squeezed her hand as the Cafcass report was submitted, which confirmed that Jackson had witnessed his father commit acts of violence against his mother.

Even though she had seemed overpowered by Greg in the witness box, she spoke up when the magistrate asked her if there was anything further. The steel in her voice was apparent to Daniel when she told the magistrate that she wanted to give evidence about an incident only two weeks previous.

'I think it's important to give testimony on this, as it shows what my ex-husband is really like,' she said, pushing her shoulders back.

'What pleading is this?' The magistrate pushed her glasses down her nose and shuffled through the papers before her.

'Something that happened outside the school gates two weeks ago. I wanted to tell—'

Sitting behind Michele, Daniel clasped his hands and allowed his head to drop. Silently, pressing his teeth together, he berated himself. He should have called Michele before today and checked with her that she didn't want to submit any new testimony that they had not already discussed. He'd allowed himself to be distracted by everything that had been going on with Sebastian and his case.

'I'm afraid this testimony is not in the pleadings.' The magistrate looked directly at Michele now, over the top of her glasses. 'I can't allow it.'

'Can't allow?' Michele whispered, turning to Daniel briefly and then back to the magistrate.

'If you wished to amend the pleadings then documents to that effect should have been lodged with the court. As this recent incident is not in the pleadings, I'm afraid we can't hear testimony on it.'

'Thank you,' Michele said weakly, sitting.

There were no windows in the courtroom. Although it was cooler than outside, the air felt trapped, giving a stale, claustrophobic feeling to the room. Michele left the courtroom briefly – he presumed, for a cigarette – and Daniel went to stand with her, in case Greg tried to approach her outside.

He found her on the steps of the courthouse, struggling to light her cigarette in the warm breeze.

'What was that extra testimony you wanted to speak about?' Daniel asked. 'Something about the school gates?'

Michele nodded. On her fourth attempt, she managed to ignite her cigarette. Her cheeks hollowed as she inhaled, exaggerating her small, pointed chin. 'Less than two weeks ago, when I got to school to pick Jackson up, Greg was already there. He'd just turned up to take Jackson even though he's not been given permission. I could tell he was working on the teacher as she was laughing her head off, like he was the funniest guy in the world. If I'd been a minute later, they'd've been off. Jackson told me later he was terrified. He was desperately looking down the road for my car.' Michele took another long drag, biting down on the smoke so that it drifted out of the sides of her mouth. 'Of course I just went right up and took Jackson by the hand, no word to that stupid teacher who was obviously fully won-over. I got to the car, Jackson in the back, but Greg ran over and grabbed my driver's door. He wouldn't let me close it.'

Finishing her cigarette, Michele let it drop to the pavement and stamped on it.

'Right there, outside the school – with Jackson in the back – he told me he was going to kill me. He still wouldn't close the door, so I just put the car in gear and hit the accelerator. I'd hoped I really hurt his shoulder, but you saw him today, none the worse for wear.'

'He said he was going to kill you?' Daniel repeated. He thought about how often that phrase wasn't meant literally, *I could kill you for that.*

Michele shrugged. 'Not like I've not heard it before. Ten a penny ... but I wanted to tell the magistrate that.'

Daniel blinked rapidly as her exhaled smoke drifted towards his eyes.

'I'm sorry about that. I didn't know that you had new testimony that you wanted to present. I should've called you to double-check—'

'I don't understand all the rules.'

It was why she needed a barrister. 'Basically, the magistrate has a list of what's going to be presented and, for new evidence to be accepted, I would've needed to amend the pleadings.' He had offered to help her, and he could have amended the pleadings for court, if he'd known – if he hadn't been busy with other things. He hoped it wouldn't matter and that the Cafcass report and safeguarding letter would speak for themselves.

*

There was no jury, and the magistrate returned within fifteen minutes.

'The matter at hand today was specifically to decide on the applicant's request to have contact with his son. Cafcass and the respondent, via police interview, notes alleged domestic violence in the home as a reason why the father, Gregory Atkinson, should have his contact with his son restricted to a contact centre. I am in no doubt that the outcome of this case would have been very different had the parents had appropriate representation. There were a number of elements that fell below expectation – in terms of court bundles unprepared and left for court staff to organise, and in the unsatisfactory cross-examination of witnesses. That said, despite the applicant's rejection of all allegations that he perpetrated violence against his wife, Michele Atkinson, I think it highly likely – as a result of the police and Cafcass reports – that such violence *did* take place. However, this hearing is not to determine the validity of violence against the mother but to determine whether the father should have access to his son, Jackson.

'The Cafcass report stresses that the father has never been violent towards the child and I have no reason to think that he would begin to be violent towards Jackson going forward. With careful consideration, I therefore rule that Gregory Atkinson *should* be allowed visits with his son in his own home and that Jackson may stay overnight. While I do not think that supervised visits at a contact centre are necessary at this time, my judgement includes a requirement that a suitable family member supervise the paternal contact for at least three months. I am aware that Mr Atkinson's mother sometimes babysits for Jackson and I am sure her supervision would not impinge on Mr Atkinson's paternal rights to the same extent as contact centre visitation.'

Daniel's chest cleaved with disappointment. He watched Michele who sat unnaturally still, her head bowed.

'The applicant requested joint custody of his son amounting to three point five days a week. I submit that, for the following three months, Mr Atkinson should have sole custody of his son – with the supervision of his mother – two days a week, including one overnight stay, to be increased to three point five if the arrangement proves successful.'

Michele looked down into her lap.

Outside the courtroom, Daniel made sure he stayed near Michele until Greg had left the building.

'All for nothing,' Michele said bitterly. 'He gets what he wants, as always.'

'You can appeal.'

'I could just not let Jackson go to him.'

Daniel sighed. They were outside now, the heat wrapping itself around them. 'If you don't comply with the order, you can be charged with contempt of court – compelled to obey. We can appeal, but you *need* to get a barrister this time ...'

Feeling dejected as he arrived back at the office, he took the lift instead of the stairs, jacket hooked over his shoulder, leaning against the metallic walls as the elevator rose to the eighth floor. Even offering to give advice pro bono, he felt he had failed Michele, who had not only been attacked by her violent ex-husband in open court, but now had to give up her child. He spent large amounts of his time frustrated by the current legal aid arrangement and how it failed to protect those who needed it, but he also excoriated himself for failing to ask Michele what she planned to present, and so amend the documents lodged at court. Would it have changed the magistrate's mind if she had heard what had happened at the school gates, or did the professional social work reports bear more weight?

It was after lunch and the office was busy. Daniel thought he had a free afternoon and was looking forward to catching up on paperwork before he went to Rene's party in Holborn. He was heading straight to the kitchen for a coffee, when Jacob – the assistant that he and Veronica shared – waved him over.

'Danny?' Jacob said. 'Your client Sebastian Croll's here. He doesn't have an appointment, but he was very insistent. I even asked if he could come back after lunch but he wanted to wait. I told him to take a seat in the waiting area.'

'Right?' Daniel said, frowning into the distance, to the waiting area. He couldn't see Sebastian.

'Is that alright? If it's not convenient, I'll go and ask him to come back another time, make an appointment—'

'No, it's fine, I'll see him. Thanks, Jacob.'

Sebastian wasn't in the waiting area and Daniel wondered if he'd left already, but as he opened his office door, he found Sebastian seated at the meeting table. He seemed very relaxed, sitting low in the chair with his ankle crossed over his knee.

'Didn't like the waiting area?'

'Sorry,' Sebastian said, blushing, sitting up. 'I'm just so paranoid at the moment. I felt more comfortable hiding in here. Your name's on the door, so I was in no doubt—'

'Yup, it's my office. Are you okay?'

'I was getting stressed out and ... I wanted to talk to you in person. I'm sorry to just turn up. I needed to get out of the house. I've been cooped up there for days, and here seemed like a safe place to go.'

As Daniel hung up his jacket, he saw a stack of opened mail resting on top of his legal pad. At a glance he could see it was mail from home that Rene was forwarding to his office when she thought it was urgent or needed attention. Daniel only noticed it because he didn't remember leaving it there. He thought he'd put it in a drawer, but knew he might've misremembered.

'Nice office – great view.' Sebastian stood with his hands on his hips, looking out over South Hackney.

Daniel took a seat at the table and, after a moment, Sebastian joined him. Noticing Daniel's black eye, Sebastian touched his own.

'Are you alright?'

'It's nothing,' Daniel said, brushing it off. 'Have there been any more developments? Were the police able to track down the person that threw the brick?'

'No, they weren't, but they said they got partial prints. There might be more news on that soon.'

'That's promising. It must've been very frightening. Someone actually breaching your home—'

'It was terrifying. I feel constantly on edge at the moment. These people seem to hate me, but they don't even know me.' Sebastian raked the fingers of both hands over his short hair. 'It's just so much stress.'

Daniel clasped his hands on the table. 'It was very unfortunate what happened, but it's good you have protection now and I'm hopeful that things'll die down as we go into the summer.'

'My father was saying, and I'm starting to think I agree with him, that we should sue?'

Daniel nodded slowly. 'Launch a civil action against Cambridgeshire Police? It's possible. You might get compensation.'

'Should we start that soon?'

'I can speak to a colleague, get someone to advise you.'

Sebastian nodded, looking down into his large hands.

'I can't see how things will go back to normal. Even people I've been close to for some time don't want anything to do with me. My friends from Cambridge, I mean.' Sebastian covered his eyes, fingers kneading his temples as if he had a headache. 'And I *hate* being in that house—'

Daniel knew he meant the family home in Islington.

'It's not because it's just me and my father there – to be honest, he's hardly home – but it's the house I grew up in. When I'm there, I think about Mum. For so long it was just me and her there, because Dad was always away travelling—'

Even though Leila had shared information about Charlotte

Croll's death, Daniel said: 'You didn't tell me what happened to your mum.'

'She'd taken some pills. She drowned in the bath, but I *know* it was him. I didn't see it, but I imagine he held her under. He always used to hurt her. I think you knew that?' Sebastian looked up into Daniel's face. 'I hate him. I fucking hate him,' he spat.

'Is there someone else you could stay with over the summer then – a friend? It might be safer as well—'

'I just told you . . . I don't have any friends any more.' He held up his hands, as if out of options. 'Could I stay with you?'

Daniel barked a syllable of laughter. 'I'm afraid not—'

'But you're the only one who understands me, who doesn't judge me for that thing with Ben. I mean . . . I was just a little kid when it happened.'

That thing with Ben.

Daniel pressed his lips together, unsure how to respond. Sebastian seemed both agitated and distracted. His body seemed sprung with tension but his eyes were almost glazed, the pale green of them strangely flat.

'I suppose, what . . . I . . . really liked about Frankie was that she accepted me for who I was—' He looked away, at the large windows reflecting their faces. The way the early afternoon light cut into the room meant that the windows now seemed opaque, reflecting the interior rather than the outside, making the large room with its London view seem intimate, almost claustrophobic. 'That was the best thing about her . . .'

Daniel wasn't sure why, but he had a strong feeling of unease at the mention of Frankie's name.

'I mean, obviously she was just using me, to get back at her husband – or whatever – but at the beginning, when it was good – I felt really *accepted* by her. It'd been a long time since I'd felt able to show someone who I really was – to feel that . . . trust.'

'You must've had other girlfriends at Cambridge?' Daniel asked, trying to change topic.

The question seemed to unsettle Sebastian further. His face assumed a strange grimace.

'Yes, there was someone else – another girl in my year, but it ended. She dropped out of Cambridge. I suppose I was still a little . . . tender after her, when Frankie came on to me. *She* seduced *me*, y'know. At that party at hers. After I spilled wine on my shirt, she took me upstairs, and helped me change . . .' Sebastian looked up at Daniel. 'It happened right there in her bedroom – in *their bedroom* – with everyone downstairs.'

Daniel didn't really want to hear this. He felt uncomfortable and it was on the tip of his tongue to ask Sebastian to leave, tell him he had a meeting.

'To think how different things were then – how free.'

Daniel cleared his throat, trying to close the conversation. 'Eventually, all this will die down. Rest assured the police won't even interview you again, unless they have new incontrovertible evidence in the Frances Owen case—'

'Evidence—' Sebastian repeated.

'Until they find the murder weapon or another key piece of evidence.'

Sebastian's eyes widened as his eyebrows raised. It made his face seem comical and sinister at the same time, almost like a mime artist – at once without feeling while exaggerating emotion. 'Oh, they won't find the murder weapon.' His voice was quiet.

Silence. A pause as long as a bar of music.

Daniel held his breath. Was Sebastian suggesting what he thought?

'Have you ever wondered ... where does the violence go?' Sebastian focused on Daniel.

Unsettled, Daniel stared back at him.

'You must work with dangerous people all the time. But then, there are people like *you and me*, making their way in the world, despite having a . . . history of violence.'

Daniel felt his stomach muscles tighten.

'I remember you told me that you were violent when you were young too – I think you said you nearly went to borstal. And that you carried a knife when you were a boy.'

There is so much darkness in you. Rene's words in her letter echoed in Daniel's mind.

He couldn't remember telling Sebastian so much about his youth, and he certainly hadn't told him about the knife. He hadn't told *anyone* that. How did he know? A guess?

Not wanting to engage with this, Daniel shrugged his shoulders. 'I believe that children have the potential to change. I think violence is a kind of acting out of the harm done—'

'Acting out the harm, yes.'

'Violence to others can be seen as a form of *self-harm*, particularly for children who have experienced abuse.'

Excitement flickered in his pale eyes. 'Yes, that's right.'

218

Daniel swallowed, disconcerted by Sebastian's electrified face.

'. . . but it's also something natural. It's like a—' fingers to his lips as if to pluck the word '—a desire, something latent that needs to be expressed, that *will be* expressed, no matter how hard you try to suppress it. Don't you think?' Sebastian seemed intellectually engrossed.

For the first time since they'd met again, Sebastian's manner reminded him of the child he had once been. The patina of charm and maturity seemed to have been stripped away and now there was an intense, unflinching callousness that was even more alarming because Sebastian was now so tall and strong.

'With Ben, that impulse was very childish, not fully formed, but with Frances I really felt . . . in control of it. As if I'd reached some kind of . . . mastery—' He smiled, a strange, askew smile like an unhooked crescent moon. The skin on Daniel's scalp prickled. 'Maybe violence is like energy. It can't be created or destroyed; it can only change.' His face was expressionless.

'What're you saying?' Daniel whispered, incredulous rather than prompting Sebastian to continue.

'I put that rock on Frances's face, but . . . she deserved it. It was needed.'

The air in the office seemed to compress, as if before an explosion.

'Sebastian.' Daniel took a deep breath in and held it for a second, sensing how Sebastian would react. 'You understand that now you've told me this, I can't represent you any longer?'

'What?' Sebastian's eyes flicked as he began to comprehend. Daniel could almost watch the anger possessing him.

'I mean, I can't act for you any longer. Legally, I can't lead a positive defence now that you've told me this.'

'You mean you're turning me in?' His voice a whisper, Sebastian stood.

Daniel was shocked to feel himself trembling. He slipped his hands into his pockets to disguise it.

'No. Our legal conversations are privileged, which means that they can't be disclosed. I can't tell anyone what you've told me. But I also can't continue representing you.'

'You're my lawyer, you have to do what I ask—'

Daniel could see that Sebastian was angry, but it seemed to be packed down inside him, only his eyes giving vent to it. It reminded Daniel of the viciousness he'd seen in Greg's eyes.

'That's a common, but incorrect, assumption. I *can't* tell the police what you've said to me . . . but I now can't represent you in interviews or in preparation for trial, should that come, knowing that you've confessed.' The stark professional talk, after what had verged upon friendliness between them, jarred. 'I'm bound by my own legal obligations as a solicitor—'

Sebastian's eyes narrowed. 'So, I'll take it back. I didn't do it. You can still be my lawyer.'

Daniel was in no doubt that Sebastian had been telling the truth. How else would he have known how Frances was killed? When someone was murdered, the police didn't reveal the exact cause of death, because there were always strange nobodies willing to admit to brutal crimes. Even though he felt somehow blindsided by this revelation, Daniel believed him.

'I'm afraid there's nothing more to say. Solicitors have to follow the rules, just like everyone else—'

Nodding almost menacingly, Sebastian looked around the room. Daniel felt steeled for a confrontation. He turned his back on Sebastian for a second as he went to open the door. It wasn't that he expected Sebastian to leave immediately but he felt better – safer? – with the door open.

'You know, I kept tabs on what you were doing,' Sebastian said. 'I knew about your marriage to Irene before you told me, and about ... your son—'

Daniel was about to cut him off, not wanting any mention of his family, but Sebastian interjected. 'I hear that Irene is now a judge. How does that change your dynamic?'

Daniel cleared his throat. 'I'd like you to leave now, Sebastian.'

Rene's appointment was now on the Judiciary website, and Sebastian could also have found out about their marriage online, but it was his tone – at once obsessive and sinister – that disturbed Daniel. Sebastian picked up his sunglasses from the table, began to walk very slowly to the door.

He paused in the door frame and waved a hand towards Daniel's desk with its papers and photographs. 'You have a nice family,' he said, with an uncanny smirk. 'Billy looks just like you.'

'Goodbye,' Daniel said, unable to stop the anger he felt at the mention of Billy's name creeping into his voice.

Daniel watched Sebastian slowly walk down the corridor and into the lift. Thoughts tumbled in his mind and all his muscles felt tight. Had Sebastian just threatened his family? He thought about how quickly Sebastian had turned, the thinly veiled aggression and the strange way he had confessed, talking of mastery and violence as if it was something that Daniel would relate to. The unforgettable image of Professor Owen's face, one half still intact with its sprinkling of freckles, flashed in Daniel's mind. He felt a queasy anxiety at the centre of him.

He remembered how he'd felt all those years ago, in the bowels of the Old Bailey, when Sebastian had confessed to Ben's murder. That time and this, Daniel had been shackled by the legalities. Once again, Sebastian was guilty, and once again, Daniel couldn't say a word.

Alone in his office, Daniel closed the door and walked towards the windows, fingers over his mouth. He didn't know what to do. He wondered if there was some loophole that meant he could pass this information on in some way.

He decided to take a chance and call the Law Society. It was just before five.

Feeling lucky when someone answered, he resigned himself to wait until he was passed to a relevant legal advisor. Listening to the music they played as he waited, he put his elbow on his desk and one hand over his face. He thought the music was Erik Satie. He seemed to remember the melodic discord from Minnie's record collection.

The music didn't soothe the anxiety that reverberated through him. Even though Daniel remembered feeling com-pletely shorn when Sebastian admitted killing Ben, somehow hearing him confess to Frances Owen's murder had felt even worse. Sebastian had been a little boy when he'd confessed to Ben's murder – a child from a terrible home who needed help, not punishment. But now Sebastian was an adult, not even charged with Frances Owen's murder, and the way he had spoken sounded so callous, pathological and dangerous. Daniel thought of the newsreel of Jon Thompson being taken to the police station in handcuffs. He thought about Frances Owen's sister, Margaret – her composed distress. He thought about Detective Constable Murphy, who had trained with Leila, but who had been sacked and might be awaiting further charges for data protection leaks after revealing Sebastian's identity. He thought about DCI Lloyd organising round-the-clock protection for Sebastian.

'Sorry for your wait ...'

'That's alright. Grateful for your time,' Daniel said, hunching over the phone. He knew what he was about to hear, but he needed to be *told* it.

After Daniel had explained everything, the woman on the end of the line sighed, almost imperceptibly. 'I understand the very difficult situation you find yourself in, but your legal position is clear. Even in these very difficult circumstances, you cannot breach client privilege.'

After hanging up the phone, Daniel realised he was still trembling. 'Fuck,' he said quietly, resignedly.

The photographs on his desk had all been moved and Daniel returned them to their usual position. As he straightened the photograph of the family together, it struck him that Sebastian had mentioned Billy by name, despite the fact that Daniel had never told him his son's name.

He picked up the mail from home, about to slip it into his

briefcase, when he noticed that one of the envelopes was empty. It had been nothing particularly confidential: an energy bill because they needed to change suppliers. He checked in the drawer but there was no sign of it. On his desk, the letters had been placed on top of a legal pad.

Now that the mail had been removed, Daniel noticed that the leaves of the pad had been turned over to one specific page: the stream of consciousness he had written the other night to Minnie. He'd continued using the pad, so that his 'therapy journal' had been somewhere in the middle with fresh notes on top.

Daniel recalled Sebastian's remark about the knife, and how he had written about Billy in that stream of consciousness letter, over and again. Anger and humiliation flashed through him: Sebastian had most likely read those private thoughts. He felt exposed and foolish to have been taken in by Sebastian – to have felt sorry for him. He had been deceived, all over again.

16

Arriving at Rene's leaving do, Daniel still wasn't in a party mood. He told himself that he could have a drink and try to forget all about Sebastian, and Cambridge, Michele and Greg and legal aid. He would have a drink and hope his wife, newly appointed high court judge, might take him back home afterwards. He realised he needed a drink very badly.

Heathcote Street Chambers tended to throw a decent party. They held a regular September event, to allow their barristers to network with key solicitors and judges, and Daniel had gone several years in a row, usually with Veronica Steele, his partner.

Tonight, he entered alone. Even heading up the carpeted, curving stairwell, in the direction of a swell of laughter, Daniel felt deeply anti-social and wondered if he should just leave. The day had left him burned out – first Michele's trauma in the courtroom facing her ex-husband, and his part in that, and then Sebastian's revelation, followed by the uneasy sense that his privacy had been breached.

He was here only for Rene and he reminded himself of that as he put one foot in front of the other. He'd been working hard over the last weeks to show her that he could be the husband and father she wanted him to be and he thought he'd made some progress, with Billy at least. Climbing the stairs, feeling fatigued, beaten, he thought he'd even submit to having his head examined if that was what Rene needed to take him back.

There was a large function suite at the top where most of the guests were already assembled. Casting his eye around the room, Daniel saw it was mostly silks and junior barristers from Heathcote Street Chambers or other sets nearby. The room was wood panelled, the original floorboards covered in Persian rugs. Black leather sofas lined the room and there were round mahogany tables with servings of champagne and canapés. The large, sash windows were all open and so, despite the number of people and the unbroken heatwave outside, the room had a pleasant temperature with air circulating. The heavy furnishings seemed to contain the noise and make it denser, so that when Daniel spotted Rene across the room, he knew his voice wouldn't carry.

He was desperate for a drink, so he picked up a glass of champagne from the table as soon as he entered. It wasn't clear what the canapés were: pastries with savoury fillings, and individual serving spoons with a bite of meat and sauce. He would have preferred some good, old-fashioned sausage rolls. Because he hadn't managed to have lunch yet again, he was starving, again, and ate three pastries before he turned back to the room and tried to make his way to Rene.

There had to be over fifty people here, some of them clearly straight from court in their white shirts and black waistcoats. Rene was wearing a red dress that was one of his favourites – high-necked but cut out at the back so that it showed her delicate shoulder blades and the beads of her spine. Her light-blonde hair was twisted into a French knot. Watching her, his heart lifted, and he started to thread through the people to reach her.

Straining over the heads of the people before him, he saw she was laughing, champagne in hand, with a QC from Heathcote called Bamber Worthington. Daniel *hated* Bamber and so, as soon as he recognised him, he paused in his navigation of the crowd. He drank his glass of champagne chatting to a clerk just as the head of chambers, Mark Pratt QC, was helped onto a chair. Mark tapped his whisky glass with a spoon to bring the gathering to silent attention, so Daniel paused his conversation with the clerk.

Daniel knew Pratt too. He'd been good to Rene, supporting her bid to become QC ten years ago and also her application to the bench. He was old-school: florid complexion; whisky-soaked with a belly big enough to make Daniel worry about the solidity of the chair supporting his weight.

'If I may take a brief moment of your time.' Pratt turned left and then right to take in all the faces around him. Daniel was sure he heard the chair creaking.

'I'd like to say a few words about our learned colleague and now ... most excellent member of the Queen's Bench Division of the High Court, The Honourable Mrs Justice Clarke.'

There was a spattering of applause and a few rowdy cheers. Daniel half-smiled at the woman he had been chatting to as he claimed each of them another glass of champagne from a passing tray. 'For the toast,' he whispered, as she seemed surprised at the offer of another glass.

'Since she joined our set, Irene has consistently shown her calibre – turning silk at just thirty-nine years old, and taking the lead on a number of flagship cases, which she has invariably won. She's acted in defence of whistle-blowers at The Hague, for detainees in Guantanamo Bay, Cuba, and at home, in human rights cases involving migrants interned at Yarl's Wood Immigration Centre. She is a leading light, not only in Heathcote Street Chambers where she has nurtured several pupils into competent and formidable barristers . . .'

Daniel had finished his second champagne and looked around the room for more. He glanced at Rene, who was blushing, a hand to her cheek. He couldn't catch her eye. As he watched and listened, he felt a complicated knuckling under his ribcage, that he realised was mostly pride. He was proud of her and always had been. She was *all* those things Pratt described and more.

The room was hot and his mouth felt dry. In the crowded room of people he almost knew, and one woman he knew deeply, he suddenly felt unfathomably lonely. He drank the last single drop of champagne from his glass, thinking how differently he would feel right now if the last few months hadn't happened; if he was standing by Rene's side knowing that he was going home with her afterwards. He saw Bamber put a hand on her back. Jealous anger stung at the back of Daniel's throat. The touch was only fleeting, but the way Rene's dress was cut, Bamber had his hand on her bare skin.

'Many of you know that Irene comes from an esteemed legal family—' Pratt added, turning to the crowd for approval. The room sounded with *hear, hear* and *point of law, m'lord* in response, which sounded to Daniel like an echo of the public school backgrounds from which so many of those in attendance hailed. Bitterness sullied the sweet aftertaste of the champagne in his mouth. Rolling his eyes, feeling impatient, Daniel managed to get rid of his empty glass and snatch a replacement from another tray.

'A little bird told me that our dear Irene was named by her father, Sir George Clarke QC, after Irene of Rome. All those keen art historians among you will remember that Irene of Rome tended to the wounded Saint Sebastian after he was shot with arrows. How fitting for Irene, a champion defence barrister, who has tended the wounds of so many – and won justice for those who have fallen foul of the slings and arrows of fortune.'

Pratt raised his glass, defiantly still standing steady on his chair despite the weight of his belly threatening to topple him. 'Irene, my dear colleague and, most importantly, my dear friend, it is with great pleasure that we come together today to congratulate you on reaching yet another pinnacle of achievement, in being selected to join the Queen's Bench Division of the High Court. I'm sure your assiduousness, your eye for detail and your innate sense of justice will serve you well in this next challenge.'

Pratt held up his glass to the room. 'To Irene.'

To Irene, the room echoed back.

'Rene,' Daniel whispered and took another long sip of champagne.

As Mark stepped down from his chair, Daniel continued to thread his way through the gatherers. Rene still had not spotted him and turned her back just as he approached. When he reached her, he opened his hand onto the skin at the small of her back.

He'd done it unconsciously, but then worried that she would startle.

She turned, her high cheekbones pink from champagne, and her face lit up. 'You made it.'

The way she spoke, the way she looked at him, filled him with joy despite his terrible day and Bamber being there. He felt the tension he had been storing in his shoulders loosen.

'I was here for the speech,' he said, deciding not to try to kiss her with Bamber lurking.

She beamed down into her nearly empty glass and then looked up into his eyes.

'You look great,' he whispered, so quietly that he almost mouthed the words, taking his hand from her back. Being near her bolstered him. Standing with her righted him somehow, as if he had been sinking just a moment before and not known it.

'Did something happen to your eye?' she asked, frowning up into his face.

'I'll tell you about it later.'

'Good to see you, Danny.' Bamber pumped Daniel's hand.

Trying to smile back, Daniel was aware that it might come across as more of a snarl. They had met once or twice in similar circumstances, but Daniel didn't know him well.

Bamber was wearing an opulent, tailored, three-piece, blue

pin-striped suit with what was obviously a pure silk yellow tie. He was taller than Daniel by about three inches, with vigorous floppy dark curls and prominent white teeth.

'Got any big cases on at the moment?' Bamber asked, speaking to Daniel but looking around the room at the same time.

'Um, yeah, a couple of murders and helping out a colleague with a family court case,' Daniel replied, disinterested. He finished his champagne and looked down into the eye of his empty glass. He didn't like champagne; it was so insubstantial.

'Are you?' said Rene, eyebrows raising and her lovely eyes brightening. 'Family court – you've not done much of that; how're you finding it?'

Bamber laughed at Rene's surprise, the fact that she was not up to speed. 'No office pillow talk with you two then?'

Anger flickered through Daniel. He wasn't sure if he was annoyed at Rene for accidentally leaking to Bamber that they were separated, annoyed at Bamber for pouncing on it, or else just slightly pissed from the champagne. Either way his mood turned, so that he pitched back into the heaviness he'd felt when he'd arrived and climbed the stairs.

'We've usually got better things to talk about,' Daniel said, attempting a recovery, pressing his teeth together, as he stretched to get another glass from a tray, taking two, one for him and Rene.

'I've still got some,' she said, as he tried to hand the champagne to her.

'Where's your accent again?' Bamber asked. 'Is it Yorkshire you're from?'

He said *Yorkshire* as if it were the ends of the earth.

'Newcastle,' Daniel said, his face deliberately unsmiling, blankly belligerent. He felt Rene's fingers on his forearm, as if sensing his mood and attempting to settle him.

'Where did you study law, then?' Bamber asked, his lips receding to show both tooth and gum.

Perhaps he was genuinely making conversation but Daniel heard it as another dig, as if all the universities outside of Oxbridge handed out Mickey Mouse degrees.

'Sheffield. And I got a grant. And I got a legal placement without Mummy or Daddy helping me. Fucking impossible these days.'

'*Danny,*' Rene said, in that voice she used when she thought he was being unreasonable.

'Shall we go?' he said, turning to her.

He didn't know what he'd been expecting. He looked into her eyes, knowing she would turn him down. He only wanted time alone with her, away from Bamber the Bastard, to tell her how sorry he was for what had happened between them and *how proud* he was of her. Of course he knew all of this was in honour of her, and she couldn't just leave, but he was exhausted and just wanted to be in her arms again, just the two of them.

That awkward, polite laugh of hers. She whispered, 'It's my leaving party. I can't just go.'

'Alright, well—' Daniel downed the remainder of his own glass of champagne and then knocked back the glass he had purloined for her '—I'm gonna head.'

She nodded once, but he could see the hurt in her eyes. He'd disappointed her, again.

He waited a moment, realising he was drunk now, feeling beads of sweat at his hairline, watching the merry swirl of dust motes caught in a shaft of late-evening sun, dancing like particles of gold above the heads of Holborn's chosen legal few. If Bamber hadn't been standing so close that Daniel could smell him – boot polish and leather and expensive cologne – he would have changed his tone and turned to her, asked her to see him out. He would have apologised then, for embarrassing her, for letting his hackles rise. He might have told her about his terrible day and everything that had happened, or maybe he wouldn't. Tonight was for her, and he'd ruined it already.

Turning, he pushed his way through the crowd, aware, before he reached the door, that he'd spilled someone's drink. He tossed *sorry* over his shoulder then almost ran down the carpeted stair, feeling his face burning.

Outside, he didn't feel so drunk but he was aware that his footsteps were heavier than normal. He could go back to the flat, but he didn't want to be alone just now. He wanted to drink more. He wanted to forget, to go back in time and change who he was and what he had done. He wanted to stop thinking about Sebastian or the fact that, if Michele complied with the court order, she would be handing over Jackson to the partner who beat her. He would forget that there might be a man called Cobain in New Zealand who was his father. He wanted to stop thinking, period.

At the illuminated mouth of the Tube, Daniel scrolled through his phone contacts. Someone was selling *The Big Issue* and Daniel gave her a fiver, but then refused the paper. The woman, dark-haired and dark-eyed, kept trying to press the newspaper onto him as he waited for the phone connection.

'This is a surprise,' she said, answering just before her answerphone picked up. 'You needing some more information?'

'No, I'm needing some company. Where are you? You wanna go get a drink?'

'Where are you?' Leila asked.

'Holborn, but I can go wherever, just at the Tube now.'

'I could meet you over in Farringdon, say twenty minutes?'

'Done.'

The sun had gone down, its light replaced by fairy lights strung across bar windows, streetlamps, car headlights, the finger strobe of delivery drivers on bicycles. They were sitting outside a bar on the border between Farringdon and Clerkenwell. Daniel was drinking beer – finally – and Leila, cider.

'Well, as an ex-cop, what I don't get about criminal solicitors is, what do you do when you think your client's guilty, particularly of something awful – like murder, or rape? How do you justify continuing?'

Daniel stiffened immediately, but he realised that Leila's question wasn't about Sebastian and so forced himself to relax. There was still an ache inside him about what Sebastian had told him, and all the champagne and the beer had failed to quell it. 'Well, firstly, everyone's entitled to a defence, but, basically, in the legal system everyone has a role to play.' Daniel was at that point in drunkenness when he was more articulate and knowledgeable than he was sober. 'My role is to defend. It's the

police's job to seek the truth and present it, the judge's role to
see that justice is done—'

'I get that, but if you *know* someone is guilty – committed an
offence, how can you justify defending them?'

'Well, it depends. If I have a client who says they didn't do
it – which is most of them – I have a duty to give them an
adequate defence regardless of whether I believe they did it or
not. However, if they actually plead guilty in court there's no
trial as you know, so I'm only preparing their case for sentencing, highlighting extenuating circumstances or whatever. But
if – which doesn't happen very often – I have an accused client
who admits their guilt to me, but insists on pleading innocent,
to the police, the court, then I have to cease to act. I can't lead
a positive defence.'

'That makes sense. But there must be a lot of times when you
defend someone and you know in your gut they're guilty, even
if they're saying they didn't do it. How can you defend them in
that case?'

'Because that's my job. We all have a role to play. Like I said,
it's not my job to seek the truth. If they say they didn't do it,
then they didn't do it.' He opened up his palms.

'But the police are trying to put someone away – protect
society – and you're in the way.'

'No, I'm not. I'm just part of the process. The way I look at it,
the police have to do their job, follow correct procedure, gather
evidence that will stand up in court. It's not a morality play. It's
not about good guys and bad guys in the end – it is just about
evidence and whether it's robust enough.'

'Hmm, I dunno. I suppose I do think it's about good and bad, right and wrong.'

It was her eyes that showed expression, intellectual interest; the rest of her face was relaxed, unanimated. The balance of that comforted him, like a touch. He thought again about neuroscience and hard-wired morality, the frontal lobes and the amygdala.

'What about before the police?' Daniel asked. 'How did you end up in the army, the military police?' They were both merry now, or at least he hoped she was too. Questions he'd always wanted to ask her came forth. The fatigue and heaviness he had felt earlier was gone.

Shrugging, she laughed. 'In a way, I feel like a cat – nine lives – maybe not quite nine yet, but sometimes it feels like at least six or so ...' She sighed, deeply. 'Where to start ... I was young when I went into the army. It wasn't my first experience of being in a man's world but on my first tour of Afghanistan, I felt very *other*.

'I was working in community engagement, and I thought I was doing a good job, because I had passable Dari – it's very similar to Farsi, y'know. It was a very complicated war, as you know, and the reasons for us being there were always in debate, but there were times when you felt you were really making a difference – I felt that anyway—'

Daniel nodded, waiting for her to continue.

'But, I ... became disillusioned.' She glanced at her nails, the smallest of frowns appearing between her brows. 'I was attached to a new battalion and ...' She looked down into her almost empty glass. She swirled the golden liquid at the bottom, peering into it, as if she could see the past in there. 'Some bullying went on . . .' Leila cleared her throat.

'I can't imagine anyone bullying you. I wouldn't fancy my chances.'

'Well, I was . . . assaulted, and then sent home on leave.'

'Assaulted?' Daniel repeated, his voice low, his smile disappearing.

Her eyes shone under the fairy lights. 'Yeah, wounded in action – that seemed to be what they wanted to call it.'

Daniel frowned, not quite understanding.

'I was raped,' she said, starkly.

Her directness, the lack of emotion and the fact that she had shared this, hit Daniel like a fist to his ribs.

'He was a lieutenant. They all rallied around him. They made out there was some sort of relationship between us that went wrong, but that wasn't the case. I was sent home as if I was shell-shocked – which I was – only it wasn't the IEDs that had got to me.'

'I'm sorry that happened to you,' he said, quietly. All the air seemed to have left his body. 'But you went back?'

Again she smiled. 'Yeah, I went back as RMP though – military police.'

'And did you get justice?'

'Justice for quite a few others, but not for me. One of those things. Some kind of warped karma, I guess.'

'I'm sorry,' he said again. He was deeply sorry this had happened to her.

'It wasn't your fault. But now you know why, when I was

investigating your man Sebastian, I was keen to look into that rumour about him and Sarah Doyle – him stalking her and her feeling frightened. I still want to find her. It still does drive me, I suppose, in surprising ways—'

Changing position slightly on the uncomfortable wooden seat, Daniel let his gaze drift. He was aware now that he was drunk, but even in this state he had enough grasp on himself not to reveal what Sebastian had told him today. He wanted to tell Leila and he was sure she would want to hear it. She would go straight to the police and Sebastian would be arrested, but Daniel would also, ultimately, be struck off. Not telling her about Sebastian's confession wasn't just about escaping disciplinary procedures; Daniel's whole life was the law. Minnie had led him to the law and he had grafted to make it his own. He wasn't about to let Sebastian or anyone else rob him of that. Leila was an ex-copper and so she saw things in black and white, but it had never been that easy for Daniel.

Shifting his focus from Leila's face to the pavement tables, the straggle of fairy lights and then the busy street beyond, Daniel was aware of the sudden lag in his vision. He took a deep breath and sat up straight, trying to counteract it.

'Talking of finding people. What about the hunt for my father?' he asked, smiling a little, even though the subject didn't amuse him at all. If he hadn't been drunk, he might not have prompted Leila at all. It said a lot about the gloominess of his current professional and personal circumstances that he was so keen to hear about the – probably greater misery – of his history.

Now Leila shifted in her seat. 'I was kind of putting off updating you on that—'

'Why?'

Her eyes were far away at first, watching passers-by laughing on the pavement, but then she looked him in the eye. 'You know the other guy who could be your father? Robert Cobain's competition?'

Nodding, Daniel said, 'Yeah, Steven Something.'

'Well...' Leila pressed her full lips together. 'Once I got a lead on who he was, it wasn't so hard to find his whereabouts. Tell me – if I told you he was in prison, would you still want to know?'

The lights and faces before him seemed to blend and swirl, kaleidoscopic. He sat up and blinked and found he was nodding before he'd really considered her question, but as Leila continued to speak he realised that, of course, he wanted to know.

'He's in Frankland Prison, in County Durham, doing time for murder.'

Pitching forward, Daniel put one hand over his mouth, felt the shadow of his stubble breaking through his cheek. 'Jesus.'

'His name is Steven Salter.'

Daniel sat up. 'That name, it sounds familiar ... Should I know him?'

Nodding very slowly, Leila said, 'You might have heard of him, his case was in the news at the time. It was a while ago. He murdered a young woman in Gateshead in the early eighties, but wasn't caught until the early nineties when he was arrested for murdering another woman in Sunderland—'

Again Daniel looked away, and again his vision slid and

slipped, making him feel queasy. He remembered the Gateshead case, partly because it had been so close to home. The woman had gone missing after a night at the pub. Her body was found weeks later, strangled and dumped on the moors. Daniel had been in foster care in Newcastle at the time – his last home before he was sent to live with Minnie in Cumbria. There, his last foster father, with the dark hair and square chin, had told Daniel that he was an *evil little bastard.* Somehow Daniel remembered being told that he was evil around the time that the Gateshead case was on the news.

Daniel had drunk so much but suddenly felt sober. Why did so many men kill women? Even after all this time in defence, he still didn't know the answer to that and wasn't sure he wanted to. He wondered what it would mean about him, if such a man as Steven Salter was his father.

'Jesus,' he whispered.

'Doesn't mean he's your father. It could be Robert Cobain after all. Or it could be someone else entirely. I'm just telling you where my investigation has led me so far: Steven Salter was seeing your mother before you were born, and Cobain stopped seeing your mother, because he was sure Steven Salter was the father of her baby.'

Daniel reached across the table and put a hand on her wrist. Her skin felt soft and warm.

'I'll get us another,' he said, knuckles on the table to help him stand.

17

Daniel woke up on the edge of the bed. He hadn't closed the blind and the sun split his head like a melon. He felt its two hemispheres severed and trembling inside his head. His mouth was dry and he struggled to swallow as he sat up. He was naked apart from his boxers and one sock. As he turned in the direction of the excruciating light, he saw Leila sitting on the edge of the bed. She was wearing more clothes than he was and was playing with Billy's Nintendo Switch. Daniel hadn't realised it was still here since Billy's sleepover. He would have to return it.

'Good morning,' he said, confused, so shocked with himself that he lay back against the headboard, reeling for a moment, trying to piece together what had happened, what he had done.

He couldn't remember sleeping with her and that had never happened to him before. It most certainly hadn't happened to him in the last decade – longer – since he had been with Rene.

'Good morning.' She placed the computer game on the nightstand. 'Sorry, it was just by the side of the bed. I was waiting for you to wake up.'

'Right.'

'You're a really quiet, compact little sleeper,' Leila offered, smiling down at him. Her hair was plaited, the tip almost touching the bedsheet, like a dark paintbrush.

Daniel sat up, rubbed a hand over his eyes. 'Um, thanks.' He didn't tell her that sleeping lightly and with minimal intrusion was something he'd taken with him from childhood: sleeping expecting to be roused; sleeping without the security of knowing that the bed he was in would still be his the next night.

'What time is it?' he said, trying to swallow.

'It's nearly ten, would you believe?'

Daniel swung his legs out of bed. He didn't believe it. He never slept this late, even on weekends. Feet on the floor, he reached down and peeled off the odd sock and threw it into the corner of the room where the washing basket had been, when he'd lived here properly.

Feeling somehow vulnerable in just his boxers, he found his jeans and stepped into them.

'I'll get us some coffee,' Daniel said, more because he needed one.

'I made a start on it. I thought I'd just wait for you.'

It might have been his altered state of mind, but he thought her voice was more polite than normal and that made him feel more awkward. In the kitchen, he saw that the cafetière had been filled but not plunged. He poured coffee into two mugs.

'Um ... what do you take again?' he called through to her – the question, after what he presumed had been intimacy, making him feel even more awful.

'I can take it black,' Leila replied, her answer indicating that she had already conducted kitchen reconnaissance and knew he had neither milk nor sugar.

Open on the kitchen bunker, obviously from last night, was the bottle of gin. Daniel screwed the cap back on and pushed it to the back of the counter, next to the tea bags.

Leila was still in the bedroom gathering up her things and he handed her a cup.

'Is it okay if I have a shower?'

'Of course.' Daniel put down his coffee to go and fetch her a fresh towel.

Nudging his forehead, Daniel felt the dull throb behind his eyebrows lessen. It was on the tip of his tongue to ask her what had happened between them, but he couldn't say it out loud. He had a memory of kissing her in the street somewhere, her full lips against his with the sweet-dough-smell of takeaway shops nearby. He remembered walking down the Grove Road together, hand in hand. He'd told her he was separated from Rene and maybe she thought there was something . . .

'Are you alright?' Leila asked.

'Yeah, why?'

'I dunno, you seem . . . upset or something.' He was very upset. He was horrified with himself and this behaviour. All he could think of was Rene and how she would never forgive him.

'I was . . . gonna go for a run.' Sipping his coffee, he wasn't sure if his body would take a run, but it was his intention to go anyway, find some balance.

She looked so beautiful with her long plait, yet his insides twisted at the thought that he'd been unfaithful. Rene was already disappointed with him, but this was seismic. Just imagining how hurt she would be filled him with pain that surpassed the ache in the centre of his head. Leila headed into the bathroom, but left the door ajar.

'Did we—?' he asked, finally, raising his voice so that it would carry through the slightly open door. Like the intelligence about his father, he held his breath, unsure if he wanted to hear the answer.

'Don't you remember?'

Daniel was silent, opened a drawer to pick out his running gear but instead stared at the contents, hanging his head. His temples and ears burned as he waited.

'Oh my God . . . the earth moved, Danny; the angels wept—'

Biting his lip, he looked up from the drawer.

Peeking her head out from the bathroom door, Leila beamed at him. Her face vanished and then he heard her laughter before the shower started up. When she spoke again, her voice was echoey as she stepped under the jet. '*Nothing* happened, for God's sake.'

Relief flooded him. He stood just outside the bathroom door, pushing it open a little further. 'I knew we didn't. I would have remembered,' he said, into the cloud of steam.

'*You bet* you would.' She laughed again. 'One thing was clear,' she said, poking her face out of the shower curtain. 'You need to sort things out with your wife . . . fast. You would *not shut up* about Rene and some guy called Bambi—'

Despite his hangover, Daniel chuckled. 'Listen, I'm going for a quick run. I'll be back in half an hour.'

*

Outside, he ran his old circuit of Victoria Park, the dehydration slowing his pace and making his muscles feel tighter. He realised when he was halfway round that he had left his phone in the bedroom. Saturday morning, and the play-park he'd taken Billy to was busy with children. He could only half-remember yesterday, but the things he did remember were the things he wanted to forget. He remembered Sebastian telling him that he had killed Frances Owen. He saw the pages of his legal pad turned to the spot where Sebastian had stopped reading. He remembered how rude he'd been at Rene's party.

When he arrived back on Old Ford Road, despite the short run, he noticed that he was sweating more than normal and so slowed to a walk as he approached his stairwell, allowing himself to cool down.

Double-parked outside, he saw the car that he and Rene owned, which had been left in Herne Hill since he moved out. Sweat drying in fear, Daniel peered inside as if to double-check that the car was really theirs. Billy's car seat was secured in the back.

Realisation brought a sudden chill to his hot skin. As if getting there quicker would soften the impact, Daniel took the steps to his door two at a time, vainly hoping that Leila had already left.

At the top of the stairs, the door to his flat was open. Breathing hard on the landing, he heard Rene and Leila talking. Swallowing, he pushed open the door. Leila was fully dressed – thank God – but her long hair was wet, combed down her back. Rene was in jeans, a brittle smile on her face and Billy's Nintendo in her hands.

'Hi.' Rene's greeting was strained and Daniel felt the chill spread to his extremities, as if seeing her had caused all his blood to rush to his major organs. 'Billy forgot this. I called but you didn't answer. He was freaking out. Just thought I would pick it up.' She held up the video game machine. 'See if it'll buy me some peace.'

Despite her artificial cheer, Daniel could see that she was trembling. He went to touch her, but she moved as if electrified and threw up two hands to keep him away.

'Okay, bye then.' Rene nodded to Leila, avoiding Daniel's gaze and starting back down the stairs.

Leila looked at Daniel, eyes wide. Silently, she put her hands on her face, imploring him to go after Rene.

By the time Daniel got downstairs, Rene was in the driver's seat and had started the engine. He opened the door to stop her pulling away.

'It's not what it looks like,' he said, hearing the phrase in his head as unbelievable, cliché.

'She opened the door in her fucking underwear, Danny—'

Daniel turned away from her, trying to swallow, struggling with his dry mouth. It felt as if he had a pebble in his throat.

She kept her hands on the steering wheel at ten and two, eyes on the road.

'I swear to God, it's not what it looks like,' he said, quieter, chastened. He could imagine it happening, Leila just out of the shower and thinking the knock at the door was him. He felt his stomach falling away from him, as if he had just stepped off a building.

'I'm double-parked. I got what I wanted. I need to get back. Billy's over at Max's.'

'Rene, *please*. You have to listen to me. *Nothing* happened, I swear to you. I—' He was about to apologise for the evening before, a tumble of regret and humble words.

As if overruling him, Rene reached out, took a hold of her door and pulled it shut. Before she pulled away, she opened the window just a little. He slipped his fingers inside.

'Nothing …' his shoulder jarred slightly as the car pulled away, *happened*.

Back in the flat, Daniel ran a hand through his dirty, sweaty hair. Leila had been perched on the couch, ready to go, and now stood up.

'I'm sorry,' she said, her face genuinely pained. 'I even thought to go when you were running – leave you a note; I should have just done that, instead of waiting to say goodbye.'

'It's not your fault.' He smiled, sadly. 'It's mine.'

'See you at work,' Leila said.

She touched his elbow lightly and kissed his damp cheek.

'Will you be alright getting back to the Tube?'

'Of course. I remember the way. I wasn't as drunk as you were.'

As he heard Leila's footsteps fade on the stairs, Daniel pressed his fist into the side of his head in an effort to stop his headache that was no longer just a hangover. He stood at the sink and drank a pint of water and then went into the bathroom and turned on the shower. He wasn't sure how this weekend could get any worse, but he knew he didn't want to face the rest of it until he washed.

He kept the water cold as he stepped into the shower. Despite his run and the heat of the day, the iciness of the water took his breath away. He forced himself to stay under the jet, enduring it, as if it was a punishment he had to suffer. *Nothing had happened.* He hadn't had sex with Leila, but he might as well have. He didn't know what had come over him – how, drunk or sober, he could have crossed that line. He gasped, although it was no longer just from the cold. It was years since he had broken down yet he buckled now under the stinging cold shower and cried, one hand on the tiles and another over his face. The fact that he considered he had been unfaithful to this woman he loved so deeply ripped through him. He didn't know how he would ever make it right.

It was over fast and then he slowly turned up the heat and let his tears merge with the shower as the breaths still spasmed in his chest.

18

Daniel felt Billy's small, damp hand tug from his. It was early Saturday morning and they were at Roman Road Market, only a few blocks from the flat.

Apart from child-handover arrangements, Daniel had not been able to speak to Rene at all, much as he had tried. Even now, a week after the Leila incident he still felt obliterated that he had let Rene down. He had no idea how he had allowed himself to be so stupid, but he hadn't given up. Now, more than ever, he was resolved to prove to Rene that they were meant to be together.

In a change to the new arrangement of parents moving around Billy, Rene had dropped Billy at Daniel's office on Friday evening. He and his son had spent another night in the flat in Bow as Rene had wanted to use her free evening to have friends over for dinner. Dropping Billy off, she had barely been able to look at Daniel. He'd tried again to explain to her, but with their son there it wasn't the right time.

There had been no word from Sebastian and Daniel was relieved. He'd told his colleagues he wasn't representing Sebastian any longer and had sent a letter confirming he was no longer acting for him. Unable to let it go, he'd specifically looked into the news about the Frances Owen investigation but nothing new had been reported. Jon Thompson had still not been charged with his wife's murder and was currently on police bail. Daniel hadn't warmed to the man, but he felt sorry for him now, knowing that he was innocent of Frances's murder. Of course he was guilty in other ways. If Leila's intelligence gathering had been correct, then Jon Thompson was an abusive spouse, a perpetrator of assault. Even so, that didn't give Daniel the right to judge him – that was why there was a justice system.

'What are *those*?' Billy asked.

As he turned to see what had snagged Billy's attention, Daniel blinked the sleep from his eyes. He'd gone to bed late – reading briefs and emails after Billy had conked out on his bed – and then stayed up even later watching sport on the laptop because there was still no TV. He refused to have it installed, or do anything which would bring permanence to the temporary separation of living arrangements. Billy had got up at six thirty and after a breakfast of Rice Krispies and a couple of hours running about the flat, then complaining about being bored, Daniel had needed to get him out.

It was a while since Daniel had been at the market and now they drifted, experiencing different sights and smells, directionless. Tiredness tugged at him as Billy bounded from one stall to another. Daniel hadn't been for a run or had a shower this morning, and so felt his responses slower, his senses dimmed, as if he was underwater or jet-lagged. The sun was swaddled behind cloud and so it was a warm, pleasant morning, without the intense heat of days past.

'I think they're peaches,' Daniel said, raising an eyebrow at the fruit on the stall and in the direction of Billy's wavering finger.

'They're squashed.'

Daniel smiled and pointed at the sign. 'Doughnut peaches, you see – so they're peaches in the shape of doughnuts.'

'They look funny.'

'Probably easier to eat – do you want one?'

Billy shook his head and they moved on.

They walked on past lengthy clothing stalls: clothes that even in the fresh air smelled musty. There were rows of leather jackets, and then psychedelic prints, racks hung with T-shirts and shirts. Daniel noticed that Billy was walking in the same way as he was: left hand in the pocket of his jeans.

'Are you copying me?' Daniel asked.

Billy grinned, lengthening his pace in mimic.

'I don't walk like that, do I? Bandy-legged.'

'What's bandy?'

'What you're doing. I don't look like that.'

'Yeah, you do, and your face looks like this—' Billy exaggerated a frown, lips protruding.

Daniel laughed. 'No, it doesn't.' Some part of him was troubled that his son saw him as frowning, stern, disapproving, while another part of him was comforted that Billy paid such attention to him. The past few months had been difficult for them all, but Billy was of an age when he was just starting to assert his independence. His language was developing and that fed his imagination. He had had nightmares the past two times that Daniel had looked after him, and Daniel knew that the split was troubling him. As grief-stricken as he'd been the past week about Rene – hopes of getting back together dashed – Daniel had done his best not to show that to Billy. It was hard enough being seven without your parents splitting up.

'Yeah, it does; your face looks like this.' Billy's sweet little face – a face with a neat allocation of features, like his mother's, contracted in a good imitation of a gargoyle.

'Well, you better watch. The wind'll blow and your face'll stay that way.'

'What do you mean?'

Daniel didn't know. It had been said to him when he was a boy. Now here he was, doling it out again, even though it had never made sense. This was part of his struggle as a parent. Other people had a consistent experience of childhood to accept or reject; Daniel was sure that *had* to make it easier. He didn't feel he had anything coherent to pass on to his son. His attempt at parenting felt like a scrapbook: cut-outs from his past, some of which were still traumatic to remember, others that filled him with shame, and some – that time with Minnie – which gave him something to aspire to. Altogether it had never felt enough. And now there were these scraps that Leila might have found, family he'd never known but with whom he shared blood.

After a stall bearing a large selection of baseball caps and trilbies, Daniel smelled beef cooking and felt his mouth flood with saliva. Letting his hand rest on Billy's head, Daniel guided him through the crowd, past a man flipping burgers – the sign on his stall read 'ostrich, lamb and beef'. All the stalls here were either cooking or selling food, and people were standing around, eating off paper plates, so that there was less movement and it was hard to pass through.

Sellers called out their wares – there were scotch eggs with unusual fillings, three for a tenner. There was a stall of jam and Daniel paused there, not wanting to buy any jam, but reminiscing. As a boy, he'd helped Minnie at her market stall in Brampton, Cumbria. They had sold eggs from their own chickens there, but also jam that she had made herself, raspberry and strawberry.

Wistfully, Daniel smiled and turned to Billy, ready to tell him again about the farm from his childhood and ask if he wanted to go up there with him. He looked down, where he expected Billy to be – next to his hip – and then down the tunnel of people that were weaving in and out of the stalls.

He wasn't there.

Frowning, more irritated than worried, Daniel peered through the crowd, but saw no little boys. There were other children here, but they were toddlers in prams or babies strapped to chests. He pivoted and looked up ahead, in the direction they had been walking. This row of stalls was soon to end and Daniel expected Billy had gone on to the next attraction. Annoyance flickered in him as Daniel pushed his way towards the next gap in the crowd.

His lips pursed as if to sound his name, but still he kept quiet, striding right to the end of the market, looking left and right, in case Billy had wormed his way into stalls, or between clothes rails, but he was nowhere to be seen.

Frowning deeply now, and remembering Billy's comical impression of him, Daniel stood on his tiptoes to peer back down the line of stalls and people, searching for a small boy wearing a red T-shirt and khaki knee-length shorts. His eyes cut to the height of four feet, Billy's height, trying to pick out his dark hair and the red of his T-shirt in the crowd.

Vanished.

A tightness now in his throat, Daniel retraced his steps. He began to weave his way back through the crowds, looking not at the people in front of him, but beyond them, searching for Billy's small, dark head weaving in between. Inevitably, Daniel bumped into someone – a corpulent older man who smelled ripe with body odour. The man was carrying a cold drink – some kind of fruit juice and it spilled a little.

'Sorry,' Daniel said, automatically, not even looking at the man as he spoke.

'Mind where you're goin'.'

Now Daniel was taking long strides almost breaking into a run. He gave up simply searching the crowd and began to call Billy's name. Daniel didn't often raise his voice and normally he would have felt self-conscious doing such a thing, but now he bawled like a lunatic, calling so loudly it rasped in his throat.

'Bil-ly. *Bil-ly?*'

He was aware of how he must seem, screaming in a public place, but he didn't care. Roman Road ran parallel to Old Ford

Road, where his flat was. Sweat breaking at his hairline, Daniel wondered if Billy would have tried to go back there, but it made no sense. He had never wandered off before, and they hadn't had an argument to prompt it. A few minutes before they'd been hand in hand. Daniel rubbed his fingerprints against his now-moist palms, as if to remember the touch of his son's hand in his. He clenched both of his fists, as if to take the small hand again and this time not let go.

In desperation, he looked upwards, at the tight, brown Victorian brick of the terraced street and the windows that looked down onto the stalls, wondering if he would see more clearly from a height. As the market once again began to thin and come to an end, Daniel turned on the street, still shouting his son's name.

'Billy!' He felt his face reddening. People stared.

The shops here were a strange mix – tattoo parlours and vaping shops next to new hipster coffee places. Daniel took out his phone and stared at its illuminated face, wondering what to do.

Two horrible thoughts yoked in his mind: someone had taken Billy; and he would have to confess to Rene that he had lost him.

He was still rattled from the events of the past weeks – protesters outside his office, threats online and then the mugging, even though it might have been unrelated to Sebastian's case. Nevertheless, he still felt primed, on high alert, as if someone was out to get him. He could handle that, he thought, but he couldn't handle *anything* happening to Billy.

Trembling, the breath rattled in his throat. As his thumb hovered over the call sign on his phone, he wondered if he should call the police before Rene. How long had it been since he'd held Billy's hand in his? It felt as if it might have been fifteen or twenty minutes, but he realised it could be as few as five. He was a panicked parent and time had slowed now he was separated from his child.

'BILLY!' he screamed one last time, turning in the direction of the flat, knowing that Billy would not have gone back there without him. There was the playground in Victoria Park, but Billy hadn't even mentioned it since they were there last. 'Billy.' This time he didn't seem to have enough air to carry it. He tasted salt at the back of his throat. Spent, Daniel turned back towards the market.

At exactly the same time, so that their images almost over-lapped in his brain, Daniel saw Billy and a tall man hand in hand, at the far end of the street.

He felt a punch in his chest, as if his heart had stopped and then been jolted back to life. The panic he had just felt – that aching vertigo, pain in the soles of his feet, as if he himself was lost, not just his son – that feeling suddenly changed, crystal-lised into something much more tangible, the fear of a specific threat. Someone was trying to take his son away. Immediately, Daniel sprang forwards, his muscles full of energy, sprinting. As he drew close, whoever had been holding his son's hand let it go.

'Billy!' Daniel said, sprinting forward, reaching him in a few paces and grabbing the scruff of his son's T-shirt. 'Where did you go? Didn't you hear me calling you?'

Only when he saw the fear and upset on Billy's face did Daniel check himself. He'd been frantic and knew he must look terrifying. If someone had hurt Billy, he would have torn them apart.

Roughly, in one sweeping motion, Daniel picked Billy up. He almost expected him to protest, but instead Billy put an arm around his neck.

'I'm sorry,' Daniel panted, 'I thought I'd lost you—'

He swore under his breath. Fuck. Fuck. Thank God. Thank fucking God.

His son in his arms, Daniel turned again and again on the street, looking for whoever it was that had been hand-in-hand with Billy moments earlier. His body felt full of adrenalin. He wanted to find this guy and beat him to the ground, but he needed to look after Billy.

'Your neck's all sweaty, Daddy.'

His chest heaving, Daniel pressed gently on Billy's shoulder blades, pushing the little body into him, relief flooding him. The smell of his son up-close soothed him deep-down. His heart was still racing, so he could feel the pulse of it in the veins in his neck.

Billy wriggled a little and Daniel set him down onto the ground. Kneeling, the buzz and swagger of the market reeling around them, Daniel took hold of Billy by both shoulders. '*Who took you?* I saw you were holding someone's hand. Who was it?' Daniel saw an image of Billy and the tall man from behind. Even as he spoke, he doubted himself, as if he had been hallucinating.

257

'I was just looking at the hats, and then that man came.'

Daniel took hold of Billy's arms. 'What man? Who was he?'

'He said he was your friend.'

'What did he look like?' Daniel asked, even though he thought he had seen him.

'He was a man.'

'Describe him? You talked to him, what did he look like?'

Billy's face was startled, confused, on the verge of tears.

'He was tall and thin and he had dark hair like yours. He just said he was your friend and that I should take his hand.'

'He's *not* a friend. You understand? You stay near me and you don't go off with *anyone* that you don't know, alright? Ever.'

Billy nodded, frowning.

Who was it? Who would do that? Daniel wiped his mouth with his hand. He knew he was on edge – paranoid maybe – but would Sebastian have done that? Sebastian had known Billy's name. Or was it one of the protesters linked to Sebastian's case, still determined to punish Daniel for defending him?

'You don't have to take anyone's hand if you don't want to. If you don't know someone, you don't take their hand, even if they tell you they're my *best* friend; you tell them to get lost, okay? You run away. You don't—' Daniel had to stop; he had no air left to finish the sentence. 'Tell me you understand.'

'Yeah. I understand.'

Still kneeling on the pavement, Daniel pressed Billy into him. 'I got a real fright there. I'm sorry, I really got a fright.' He nudged a lock of hair from Billy's brow. 'I thought I'd lost you. What would I do?'

Billy half-smiled at Daniel, unsure, watching his face.

'I won't *ever* let anything happen to you—' Daniel got up and dusted the knees of his jeans and then took Billy's hand again as they headed back to the flat. As they walked slowly back, the breaths sagged and snagged in his chest. A contortion of relief and fear rippled through him.

That twist of fear that Daniel had felt deep in his gut when he saw Billy hand in hand with a stranger remained. It stayed with him as he climbed up the steps into the apartment and lingered while he prepared them sandwiches for lunch. It stayed until later in the afternoon, when he took Billy back home, south of the river. Someone had taken Billy's hand, but Daniel didn't trust his panic-stricken memory.

Rene was still barely speaking to him. There was too much pain between them and everything he said seemed to come out the wrong way. At the door, he handed over Billy's bag, but she didn't let him into the house. Billy had already disappeared inside. It really had become that bad between them and Daniel knew it was all his fault.

'I lost Billy at the market today,' he blurted out, rubbing a hand over his cheek, hoping he didn't look as worn-out as he felt. 'I was terrified. I think it was only for five or ten minutes, but I thought—'

A flicker of understanding on her face. 'You remember that happened to me with him—'

He nodded, frowning into the distance, not wanting to do this here on the doorstep. 'Yeah, when he was three. I remember.' She'd been in Richmond Park with a friend and Billy had toddled off on his own. An older woman had found him and taken him to a police officer, where he'd wailed so loudly that Rene had found him before they'd even tried to contact her.

'Yeah, someone actually—' Daniel put a fist to his head, frowning into the distance, still struggling to get everything in sequence '—had him by the hand, and I panicked, but then – I found him. I got him—'

Heart squeezing with the pain of being near her but also feeling so distant from her, he realised he couldn't articulate just what had happened at the market.

'I've got to go—' she said, looking over her shoulder, into the house.

'Listen, we need to talk—' His words came in a tumble. He'd told her about the police leaking Sebastian's identity and made sure she hadn't been subject to online attacks, but he hadn't had a chance to go into everything since. 'So much has happened and I know I should've tried to tell you about it before, but with everything that happened with Leila—' as soon as he said her name, he choked on it. It stalled him as he realised that she was closing him down.

'Not tonight, Danny, I'm tired.'

He put a hand on the door as if to stop it closing. 'You know I can't be telling you this, but Sebastian confessed to the murder of Frances Owen—' He blurted it out. Even though she was his wife, he was forbidden from sharing this client-privileged information, but he wanted her to know. She was a barrister, a judge, and he knew she would keep it to herself.

'To you or the police?'

'Just to me.'

'Just like before—'

Their eyes met for the first time since he'd arrived. He wondered why he'd been so keen to tell her that information *right now*. Was it important to her, or did he just not want her to close the door on him?

'I've ceased to act for him, but—'

'Well, of course, you have to – that's all you can do—'

He nodded. He'd wanted some other reaction from her; her response seemed distant – one legal professional to another.

'I suppose you just have to hope that he confesses to the police soon.' Her eyes were narrowed, as if she had a migraine, wincing out the light – or him – he couldn't be sure.

'I doubt he will. I know you won't, but don't say anything—'

'I won't say a word.'

'I'm worried about so much—' He stood on the doorstep, trembling. Losing Billy had left him fraught. He just wanted to be inside with his family. He felt an enormous shadow over him, as if there was imminent danger that he couldn't describe or articulate. All of his senses felt over-exposed. He hadn't been eating or sleeping enough.

'Try and move on, Danny,' she said.

He was aware that she wanted to close the door. He took a step back, said goodnight. It was only after the door closed that he wondered what she'd meant.

Had she meant he had to move on from Sebastian – *or from her?*

CRIMES

19

Monday morning, he got up just after dawn and ran ten kilometres along Pavers Way – the pathway that tracked the Regent's Canal. The long hot swell of the early summer had burst like a blister the night before, bringing thunder and hard rain. The pavements were still darkened from the thrashing, penitent.

His body felt light but his heart was heavy. His breath quick in his chest, he thought again about losing Billy and the panic that had risen in him. He thought about what Leila had told him about Steven Salter – whether or not he could be his father. There was no way she would be able to verify that one way or the other, the only certitude being a paternity test. It wasn't as if he had lived a life insulated from people who killed. He had defended so many murderers, but what did it mean when your *father* was a murderer? What did it say about himself?

On the home stretch, he pushed himself, sprinting almost the full length of Old Ford Road before he stopped at the steps outside his flat. Blood pulsing through him, he sank down onto the stone steps, looking out towards the park.

Even though the rain had broken the humid heat, it was still going to be a warm day and he thought he could see steam beginning to rise from the wet pavements as the concrete began to heat.

As he sat on the bottom step, elbows on his knees, he heard a tap-tapping sound and turned to see a blackbird, only a few feet away. It had found a snail on the wet pavement. The shell was almost as big as the bird's head and yet it lifted it and smashed it off the pavement again and again with callous determination. Daniel knew from his time at the farm that this was a male bird – its golden beak glinting in the early morning sunshine. Cruel force, and finally the shell cracked open. The yellow ring around the bird's eye shone wickedly at Daniel as the beak dipped into its soft prey.

Such premeditation! Just a little blackbird, Daniel thought – not even a kestrel, or the birds of prey he had been used to seeing up North. Just a little garden bird, yet capable of such precise, intent violence.

As the bird enjoyed its breakfast, Daniel headed upstairs. He would shower and get dressed quickly, so that he could be at work at seven – eating breakfast at his desk. The campaigners were unaware that he had ceased to act for Sebastian, and so he was still garnering unwanted attention, but he'd found that the campaigners weren't early risers and getting to the office promptly meant that he could get to his desk without being hassled. Even with the endorphins of his run pulsing through him, he still felt heavy. Sebastian's second confession still burdened him, as if the words themselves had been small weights hung around his neck. It was an onerous thing to have to carry, particularly with a live murder enquiry ongoing.

Mid-morning, he was clearing his inbox when there was a knock at the door. It was Leila. Without meaning to, Daniel startled. They had barely spoken since the sleepover, although they'd sat in firm meetings together, each of them gravitating to opposite ends of the large boardroom table, like magnets repelling each other.

'Do you have a minute?'

Her face was serious and Daniel couldn't read in her eyes what she might want to speak about. Avoiding Leila had been a mixture of self-protection and shame. He had such admiration for her, and still found her so attractive, but admitting that fact necessitated avoiding her. He still loved Rene completely, and the thought that he had jeopardised that love by his actions terrified him. Leila didn't seem as uncomfortable or embarrassed as he felt.

'Sure thing,' he said, feigning casualness, shocked to feel heat rising on his face. He got up and moved to the meeting table in the hope that she hadn't noticed the flush on his skin.

'It's just, I've made a few discoveries that I wanted to share with you – mainly about Sebastian's case – but also—'

Palms on the table, Daniel said: 'I should have told you, I'm sorry. Sebastian and I had a parting of the ways—'

'Right?' Leila raised her eyebrows. 'What—'

'A disagreement about how things should be handled with his case. You know how it goes. He may or may not get another

267

solicitor. I suppose it will depend on whether Frances Owen's husband is charged—' Another wave of nausea drifted over Daniel, thinking of everything he knew and could not reveal.

'That's unlikely now.' Leila crossed her legs. 'It's partly what I wanted to tell you. Jon Thompson has been released without charge and I would be very surprised if he's arrested again. Despite the great embarrassment of leaking Sebastian's name and putting him in danger, I think DCI Lloyd's team are focusing in on him again. I think Sebastian might need a solicitor after all.'

She swallowed. She was wearing a thin necklace that sat just above her clavicles, so that the tiny silver pendant attached trembled when she spoke. Daniel tried to push from his mind images that came to him from the night they'd spent together, her chin rising up to allow him to kiss her throat.

Leila brushed a strand of hair behind her ear, and looked down at her notes twice, even though Daniel knew she would have everything memorised. It occurred to him that perhaps she *did* feel uncomfortable. He knew he had to say something now to clear the air. He had too much respect for her to allow this awkwardness to continue. He inhaled, about to launch into an apology, when she began to talk over him.

'The police have Sebastian on CCTV – two significant sightings. It's still not enough to charge him, and I'm sure they won't arrest him unless they find incontrovertible evidence that he killed Frances Owen. Especially after what happened – with Sebastian's identity being leaked – they won't even *speak* to him again unless they're sure—'

'What kind of significant sightings?' Even though, technically, it had nothing to do with him any more, Daniel was intrigued.

'Remember, one theory was that Frances Owen's murderer went into the building the day *before* her murder and stayed there until she came to work?'

Daniel nodded.

'Well, DCI Lloyd's team have film of someone wearing a hoodie, but who bears a great resemblance to Sebastian, entering the Classics Building at three thirty p.m. on the day before the murder, and have no film of this hooded person exiting . . .'

'I see what you mean. It's not strong enough for arrest.'

'I also told you before they were very focused on finding the murder weapon and other material from the scene of the crime?'

'Yeah, you said, dredging the Cam—'

'And, if you remember, I said they were looking into whether either of the suspects had a lock-up or garage . . . well, Sebastian has recently made three calls to a storage facility in King's Cross—'

'So what, the police . . . are tapping his phone?'

'No, not tapping it, but they contacted his provider and got a list of calls.'

'How recently was this?'

'Past couple of weeks.'

Daniel leaned back against the chair. 'Don't those big discount places do student storage, and he's had to move out of Magdalene College – he's been talking about dropping out altogether—'

'I know. It's thin. I just thought I'd make you aware,' Leila said, standing. 'That's what the police are looking into—'

'Listen . . . hang on.' Daniel felt his heart rate increase. 'Sit down a minute . . . if . . . if you have time?'

She sat.

'I'm *so sorry*,' he said.

She shook her head, reached a hand over the table but didn't quite touch him.

'No, I mean it. I feel like I'm apologising all the time just now. To you, Rene, my son, everyone. And . . . that's probably right. I'm so sorry about the other night. I didn't mean that to happen, and I know I was drunk or whatever, but that makes it worse. Total prick—' He put his hands on the back of his head, as if surrendering to her.

'You're not, you've got a lot on your plate – it's fine. We're cool. You were blowing off some steam. For what it's worth, I enjoyed my night with you.'

Heart suddenly in his throat, Daniel said, 'I thought you said we didn't—'

She smothered laughter, waved her hand as if to disabuse him of that notion one more time. He relaxed.

'I don't want to joke about it. I have so much admiration for you, as a person, as a colleague, as someone who's done *so much* with your life, and you're still only, what, thirty—'

'Thirty something.'

'I value your friendship and I don't want to jeopardise that—'

'It's alright.' She touched him now, stretching across the table to put her fingers on the back of his hand. 'You haven't jeopardised anything. We're still colleagues, we're still mates—'

Despite everything, Daniel winced a little at *mates.*

'So we're okay?' He took a deep breath.

'We're okay.' Leila grinned, but then made fists with her hands on the table. 'This is a bit random, but it's been bothering me—'

'Go on.' He felt his jaw tighten, wondering what she was going to say.

'Well, remember I told you I wanted to find Sebastian's ex-girlfriend, Sarah Doyle?'

'Yeah.' Daniel put a lot of effort into not showing the relief he felt flushing through him.

Frowning, Leila folded her arms, only she didn't quite cross her arms, but instead held onto each of her elbows – just the way that Billy crossed his arms. It made her look suddenly vulnerable, as if she was trying to comfort herself.

'Well, I found Sarah, but ... she's dead.'

Daniel waited for her to continue.

'When she left Cambridge, she enrolled at UCL but only for a semester and then she seems to have had some kind of breakdown. Her mother died of breast cancer around this time; I don't know if that was significant or not. But anyway, she seems to have started doing a little bit of drugs, and fallen out with her wider family. It's not so uncommon. She lost the flat she was staying in and then—' Leila shrugged, but not in a casual way, as if to release tension in her neck '—she ended up on the street. I spoke to her brother, who talked about trying to reach out to her, persuade her to come home, but the way he described it, it sounded as if she had serious mental health problems that obviously weren't being addressed. She was homeless for nearly a year, and then . . . she went missing—'

'Missing?'

'Yes, that was what first prompted me to want to find her. She was on the missing persons register, and I suppose I . . . identified with her a little, after speaking to her friend in Cambridge. I felt determined to find out what had happened to her—' Leila took a deep breath, placed her hands on her lap.

Daniel blinked at her. 'So what happened?'

'Well, for a while she was just another young homeless person, out of touch with her family on the missing persons register. Then, nine months ago, a body was found in the Regent's Canal. It took a while to identify it, but they did, and it was Sarah—'

'Are you telling me she was murdered?'

'Yes, she'd been beaten and left to freeze to death.' Leila paused, bit her thumbnail for a moment. 'Including severe facial injuries.'

'Right.'

'It's an open case. Open but not going anywhere. To date there's been no leads on who killed her—'

'Why's that? Because she was homeless?'

'Well . . . I don't know where the investigation got to, and I wouldn't want to pre-judge. It pains me to say it, but perhaps Sarah's death wasn't a priority. I don't know. Either way, she has been moved from the missing persons register, to another database for unsolved murders. In a way, that's a positive, that it's listed as an open murder. I suppose Sarah might easily have been swept under the carpet as another homeless person who was intoxicated and fell victim to the cold after an attack. She had severe contusions, which might have killed her, but the post-mortem said she froze to death.'

Daniel stood and walked towards the windows. He stood really close to the glass, so that he almost had a sense of vertigo looking down.

'I know it's not really relevant for you any longer – now that you're not representing Sebastian – but I feel better knowing what happened to her, partially at least.'

'It's very sad,' Daniel said, sliding his hands into his pockets. 'I suppose it's always better to know—'

What he knew about Sebastian and Frances Owen again resonated inside him.

Leila had placed her bag on the table and now rooted around inside, taking out a polythene bag with a white plastic cup inside.

'Well, you can be the judge of that now—' Leila held out the bag with the cup.

'What do you mean? What's that?'

Her face was impassive, chin tilted slightly upwards. He couldn't read her.

'I went to Frankland Prison. I met Steven Salter—'

Hands still in his pockets, Daniel felt his jaw slacken. Leila stood very still, holding out the bag with the plastic cup enclosed. Daniel suddenly knew what she meant.

'He accepted my request to visit. I admit I wanted a hair from him – no idea how I planned on getting it, but anyway—' she

tried a laugh '—turns out he doesn't have that many to share.'
Leila's smile fell from her lips. 'Anyway, this is your chance to
find out, either way, if he's your father or not. He drank from
this cup on my visit. You can send it away. I have the form and
the envelope here. You're in control. You can decide whether or
not you want to find out—'

Daniel felt himself shrinking catastrophically, like a balloon.
He didn't know what to say. He turned back to the window,
feeling the heat coming through, so that he was almost basking
in it, protected from the rays yet exposed.

'Would *you* do it?' he asked, quietly, over his shoulder.

She was silent and he knew why. She was from another big
loving family. She couldn't understand being really alone and
needing to know your identity. No one wanted to find out that
their father was a convicted killer, a multiple murderer, but
needing to know who you were and where you came from was
such a powerful, basic drive.

'It's up to you,' she said, placing the bag with the cup on
his desk. 'Some things you just need to know. I felt that with
Sarah Doyle.'

'You still don't know the answer to that—'

'Neither do you,' Leila said, shouldering her bag.

Just then, on his desk, beside the Steven Salter DNA cup,
Daniel's mobile began to flash and vibrate. It was Rene.

'See you,' said Leila, slipping out of the door.

'Hey, it's me.'

Warmth pulsed through him at the sound of her voice, but she
was business-like, ticking through items on the list: when would

he pick up Billy; would he stay over in Herne Hill as planned, or should she pack a bag for Billy for the weekend? Daniel understood. There was a noise in the background, like a power drill.

'Whatever's easiest,' he said in answer to her question. He was still trying to make amends. 'What's the noise – your chambers under construction?'

'No,' Rene replied quickly, moving to a quieter space, 'I'm working from home at the moment. I don't have court until tomorrow. Just as well. We had a break-in, so I'm having the locks replaced as a precaution.' Daniel sat up straight. 'That was the other reason I was calling – I'll get you a new key.'

'What d'you mean we had a break in?'

'Don't worry, nothing was taken. Nothing obvious anyway. I think they got in through the living room window – one pane was broken – so replacing the locks is probably unnecessary, but I just thought—'

'No, you're exactly right. You called the police?'

'Yes, I reported it and scenes of crime were here dusting for prints.'

Petals of fear unfurled at the centre of him as if somehow this was connected to him being mugged the other day, and then almost losing Billy to a stranger at the market. As his thoughts began to run away from him, Rene said:

'Just bad luck on our part. There's been a couple of other break-ins on our street.'

'Has there?'

'Yes, you know Betty? That lady a few down from us? Her front door was forced open and they took her meds, but . . . get this.' Rene began to laugh. 'They stole her painkillers but left a beanie hat right there in the middle of the crime scene.' Again she laughed. 'Colonel Mustard … with the beanie hat … in the kitchen.'

Frowning, Daniel rubbed the tendons that ran down the back of his neck. It was funny, the way she described it, yet he still felt concerned.

'Do you want me to do anything? I have a friend that's in the police who would happily check the place over—'

Even as he said it, Daniel realised that the friend was Leila, technically ex-police and probably not appropriate since Rene had last seen her in her underwear answering the door to his flat.

'No, that's not necessary. Like I said, the place was checked over. If they come up with anything, they'll let us know. They advised getting the locks changed and I have. I'll leave your new key on the hall stand—'

Daniel sank into his chair. 'Don't you want me to stay over for a couple of nights, just in case?' He asked entirely because he was worried about them; he wasn't motivated by trying to get back together, although of course he wanted that too. He didn't know how Rene would have heard it.

'I think we'll be okay, thanks.'

'It's just—' He took a deep breath. 'I mean, I hope it's not related – but does it mean something that all these bad things are happening all at once?'

'What bad things?'

'What bad things … I got blood thrown at me outside my office, I was mugged and had fifty quid stolen, I lost Billy at the market and he was holding another adult man's hand, and now this . . .'

'I doubt it's related, don't you? I mean, those people are trying to make a point, not sneak in and steal drugs. I think this was a clear-cut break-in and they didn't find what they were after—'

'Rene, please—'

'Please, what? Danny, you're not making any sense.'

'I just think it might be best if I stayed for a couple of nights—' Again, he heard his words come out wrong. It sounded as if he was using what had happened to him as an excuse to move back in.

'Thank you,' she said, with crushing civility. 'We're okay.'

20

Standing at the school gates waiting for the children to be released, Daniel nodded at the other parents whom he vaguely knew. Since the rain had come, the temperature had dropped slightly and it felt more comfortable. Scrolling through his emails, he noticed that Michele Atkinson wanted to appeal against the custody decision. It was within the twenty-one day time limit; Daniel would reply to her as soon as he had Billy home and settled. With the right judge, an appeal could overturn Greg's right to unsupervised contact.

The school bell rang and a large chatter of children burst out into the playground. Almost every other child had been collected before Daniel spotted Billy, almost the last to appear, looking so small in his uniform of grey shorts and polo shirt. Daniel drew closer to the railing and waved, but his son didn't see him. He seemed lost in his own imagination, not walking with friends or paying much attention to his surroundings. Before he thought better of it, Daniel put thumb and forefinger into his mouth and whistled.

The parents nearby turned to Daniel – taken aback – but Billy looked up at the sound, smiled and began to run full-pelt towards him, school bag bouncing on his shoulders. It made Daniel's heart swell.

'How was your day?' Daniel asked when they were away from the other parents and making the short walk back to the avenue, hand in hand.

'It was okay. Marcus showed me how to do a fly kick.'

'You and Marcus friends now?'

'Sort of, yeah.'

'And what's a fly kick when it's at home?'

Billy launched himself across the pavement: a comical, palsied star-shape. 'It's a taekwondo move.'

'Right.'

'It's for self-defence, like if someone comes at you and you're not expecting it.'

Daniel smiled as he followed Billy, who was now karate-chopping the air in front of them.

'Hey, Bruce Lee, gimme your hand till we cross the road.'

'Who's Bruce Lee?'

As they reached the door, Daniel put his key in the lock, but it stuck when he tried to turn it. It was only then he remembered that Rene had had the locks changed. They used Billy's key to get in, and then Daniel found his newly cut set of house keys on the hall stand just where she'd said they'd be.

The antique china vase that he'd smashed the time before had been replaced with something equally large, most likely crystal, but modern – clean simple lines and a thick cut lip. Just looking at it, Daniel knew it was heavy and expensive. As he looked at his new set of house keys, he thought about an intruder being in his house and the scenes of crime officers dusting for prints, looking for some trace of who had been inside.

Following Billy into the house, Daniel inhaled the familiar scent of home. The sense of loss inside him contracted and then expanded again. Billy was ready to run outside into the garden, but Daniel told him to go upstairs and change out of his uniform first.

With sadness, he moved around the kitchen, touching receipts on the noticeboard – a business card for the man who had changed the locks. Rene's scarf was slung over a chair by the table and he picked up and sniffed it briefly. There was a shopping list half-written on the kitchen counter: hand soap, Jaffa Cakes, washing powder. These small, inconsequential things saddened him.

Listening to Billy's thumps upstairs, Daniel called Michele to tell her he would lodge her appeal, but it went straight to answer phone:

'Michele, hi, it's Daniel Hunter here, from Harvey, Hunter and Steele, just phoning to let you know that you're well within the time limit to submit an appeal. I can prepare it and send it to the magistrate for you. Let me know if you have any questions. I'll email you over the details. We can meet to discuss.'

As he hung up, Daniel noticed a text from Leila to say DCI Lloyd's team had a further lead about the King's Cross storage unit that Sebastian had been calling.

I know you don't rep Seb any more, just letting you know as I heard . . .

Daniel sent a return text to thank her, then switched his phone to silent, so that he could focus on being with his son.

Billy clumped down the stairs, wearing a T-shirt with a skeleton graphic, white on black. He opened the doors onto the garden – noticing that the glass panel Rene said had been broken had been repaired. He followed Billy out into the garden. The grass here was overgrown now, and Daniel considered cutting it. There was a trampoline, but Billy went straight for the Tarzan swing at the foot of the garden that Daniel had made for him.

With great athleticism, Billy launched himself onto the knotted strand of rope and winched himself up, coiling his legs beneath him to support himself.

'Push me, Dad.'

Daniel swung him in a circle so that he was in no danger of crashing into the trunk of the laburnum. The tree's golden but poisonous blossom had faded now that summer was in full swing, but the corn-coloured remnants still wafted in the breeze above their heads. Not content with his father's half-hearted turn on the rope, Billy used his body as a pendulum so that he moved back and forth.

'Can you get up any higher?' Daniel asked. 'You need good arm muscles to do that.'

'Yeah, I can.'

As if determined to prove his strength, Billy managed to wiggle up the rope about a foot or so before sliding exhausted to the grass. As he lay there, prone, arms and legs splayed, Daniel took advantage by sinking to his knees and tickling him, pinning him to the grass as he screamed with laughter.

'You two are having fun.'

Out of breath, Daniel got to his feet. Rene was in her work clothes but barefoot on the grass behind him.

'Hey.' Daniel ran a hand through his hair, smiling shyly at her, trying to judge her mood. He was determined to talk to her today, but he would need to find a moment when Billy wasn't there. He hoped he would be allowed to stay until bedtime. With Billy in bed, he would have enough time to plead his case.

'Push me again,' Billy said, launching himself back onto the swing.

'I'll be back in a bit. I want to talk to Mum first.'

In the kitchen, Daniel realised that Rene had brought shopping home with her. As if they were still together and meeting at home after long days in the city, they put away the shopping and emptied the dishwasher. There was something in their synchrony, the combined rhythm of these mundane tasks that nourished him.

'Listen,' he said, reaching out and putting a hand on her shoulder, 'we need some time to talk.' He swallowed. 'I'm so sorry for everything. I just feel—'

Gently, so that he couldn't be sure if it was deliberate, Rene moved slightly so that his fingers fell from her shoulder.

'Daddy, are you staying for dinner?'

Beaming, even though it felt as if his heart was breaking, Daniel turned to look at Billy, who had just come inside, arms tucked underneath his T-shirt. 'What happened to your arms? Did they get so tired you left them hanging on the tree?'

'Don't be silly, here they are.' Billy pushed his arms back into the sleeves. 'So are you staying for dinner?'

Rene had her back to him, both hands on the counter. 'You can stay if you like. It's spaghetti.'

Much as he wanted to stay, he didn't want to upset her. He knew that Billy's words amounted to blackmail. Reading her lack of eye contact as reluctance, he was about to make an excuse to Billy, but then she turned and said, 'There's plenty, really.'

'Okay, I'll stay,' he said.

'Yay.' Billy launched himself across the floor, and Daniel caught him, setting him on his knee.

They put Billy to bed together. The sun was still shining brightly outside and Rene drew the thick curtains and turned on Billy's bedside light with the ladybird shade. Even though it was still light outside, the curtains plunged the room into darkness. Both parents looking after him made Billy seem extraordinarily happy and well-behaved. He got into his pyjamas without protest and slipped under the covers, not seeming tired at all, but settling quickly.

'Do you want to choose a book?' Rene asked, flicking through the stories that were in Billy's bookcase.

'Dad, we haven't finished that football one.'

Daniel lay on top of the covers and flicked through the pages, trying to remember where he had left off reading. The main footballer character was a girl, but Billy had seemed to like it. He was sure that Billy couldn't remember where they had finished either. It was a book that Rene had put in his overnight bag on the last weekend he'd stayed at Bow.

On the wall of Billy's room was a poster of the striker Andy Carroll and then another poster of Monty Magpie, the Newcastle mascot, because of their black and white strip – both of which Daniel had bought him and tacked onto the walls. Even though the club was in a dire situation, Daniel was still an avid supporter and had successfully managed to indoctrinate his young son.

As he broke the spine of the football book, Daniel felt the need to check Billy's loyalty was still strong: 'What's the best football team in the world, then?'

'Newcastle United.'

As Daniel crossed his ankles one over the other and began to read, he was aware of Rene lingering at the door, listening, watching them for a moment before she bowed her head and slipped out into the hall.

'You smell nice, Daddy,' Billy muttered, snuggling.

'Thank you, so do you.'

Even as he continued with the story, Daniel hoped that Rene saw the progress he had made with Billy. The time he had spent alone with Billy of late had changed their relationship, so that Daniel felt different around him – less afraid of a disagreement and more able to enjoy their time together. He only regretted that he had needed this separation to understand what they needed of him and how he could be a better husband and father. He was prepared to be honest with Rene about all of this.

Despite the fact that he had seemed so excited when they first put him to bed, Billy began to tire into the second chapter of his book, squirming around in an attempt to fight off sleep.

Daniel deliberately began to read with less expression, in the hope that the monotony of his voice would help Billy slip over. It worked. Daniel eased himself off the bed and put the book on the nightstand. Pulling the duvet over Billy's shoulder, he kissed his hair.

'Sleep tight.'

Daniel left the bedroom door open about two inches to allow in the light from the hall. Stretching his arms upwards to relieve the strain from the position he had been lying in, he prepared himself to go down and talk to Rene. Inside, he felt a strange dichotomy of despair and hope when he thought about persuading her that he deserved a second chance.

In the bright hall, he glanced up at the plate rail that ran along the landing. The rail was usually empty, but now there was a small dark object, round as an eyeball, staring at Daniel. He had to stand on his tiptoes to take it down. Confused as to what it was, and why it was there, he reached for it, but as he did so, he felt a gentle prick at the centre of his palm. It seemed to be some kind of brooch, and the pin on the back had drawn the smallest dot of blood. Smudging the blood with his thumb, he took the brooch downstairs.

To his surprise, Rene had opened a bottle of wine and was standing, glass in hand, looking out onto the garden, shaded now, dusk falling.

'Is he asleep?' she asked, moving away from the patio doors.

Daniel nodded, hands on hips, ready to ask if now was a good time for them to talk.

'Do you want a glass of wine?'

'Sure,' he said quickly. He didn't drink a lot of wine, but it was Rene's tipple and so they shared a bottle occasionally.

As she handed him his glass, there was a terrible finality in her eyes, as if this was it: a glass of wine before the divorce papers.

As a distraction from their problems – a childish attempt to delay their conversation once again – he handed her the brooch.

'I found it on that plate rail upstairs?'

Rene turned the brooch over in her slim fingers. 'I'm sure my mother had one of these. It was upstairs? How did it get there?'

Daniel shrugged. 'I've never seen it before.'

Rene looked closely. 'The hair on my mother's brooch was woven differently.'

'What do you mean, hair?'

'See?' She held it up to show him. 'That's *real hair* in there. It was popular in Victorian times.'

'But what's it doing here?'

'I don't know.'

Rene set the hair brooch on the kitchen table and Daniel stared at it. He knew Frankie had had a small patch of hair removed after she was killed and it made him feel uneasy. They'd recently had a break-in and nothing had been taken. But had something been left behind?

'You said they dusted for prints after the break-in. Did they find anything?'

'No, they didn't find any usable prints. There were some marks around the door but that was it – said whoever broke in probably used gloves.'

Again Daniel frowned. 'And I suppose scenes of crime would just have dusted around the point of entry anyway. They wouldn't dust the whole house—'

'No, of course they didn't dust the whole house.'

Because houses are full of fingerprints, Daniel knew. There would be no way for the scenes of crime officers to discern one print from another over such a large area.

'What are you saying?' she asked.

He didn't want to obsess over it, but Rene's theory of opportunistic addict burglars seemed unlikely now. 'Down the road, you said they left a hat behind ... what if someone broke in here and left this?'

Rene's face blanched. The beanie hat made sense, taken off and left behind in frustration or jubilation, depending on the drugs found. This random jewellery seemed more deliberate.

'Surely not,' she tried. 'I think it's probably a bit esoteric for your random burglar to have left behind – and why would anyone break in and leave this? There's no point to it.'

'What if the point was that we find it?'

'I know you've been under a lot of stress lately,' she said. 'What with everything that's happened with Sebastian.'

She thought he was overthinking things and being paranoid. He thought she might be right. It made no sense for someone to break in and leave a brooch behind, and so he acquiesced.

'I like seeing you like that with him,' she said, cocking her head to one side as she raised her own glass to chink his. 'Shall we sit outside for a bit?'

In the garden, he moved the chairs from the patio table, positioning them to reach the last of the evening sun. The garden had a heavy, lingering, musky scent of fox. When he lived here, Daniel had liked to watch them skulk and play in the grass and in the trees at the bottom, rooting out bulbs or slugs. Rene had wanted to feed them, but he'd said no, that they were wild animals and should be left that way. Yet he liked the electric sense of connection when the fox saw him in the window and stared at him, as if with a mutual sense of fascination, the silvery-flat eyes shining, as if overexposed.

'I want to start by just saying how sorry I am about the other night,' he spoke quietly, looking at the sun bleeding through the leaves of the tree. 'I was an arsehole at your party.'

'I don't care about the party,' she whispered so quietly that he had to sit up to make sure he heard her. She slipped her hand under the collar of her shirt and rubbed her throat.

'And afterwards. I'm so sorry about afterwards. Leila's a friend, you know that. I was drunk. I swear to you, nothing happened,' He turned to look at her, wanting her to see how honest he was, how he meant every word, but she wouldn't meet his eye. 'However it looked—'

'A very beautiful friend . . . and younger—'

It wasn't something mentioned often, but Rene was four years older than Daniel. She would be fifty later this year. The slight age difference had never mattered to him, but he understood now how *she* might feel about it in relation to Leila.

He got down on his knees in front of her, rested his forearms on her thighs, clasped his hands around her waist. 'Nothing happened. I wouldn't have wanted anything to happen. I love *you*. I want to be with *you*. You have to believe me—'

Sitting right back in her chair, creating the maximum possible distance between them, she rubbed the back of her neck. Chastised so silently, he returned to his chair, took a gulp of wine that burned at the back of his throat, bringing tears to his eyes.

'I think—' her face crumpled for a moment '—I believe you, but the thing that hurts is ... I don't know what difference it makes.'

His mind felt electrified, as he tried to fight through his emotions and work out what she meant. 'Of course it makes a difference. Leila wasn't the reason why we separated. The reason ...' Now it was his turn to fight tears and he cleared his throat. 'The reason was that I was letting you down. You said it best in your letter. You didn't feel supported by me and, that ... is absolutely not what I want. I was selfish. I was just thinking of myself. You've got enough to deal with without trying to manage me and my ... darkness,' he said, repeating her word for what was wrong with him. 'I can do better. I will ... I'm your husband and I love you—' he turned to her '—so, so much, and the fact that I let you down makes me feel just ... *ashamed*.' He could barely get that last word out.

Eyes shining, she stared at the laburnum tree at the back of the garden, its blossom ghostly now, in the fading light.

'I know now what you were going through with me. I get it now, I do. I was frightened of Billy – actually frightened of my own son. I left so much for you to do— But really, y'know, at the root of it all, I was frightened of *myself*—'

'You don't realise you're doing it. You push us away. It's like you have this emotional shutdown, the screens come down and neither of us can get in—'

'I'm sorry. I don't know if you'll believe me, but I think I've learned a lot these past few weeks—'

She turned to him.

'I have. I don't think I've spent so much time alone with Billy than since we've been apart. It's been good for me. I've had to confront a lot of things, about myself. You don't understand that I'm not like you. I'm not wonderful, and wise and beautiful and kind and loving—'

'You are,' she said, tears spilling. 'You are, but you just—'

'*I'm not*. You were right about my upbringing. Probably I do need fucking therapy. Things don't come naturally to me. I have to think them through, and the things that do come naturally – like getting angry, losing my temper – it scares me because I don't really know where it comes from, what it means.' He wiped a hand over his lips. 'And I know that it must seem like I'm pushing you and Billy away, but in my head I'm just protecting you . . . from me—'

Hugging herself, as if she was cold, she spoke into the garden, the colours of which had changed as the dusk relented into darkness and moonlight.

'I know now how much damage that strategy has done to us as a family. And this time apart I've learned to just be myself with Billy, not be so guarded all the time . . .'

She was nodding. 'Up there tonight . . . you were so lovely with him, and it just—' She put a hand on her chest. 'I dunno, I want you two to have a good relationship. It's important to him, to me. I know it is to you too.' She took a large sip of wine and a drip rolled over her lower lip and she caught it with her forefinger.

'Of course it is, but I want *us* to have a good relationship. I want *us* to be close again. I fucking hate myself for taking my eye off the ball and letting you believe that I don't love and adore every single fibre in you—' His breath was rough in his throat as he struggled to control the emotion.

'It's not that.' Rene stood up. She *was* crying now. She carried her empty glass inside, set it on the counter, her face wet with tears. 'I know you love me. I've never doubted that, it's just, it's just . . .'

He went to her, putting his hand on top of hers on the counter.

'It's just—' the neat blades of her shoulders were visible through her shirt '—I've felt so alone these past few years. So lonely, even though you were there.'

'So let me try again. Let me show you that I can be better—'

'I don't know, Danny.' She wiped her face briskly with the fingers of one hand.

'Hearing that you feel lonely in our marriage breaks me apart. Please give me another chance. Let me show you that I can support you and Billy, just as you've supported me—'

He felt as if he'd run a marathon. His muscles, his heart were aching. He dropped to his knees in the kitchen and pulled her into him. 'Please, Rene, please let me show you,' he said, pressing his face into her stomach.

After a moment, he looked up, felt her fingers run through his hair.

'I need time.' Sniffing, she leaned back, putting her hands on his shoulders to break the embrace.

How much more time? Defeated, he got to his feet.

Feeling chastised, he looked over his shoulder, and saw the fox slinking in the back of the garden. The fox saw him too and froze, staring at him with the locked-in gaze of a hunter.

'We've had so much time apart already,' he whispered. 'It's like I said before, unless you let me back in, I can't prove myself to you.' Just once, quietly, he pounded the counter with his fist. 'I've *not* been unfaithful to you. You have to believe me. I've listened to you and I've tried. Don't give up on us. Let's try again, just one more time.' He couldn't keep it together a moment longer, tears breaking through him. He turned to leave, feeling destroyed, looking about for his things – his jacket, his phone.

She put a hand on his cheek. 'Let me sleep on it, okay? It's late, I'm tired.' The thought that he had to make the journey back to Bow brought a sudden depression that closed over him like a lid. All he wanted to do was go upstairs with her and hold her, allow the smell of her to reach deep inside him.

Breath snagging in his throat, he wiped his eyes with the crook of his elbow. 'Fair enough.' He swiped at the counter to pick up his phone and knocked the mourning brooch onto the floor. Where the brooch had come from still made him uneasy, but he was too shattered to think right now.

She walked him to the door.

'It's nearly the school holidays. I told Billy I would take him up to the farm in Cumbria,' he said on the doorstep, looking in the direction of the station. His voice sounded rough. 'We should all go together. Let's be a family again—'

'Maybe.'

He mouthed *love you*.

'Text me when you're home,' she said, before she closed the door.

Walking to Loughborough Junction, he felt weighed down; it slowed his pace. *Home* wasn't where he was headed.

21

Monday morning, Daniel was on the Central Line. It was a short journey from his flat to his office, but there were no seats and he stood, swaying gently, staring at the back of a newspaper being read by an older man seated in front of him. It was the school holidays now and there were fewer children but more tourists. There was a little boy Billy's age standing near the doors who obviously wasn't from London. He stood staring at everyone as if transfixed.

Daniel felt hot inside his jacket. He loosened his tie, glancing at the newspaper before him, reading the headlines to take his mind off the cramped heat. It was the child's name that caught his eye.

. . . and her eight-year-old son, Jackson . . . in cold blood.

He didn't want to stoop to actually read the man's paper, but he squinted to try and see more of the article. It was then he read the surname 'Atkinson'. He took his phone out of his pocket and was about to search for the news article, but the Tube was arriving at Liverpool Street and so he made his way to the exit.

Daniel waited until he was outside on the pavement – finding the article on his phone even though he was only a couple of blocks from the office.

The bodies of a woman and her eight-year-old son were found at a house in a quiet Bromley cul-de-sac. Michele Atkinson and her son, Jackson, were found stabbed. Greg Atkinson was taken into custody following treatment in hospital for a self-inflicted knife wound to the neck.

Neighbours reported that Michele Atkinson had arrived at the property to collect her son after a scheduled visitation with his father.

Daniel pressed his knuckles against his lips as he read. On the busy street corner, people pushed past him: couples trundling cases towards the station, office workers making their way to the city. The usual cacophony of the street surrounded him – wail of sirens and the traffic overlaid with passing conversation – but he closed it all out.

The shock of what he read shook the tension from his body and he leaned back against the brick of the building he was huddled against.

Neighbours heard a woman's scream and then shortly afterwards Michele Atkinson could be heard calling on her son, 'Run, Jackson, and don't look back.'

Greg pulled Michele back inside and then went out after Jackson. He had a knife that witnesses described as being red along the blade. Before neighbours were able to go to his aid, Jackson waited at the gate.

The same neighbour who had heard Michele's cries, reported that she heard Jackson, say: 'No, Daddy, please, please stop,' as Greg dragged him inside.

Jackson was killed instantly, with a knife wound to the chest. Michele Atkinson suffered eighteen stab wounds and was still alive when paramedics arrived, but died at the scene. After attempting and failing to slit his own throat, Greg Atkinson was treated in hospital and then remanded in custody.

Trembling as he went up to his office, Daniel tried to shut out sense memories of Michele that came to him in a rush: her ribcage through her jacket when he put a hand on her back to comfort her; the light floral scent of her perfume, her small, child-like face and body aged by fear. That way she had of sitting, as if she might startle and fly away seconds later. The way her face had changed completely when she laughed that one time.

Pushing back his shoulders, Daniel entered the office. He had failed to protect Michele and her son. Others would say that it was the justice system that had failed, or the government for its cuts to legal aid, but Daniel felt responsible. He had been distracted, his caseload too heavy. Offering to give her legal instructions pro bono had been his way to try and compensate for the deficits in the system. He might have helped her but he could have done more. He could have been more conscientious in following up her case before it went to court. If only Michele had been able to afford a barrister to fight for her and Jackson.

Stopping at his assistant's desk, Daniel waited for Jacob to hang up the phone.

'Good morning,' Jacob said.

'I didn't know if we've had word about one of Polly's clients I was looking after? Michele Atkinson? I read an article this morning; I think she's been murdered.'

'I'll look into it.'

'Thank you.'

In his office, Daniel sat down at his desk and pressed the heels of his hands into his eyes. They were interviewing for new trainees today, and Daniel was on the panel. He whispered that he was sorry, although Michele could not hear him. She'd warned him this would happen. She was yet another person he needed to apologise to. And little Jackson, almost Billy's age – Daniel hadn't met him, but he felt deeply sorry.

Even through his guilt, he considered how for many years he had been seeing things the wrong way round. For most of his life he had blamed the social care system for all of his problems. He had thought that being removed from his mother and put into care had caused all of the distress that followed: his aggression, his failure to bond, his delinquency, and later his depression, his failure in relationships, his difficulty in expressing warmth and love. All this because he had been a *cared for* child.

It wasn't as simple as that. Minnie had been part of the system and until Minnie he had not been loved. In so many ways, being taken from his mother and put into the system had saved him.

Just as he was about to turn on his computer, Jacob knocked at the door – his usual triple knock – and then entered without waiting.

'Just to let you know that unfortunately Michele Atkinson's dead, like you said. I didn't know if you were aware, but her son . . . was also killed.'

'I was aware, but thanks for confirming.' Daniel swallowed.

Nodding, retreating, Jacob added, 'Here's your mail,' as he placed a few envelopes on Daniel's desk.

'Thanks, Jacob,' he said, not even glancing at the mail.

He tried to shake off the feeling that covered him like a layer of frost.

As he gathered together candidate notes for the interviews, he thought about Greg and the compressed energy of him, so that even with his smile and deep laugh lines, Daniel had been able to read the potential for violence in him.

Where does the violence go? Daniel wondered what Sebastian was doing now.

As he was about to head to the boardroom for the interviews, a call came through from DCI Lloyd. Daniel was surprised to hear from him, even though Leila had warned him that the police were focusing in on Sebastian again.

'How are you, Mr Hunter?' His deep Yorkshire voice sounded tired.

DCI Lloyd wouldn't be aware that Daniel was no longer representing Sebastian Croll. He wondered if it was another courtesy
call about Sebastian's protection arrangements.

'Very well, thank you. How're you?'

'Well, there's been a development in the Frances Owen investigation. I wondered if you might be able to help us—'

Again, Daniel thought of everything he knew about Sebastian
and how he could not breathe a word of that to the DCI.

'I should probably mention that I'm not representing Mr Croll
any longer—'

'Right. This was a question for you, actually. The inves-
tigation has led us to a storage facility in central London.
It seems you rent a ten-foot-square space in Secure-Store at
King's Cross?'

'Me? No, that's not the case. I don't . . .'

Daniel remembered Leila telling him that Sebastian had been
tracked calling a facility in King's Cross.

'Well, Mr Croll seems to have been very interested in this
particular storage facility and we went to check if there was
a space rented in his name. We found nothing, but there is –
bizarrely – a space rented in *your name*—'

'It's a common name, I suppose—'

'No, it's definitely you. They require a couple of types of ID
to rent the space. I think a utility bill from your Herne Hill
address was used—'

Suddenly, Daniel felt his throat dry.

'One hundred per cent convinced, that I don't have a storage
space at King's Cross, or anywhere else for that matter.'

'Well, obviously we're applying for a warrant to search, but I wanted to check with you.'

'I'm certain,' Daniel said, his mind turning over as he remembered Sebastian's confession and then finding the energy bill missing from his desk.

'We'll keep you updated,' DCI Lloyd said.

Daniel took a deep breath.

As he was hanging up the phone, he noticed that in the pile of mail on his desk, one of the white envelopes was from the DNA testing clinic where he had sent the cup sample from Leila.

After thinking it over, he had decided that he would prefer to know, rather than not know and so, with a sense of impulsiveness, he had sent the cup along with a strand of his own hair.

It was turning into an ominous day. He tore the letter open, thinking that things couldn't get much worse. Reading, Daniel let the results letter flutter to his desk.

'Hey, we're waiting for you.' Veronica peeped her head around the door. 'Panel assembled apart from our Senior Partner – get a move on.'

'Just coming.' Daniel got to his feet, slipped on his jacket and straightened his tie. As he picked up the file with the candidate summaries, he glanced again at the result of the paternity test, as if he'd been hallucinating just a moment before. There was no doubt. It was positive. His biological father was Steven Salter.

22

It was well after eight when Daniel finally made it back to the flat in Bow, needing a run to help him shake off the day. There was so much going round in his head and movement helped him to think things through. He undressed quickly and changed into running gear.

As he ran, listening to music on his phone, all of his worries circled in his head: the results of the paternity test; the mix-up about the storage space; Sebastian and 'Justice for Ben'; Rene and Billy; the break-in. All these pressures spun in his head as his feet hit the pavement, heading towards the glow of the late sun in the distance. It was almost nine and the aching summer heat had relented.

Sprinting towards Bethnal Green, he kept his pace tight. It was one of his standard ten-kilometre runs. He liked to finish a ten K in under forty minutes. If he pushed himself, he could get closer to the thirty-five minutes he had run as a younger man. His body felt warm, his breath just starting to even out, that place in a run when he felt energised and steady, as if he could keep running forever.

Zipped into the chest pocket of his running shirt, his phone began to vibrate – a sensation like an electronic heartbeat. Slowing his pace to see who was calling, he saw it was Rene. Answering, waiting for her to speak, sweat broke from his pores. If only she was calling to say she'd slept on it and she wanted to try again with their marriage.

'Are you out somewhere?' she asked, hearing the traffic sounds around him.

'I'm just on a run.'

'Right ...'

He heard anxiety in her voice. 'Is everything alright?'

'Yeah, probably. I might be going nuts, but there's a guy standing across the street, underneath one of the avenue trees. He's been there for about twenty minutes and he's just standing there staring at our house. I'm probably paranoid, but I wondered if it's someone casing the house again, waiting to break in after not getting what they wanted last time.'

Frowning, Daniel waited for her to continue.

'I turned the lights out so I could look without him seeing me. He's wearing a hoodie, so I can't really see what he looks like. It's just he's been there in the same position for a while and he's staring *straight* at our house – it's not like he's looking around waiting for someone. What d'you think? Am I getting carried away? It might be just a random drug pick-up—'

The pavement was busier here and he stood in the doorway of a block of flats to allow pedestrians to pass. 'Apart from a hoodie, can you describe him at all?' he asked, feeling the pulse in his throat.

'He's slim, pretty tall. Nothing remarkable. He's just standing

there. Billy's in bed already. I just thought I'd let you know.'
Despite what she said, he heard the worry in her voice.

The man sounded similar to the guy who had mugged him at
the cashpoint, but then, too, Daniel had only caught a glimpse.

'I'll come over.'

'Are you sure? It might be nothing.'

The fact that she wanted him to come bolstered him.

'I'll be there as quick as I can, okay?'

'Thank you.'

'Call me back if anything changes.'

Sweat began to sting Daniel's eyes. A fine rain had started and
cars splashed past, headlights on. People were starting to go out
for the night and Daniel huddled in the doorway as he finished
his conversation with Rene. 'Make sure all the doors are locked
and if you're worried at all, just call the police—'

'The doors are already locked. I'm just spooked a little and
thought it would be easier if you were here.'

All of a sudden he felt the distance between them; the effort
of transport and traffic. 'I'll jump in a taxi. I'll be with you before
ten thirty,' he said, standing on the kerb and watching for the
light of a cab coming his way; there were none.

'See you soon.'

Again he heard the strain in her voice. She didn't scare
easily. He thought again about the burglary and finding that
strange mourning brooch – a foreign object that neither of
them remembered. He thought about Sebastian going through
his mail and knowing Billy's name even though Daniel was sure
he hadn't mentioned it.

Daniel looked up the street and down, calculating how long it would take him to get to Herne Hill on the Tube or in a taxi. He had his credit card with him in the cover of his phone, but Daniel knew that, even in a taxi, it could take nearly an hour. He wanted to teleport there *right now*. He wanted to be there *now*, to protect them, even if this threat proved to be a hoax of some kind. He knew it was only six and a half miles or so from where he was now in Bethnal Green to Herne Hill. It was just over ten kilometres, which in his younger days he could run in just over half an hour. The realisation dawned that the quickest way for him to get to Herne Hill was just to *run* there.

Without giving a taxi another thought, he set off, navigating pedestrians and cars, skipping through traffic lights. He kept one eye out for a taxi but he was travelling faster than the traffic, which crawled from block to block. Whenever he had a clear pavement in front of him he sprinted, forcing himself to go as fast as he could, feeling the momentum in his torso as it twisted left and right and the heel-toe action of his feet. He was barely aware of the landmarks he passed: the mosque in Shadwell, its dome glowing like the body of a spider; the Docks; running flat-out over Tower Bridge only vaguely aware of the metallic smell of the Thames, its water like molten pewter beneath the glow of the moon. South of the river, in the business district, he kept to small pathways, the glint of The Shard taunting him, like a chunk of quartz lit from within. Breathing hard, feeling the strain now, the tightness down his hamstring and the heat in his body, he went through Southwark and the outskirts of

Lambeth. He ran through Camberwell Green and right down Denmark Hill.

When he saw the green of Ruskin Park, he felt hope flare in him, knowing that he was finally entering his old neighbourhood and would be home in a few minutes. He slowed his pace just slightly, allowing his breathing to deepen. As he joined the avenue from Ferndene Road, he slowed to a walk. The street was dark in places – the trees shrouding the streetlamps so that the pavement was in shadow. Looking at it now from this angle, on foot, in the new dark, he realised it was a good street to burgle, doorways hidden by brick awnings set back from the pavement. Daniel looked along both sides of the street for a man lurking under a tree, a hooded figure alone, but there was no sign. There was no sign of anyone; the street was quiet.

He didn't have his key so he knocked on the door and waited, sweat pouring from his forehead, making his eyes sting.

Relief lit Rene's face as she opened the door. In the small space of the hall, they drew close.

'Thanks for coming. My God, you're all sweaty. You didn't—?'

'I ran here. I thought it would be just as quick—'

Rene reached up and touched his cheek. He clasped his hand over hers, his heart beating hard inside his chest.

'Are you both okay?'

'Billy's asleep. I think I might have been over-reacting. I'm sorry if I worried you. I know I wasn't listening to you properly the other night when you were trying to tell me about what's been going on with you . . . all that campaign stuff.' She turned away from him in the hall, running a hand through her hair.

'Then when I picked up Billy from the childminder, I had the strangest feeling that someone was following us, but maybe I was just imagining it. I'll admit I got spooked. You'll have noticed he's gone now. I think I just got a bit paranoid.'

She led him into the kitchen. Only when they stepped into the bright space did he realise that they were still holding hands. All the lights were on and the garden was in darkness, so that all they could see in the windows that opened out onto the patio was their own reflections.

'Do you want a drink?'

He shook his head, helping himself to a glass of water. Already there was a chill on his skin, goosepimples on his upper arms.

'It was when I was putting Billy to bed. I drew the curtains and looked out onto the street. He just ... looked not right, y'know what I mean? He was standing on his own beneath one of the sycamore trees, his arms folded. It was his focus – he was just staring straight at the window. It creeped me out, I'm sorry—'

'Don't apologise. That's what I've been going through these last few weeks. It's what I was trying to describe to you. It's better to be safe than sorry. I'm so glad you called me.'

A hand to her mouth. 'And you ran all the way here.'

'Yeah,' he said, putting his hands on his hips. 'At your service ... my lady. You just have to say the word.'

'I love you,' she said, staying where she was, not making a move towards him. 'Thanks for coming. It feels better now you're here.'

Even though he was frightened he was reading her wrong, he kissed her properly for the first time since that night when she asked him to leave. He pressed her into him until she giggled and pulled away, wiping his sweat from her face.

'I'll go and have a shower, shall I?'

'Please.'

Grinning, he turned for the stairs, joy surging inside him. 'I'll go and have a wash, and then we'll have a cup of tea and go to bed.' As simple as that, a shower and then bed with his wife in his own home; tonight it felt like an achievement. Nevertheless, he was still on edge and felt something snag. 'Shall I? Do you want to?' He paused at the foot of the stairs. 'Given that we're both paranoid, shall we just check everything's all locked up?'

Methodically, they went round each of the windows and doors, starting with the French doors that led out onto the patio, checking that everything was locked and secure. Together, they worked their way upstairs, checking the windows in the bedrooms and the upstairs bathrooms. Everything was as it should be.

'I'm sorry for freaking out before,' she said, on the landing.

'You did the right thing, but—'

'But what?'

'I want to stay here tonight.'

'*Please* stay.' She reached out, put a hand flat on his chest. Daniel laid his own hand on top of hers. He felt close to her again, and she and Billy were safe, and that made his frantic run from Bow seem worthwhile. 'I think we should put Billy in our bed, all of us sleep together. I think I'll feel better in the morning. I don't know what got into me.'

'Good idea. When we're ready to go to bed, I'll carry him through.'

Without saying a word, Rene stood on her tiptoes and kissed his lips. Daniel ran his hand up her neck, brushing his thumb along the line of her jaw.

Just out of the shower, Daniel pulled on an old pair of jeans and a T-shirt. Even though he shared Rene's sense of anxiety, in that moment he still enjoyed reaching into drawers to find his own clothes. Turning down the duvet of their large king-sized bed, he went into Billy's room to carry him through.

On the landing, he ran his hand over the plate rail shelf. Another act of paranoia, but nothing was there. Reaching up, his fingers didn't find any strange antiques or indeed anything at all.

It was easier than Daniel had imagined to lift Billy without waking him; he was asleep on his back and sound, a gentle little snore audible. Daniel slid his hands underneath and then pressed the body into him as he went along the corridor to the main bedroom, careful not to bang Billy's head against the door, feeling the heat radiating from the small of Billy's back. Laid down in the cool bed, Billy's eyes fluttered open for a moment.

'Wshhh, you go to sleep.' Daniel kissed the little boy's hair, relishing his rich nutty smell. The baby hairs at the nape of his neck were damp with sweat. As Daniel raised the duvet up, Billy turned, the tip of his thumb slipping into his mouth. Daniel waited, sitting on the edge of the bed, stroking Billy's back until he was sure that he was asleep again.

Making his way downstairs, Daniel stretched his arms up and pressed them against the ceiling of the stairwell. At the foot of the steps, he checked again that the front door was double-locked.

In the kitchen, Rene was tidying up papers on the table and switching off lamps ready to go to bed.

'Are you okay?'

She slipped her arms around his waist and he drew her close. They stood like that for a moment in the partial darkness, the only light coming from the cooker hood.

Pressing her into him, looking over her shoulder at the glass doors that led out into the garden, he saw only their reflection, not the trees and plants that lined the patio outside. As they swayed together gently, Daniel noticed that their image was incomplete, a panel of darkness where he would have expected to see the reflection of Rene's shirt tails.

Frowning, Daniel gently broke free of her embrace.

'What's the matter?' she asked.

'Fuck.' The panel near the lock was missing. As if disbelieving, he reached out to touch it and cut himself. 'This wasn't broken earlier, was it? We checked, right?' he said, sucking blood from his finger.

Rene's face drained of all colour. 'We checked everywhere.'

Turning the handle on the patio doors, Daniel was pleased that the door was still locked, but the glass was missing near the lock and handle. The space was clearly big enough to allow someone to reach inside and unlock the door.

'We should call the police,' she said, picking up her mobile.

'Do you have the crime number from the burglary?' Daniel asked.

Rene nodded, taking a Post-it note from the noticeboard as she waited to be put through to the operator. With the phone on speaker, Rene gave the crime number from the previous break-in and reported that the glass near the lock had been broken.

'So you discovered it broken when you came home?' the operator said. Daniel could hear her typing information into the computer.

'No, everything was secure, we are both at home, but we've since discovered that there might have been some kind of breach. Also, someone seemed to be watching our house earlier this evening—'

Rene began to give a description of the man she had seen.

'We'll send a car over.'

'When will they be here?'

'I can't give an exact time. We have a major incident ongoing in Camberwell. It'll be as soon as possible.'

As Rene finished the call, Daniel turned for the stairs, wanting to check on Billy. He was glad that Billy was in their bed, but he felt a strange, anxious need to be near him, as if sensing he needed protecting. Just behind him on the stairs, Rene slipped her hand into his. He felt his heart thumping inside him, stronger than it had on the run here. Rene's hand was a tense little claw in his and he knew it would be at least twenty minutes before the police arrived. There was a horrible feeling on his skin. Nothing was amiss as they climbed the stairs, but it was as if his skin was aware of a presence that defied his other senses.

Daniel had left the hall light on for Billy, in case he woke in the middle of the night. On the bright landing, there was no noise, nothing out of place to suggest an intruder. Everything was as it should be. In the silence, Daniel could only hear the thud of his own heart. His mouth was very dry.

Rene shook her hand loose from his. 'I'll just check these rooms,' she said, peering into the bathroom and then going to check Billy's room. He could see from the stiff way that she walked, intently focused, that she was as frightened as he was. Daniel went for Billy, breaths fluttering in his mouth, needing to make sure he was safe.

In the darkness of their bedroom, it took a few moments for Daniel's eyes to adjust. Billy was sound asleep, oblivious, positioned right in the middle of the bed where Daniel had placed him, so that they could sleep on either side of him. Relief pulsed through him. He let out a sigh and bent over, not wanting to wake him, but needing to touch him, to reassure himself that he hadn't come to any harm.

Perhaps it was the fact that he had run so fast and so hard, and then allowed his body to cool down too quickly, but Daniel's skin still felt chilled, all the hairs raised. He reached out and laid a hand on Billy's shoulder, gently, careful with the weight of his hand so as not to wake him. The little boy's chest rose and fell.

A door gently closed in the hall and Daniel heard Rene's footsteps approach.

Straightening, looking across the bed, Daniel noticed a dark shape shift in the crepuscular space. Squinting, confused for a moment, Daniel suddenly felt his stomach drop, as if he'd swallowed a stone. The black shape moved again and then took a step forward. Daniel became aware of eyes peering out of the blackness.

It took a while for his eyes to focus and realise that the dark shape was a man wearing a black mask.

Behind him, he heard Rene's sharp intake of breath.

Instinctively – some part of him sure who it was – Daniel whispered, '*Sebastian?*'

23

Slowly, Sebastian peeled the mask from his face. It was some kind of thin balaclava, holes only for his eyes.

In the half-dark of the bedroom, the only sound the gentle breathing of his son and the thud of his heart, Daniel thought about Frances Owen. He imagined how she had felt turning up at work that morning to find Sebastian somehow inside her office. Daniel felt the same shock, the same disbelief as to how Sebastian had breached the house, slipped unnoticed into the bedroom where their young son slept. Daniel expected that Frances would have felt so alone, facing Sebastian – no one to call; no point crying for help. Daniel felt a greater fear just now, because he was *not* alone. He felt as vulnerable as his sleeping son who lay between them. Sebastian was in reaching distance of Billy.

'What are you doing here, Seb?' Daniel asked, trying to keep his voice even.

Daniel couldn't see Rene's face, but sensed her just behind him, at the bedroom's threshold. Sebastian didn't seem to have any kind of weapon, but Daniel didn't want to risk a fight.

Sebastian loomed at Billy's bedside, an animated shadow, like a nightmare come to life. 'You were supposed to protect me.' The tone of Sebastian's voice was strangely devoid of emotion – flat – neither threatening, nor pleading. The measured way he spoke made his words seem more menacing.

'I *did* defend you, before and this last time.' Daniel's breaths were in his throat. He struggled to keep his breathing even, not wanting Sebastian to hear his fear.

'You abandoned me. You cast me out—'

'I ...' Daniel was about to say that he hadn't abandoned Sebastian, but feared that disagreeing would anger him. 'I'm sorry you feel like that. I didn't mean to; it was a point of law. You *can* trust me.' Daniel heard the rattle of his breath in his throat. His mind was a shifting kaleidoscope of dread and terror as he imagined what might happen.

'Trust?' Sebastian spat the word and the harsh consonants, although whispered, caused Billy to stir. His small dark head shifted on the pillow.

'I took you into confidence—'

'I didn't break that confidence. I haven't told a soul. I promise.' Daniel clenched his fists at his side, wondering if he should try to grab Billy. Because he was in the middle of the large bed, Sebastian could reach and grab him just as quick.

'You don't understand what you've done to me—'

'Of course I understand you,' Daniel said, pacifying. 'It's like you said before, we have so much ... in common.'

Sebastian's eyes flashed in the dark as Daniel dared to take a step forward.

'I don't believe your promises. I told you that I murdered

Frances and suddenly the police are now searching Barnard Park and the grounds around my father's house. Even though they're nowhere near, they're trying to close in—'

Barnard Park was the small green area near the Crolls' Islington home, where Ben had been found dead all those years ago. Daniel knew that the Major Investigation Team in the Frances Owen investigation were getting a warrant for a London storage facility, but hadn't heard about the wider Islington search. He knew they were looking for the murder weapon and blood and clothing from the Cambridge murder scene.

'I absolutely did not tell the police what you told me.'

'Frances was just like you, y'know. Trying to push me away. She deserved what I did to her. I waited patiently all night for her. She came in just after dawn and the first thing she did when she saw me was smile. I almost forgave her for that—'

Daniel's eyes had adjusted to the darkness and he could see Sebastian clearly, standing by the bed with an oily smile on his lips.

'Almost. She knew what was coming to her. Just like you, she wanted rid of me, so I got rid of her.'

Daniel could see that Sebastian's eyes were focused into the distance somewhere as if remembering.

'I hit her so hard with that old rock she kept in the office. I turned her into a thing. No more Frances—'

Billy began to stir, shifting onto his side.

Sebastian focused on the little boy 'Shhhhhh . . . there now,' he soothed.

It was such a parody of comfort, so synthetic, that Daniel felt suddenly terrified, a prickle of goosebumps at the back of his head.

'No more Frances,' Sebastian repeated, a strange electrified smile lighting his face. 'No more Danny . . . no more Billy—'

'Listen, this is between you and me, Sebastian. I know, I let you down—'

Rene stepped forward into the room. 'Sebastian, I want you to leave *right now*. You have no right to be here. The police are on their way.' Her whole body was trembling.

'It's nice to see you again, Irene. Or should I say my lady?'

'Leave, *right now.*'

Reaching back, Daniel found Rene's fingers and squeezed them: they were icy cold in his hand. She sounded full of authority, but he knew she was terrified, like him, for Billy. Suddenly, Daniel saw that Sebastian was holding something long and black in his right hand, keeping it flush against his leg.

Seeing the weapon, thoughts about what to do began to shift and crack in Daniel's mind, like plates of ice. Pins and needles in his fingertips as he again thought of reaching for Billy, trying to cover him with his own body. He felt sure that Rene hadn't seen the weapon.

Sebastian stepped further into the room, to the side of the bed. His face was now fully illuminated. He was close enough to touch Billy now and he seemed huge, his height and the power of him somehow magnified.

At first Daniel thought that Sebastian was holding a shotgun or a sword of some kind, but, as Sebastian moved closer to Billy, he realised that it was a black, metal baseball bat. Of course. Both Frances and Ben had been beaten to death.

'Go downstairs,' Daniel whispered over his shoulder to Rene. She didn't move.

'It's me you want, Sebastian,' Daniel tried again. 'Let's you and I go downstairs and talk.'

'You don't mean it. You just want me out of here. You want to push me away.'

Sebastian had been whispering before but when he said, *push me away*, he raised his voice.

Billy woke and propped himself up on one elbow. 'Daddy?'

Only when Billy saw the look on Daniel's face did he turn and see Sebastian. Billy flattened himself on the bed.

Adrenalin pulsed through Daniel's body, realising he had to act now; that he had to shield Billy from Sebastian. In a single movement, he bent over the bed and took hold of Billy. The little boy sprang into his arms, allowing Daniel to turn for the door, hunching, cringing, ducking his head; just aware in his peripheral vision of the dark bat swinging. He curled his whole body around Billy, then – in the doorway – passed him to Rene.

Time seemed to move so slowly, each second ushered by a flurry of heartbeats, his senses overexposed.

The rush and smart of the air as Sebastian swung the bat.

Billy's ankles and bare feet in Rene's arms.

The clutch of her hands, veins standing out on her forearms.

Pushing them out of the room, Daniel ducked and then stood against the door, closing it. Even though he knew he was in great danger, Daniel preferred this equation. It was just him and Sebastian now.

Looking around for something to protect himself with, Daniel saw the antique wooden chair by the window, behind Sebastian, knowing there was no way for him to reach it. He thought about a pillow to lessen the impact but that seemed absurd.

'Let's sit down and talk about this, Sebastian,' he tried again, desperate now, the words sticking in his mouth, hard to spit out from his fear-dried lips.

'Enough talking.'

With a muscular athleticism, Sebastian swung the bat again. Daniel jumped backwards, pressing himself against the door, as Billy had flattened himself against the bed earlier.

Missed. Daniel panted, heartbeat skipped, only now realising that Sebastian had been deliberately taunting him.

Again Sebastian swung, deliberately just in front of Daniel's face. A breeze on his forehead from the friction of the bat through the air. His fingertips touched the wall. He thought about the kestrel at the farm in Cumbria, the strong wings rising up on a thermal. He thought about little Jackson, dragged back inside the family home by Greg wielding a knife. Daniel had no means to protect himself. He knew, like Frances, he would have to use his arms, hands, his back.

A wide grin split Sebastian's face, his straight white teeth illuminated in the dark. 'Do you still sleep with a knife under your pillow, Danny?'

Daniel kept his eyes on the tip of the bat, all of his senses heightened, his muscles sprung.

He wondered if he would be able to hurl himself at Sebastian, grab him by the waist to take him down. His heartbeat in his ears was like thunder.

Sebastian swung the bat with all his force at Daniel's face. He defended himself, with his arm, as if there was an invisible shield attached to it.

Bone-cracking pain ripped through him, bringing him to his knees. Lower teeth to his upper lip, he growled out the agony. He knew his forearm was broken, the pain yawning up his arm. Sebastian lifted the bat above his head, two handed. On one knee before him, Daniel tasted blood in his mouth.

He tried now what he'd meant to attempt a moment before, lunging at Sebastian's torso, taking him off balance. Sebastian grabbed Daniel's injured wrist as he fell. The pain of the touch, that twist of bone before the impact of the fall was excruciating.

Scuffling in the centre of the bedroom, Daniel tried to reach for the bat with his good hand, but it kept slipping from his grasp. He must have cried out, in pain, for help.

All of a sudden, there was an explosion of glass. It burst all around Daniel, as if he was in a snow globe filled with shards.

24

Through the blur of pain and fear, all Daniel could think was that Sebastian had broken the window with his bat, but then he saw the bat resting in a pool of water on the floor.

Gasping, Daniel realised that his hair was wet and Sebastian was unconscious on the floor beside him, bleeding onto the pale-grey carpet from a gash at the back of his head. He had no idea how it had happened. In the darkness, Sebastian's blood on the carpet seemed black.

'Oh God, are you okay? The police are here. Let me help you up. *Get up, Danny,* let's get outside.'

It was Rene. His body was filled with heat suddenly, his arm swelling up but burning hot as he got onto one knee and then made it to the edge of the bed.

'What did you do? How did you . . . ?'

'I hit him with the vase from the hall. Come on. Let's get out of here in case he wakes up.'

The brand-new lead crystal vase had shattered on contact with Sebastian's head. The pieces covered the carpet like dropped diamonds.

The front door was open and a patrol car was parked outside.

Billy was crying; barefoot in the front garden in his pyjamas, he launched into Daniel's arms. Lifting Billy, pain ripped through him, a horrible crunching agony anaesthetised by holding his little boy safe in his arms.

'You're alright. Don't cry. You're okay.' Gritting his teeth, Daniel transferred Billy's weight to his good arm. He knew he was full of adrenalin, the pain he was feeling now lessened by the shock.

'No ... I'm worried about *you*,' Billy gulped. 'I'm crying for you. You're hurt.'

'I'm okay. You don't need to cry for me. We're going to be just fine.'

Rene was briefing the police officers, one of whom took out his baton and PAVA spray as he went upstairs to find Sebastian. Daniel kissed Billy's hair and drew back, sitting on the wall of their front garden, setting Billy onto his knee. All the neighbours were out now, pulling on sweatshirts over pyjamas or hanging out of front windows. As if chilled to the bone, Daniel felt his whole body trembling.

As paramedics carried Sebastian out on a stretcher, blood streaked over his face from the wound on his crown, Billy flinched at the sight of him.

'Let me take him,' Rene said as he buried his face into Daniel. 'Your arm looks terrible.'

When Rene took Billy from his arms, Daniel stood and went to the back of the ambulance, where the paramedics were securing Sebastian for the journey. His eyes were closed, an oxygen mask over his mouth and nose. There was a large blood-soaked dressing at the back of his head.

'What's his condition?' Daniel asked the paramedic.

'Head injury, very hard to tell. He'll need a scan as soon as we get to the emergency room.'

Another paramedic took time to look at Daniel's arm. It was broken without doubt, she told him. Strapping it up, she told him he had to go to A&E and get an X-ray as more information was needed about the placement of the bone. It didn't sound good. Daniel knew his arm had twisted after the break and so didn't ask any more.

The police officer who'd found Sebastian unconscious upstairs was talking on the police radio, leaning on the roof of the police car, so Daniel went to speak to him. The siren was silent now, although the lights from the ambulance and police car reflected off the road and dark pavements, like reflections of petrol.

'This isn't a random incident,' Daniel said to the officer. 'This man's a suspect for the murder of Frances Owen. He meant to kill us too. You need to contact Cambridgeshire Police, Detective Chief Inspector Lloyd—' Daniel held his fractured arm with one hand. Even strapped up, it was now grossly swollen, bruising had blossomed, red with fresh blood trapped under the skin. 'I'm a criminal solicitor. This man was my client.'

'Don't worry. There's already an alert out on him. If he wakes up, he'll be arrested. Cambridgeshire Police tried to arrest and charge him earlier but he couldn't be found—'

'So you think he'll definitely be taken into custody tonight?'

'We'll need to wait for a medical assessment on his condition—'

The police officer gave Daniel a card for the Victim Support Officer who would be in touch with them throughout the week.

As Rene took Billy back inside to try and settle him, the ambulance left with the police car trailing it. Daniel called Detective Chief Inspector Lloyd, expecting an answer phone and preparing what he would say when it started recording. Adrenalin was still coursing through his body. Each time he blinked he saw again the coldness of Sebastian's eyes. Daniel realised that he had triggered Sebastian's rejection issues by dropping him as a client. In his childhood confession, Daniel remembered Sebastian saying that Ben hadn't wanted to play with him any more. Frances Owen had been murdered because she had also said *no*.

Daniel was surprised when Detective Chief Inspector Lloyd answered.

'Mr Hunter, I was just about to call you myself. Myself and Detective Inspector Burrows are on our way to King's College Hospital right now. I hear he's unconscious—'

'It seemed so.'

'You doubt it?'

'I dunno. We're just, we're just . . . blown away. The paramedics said it was serious, but—'

'Don't worry, Sebastian won't be going anywhere—'

Daniel had so many questions; he paced back and forth on the pavement, his broken arm tucked into his body.

'That storage facility I mentioned, under the name of Daniel Hunter, address in Herne Hill?'

Daniel waited for more, saying nothing, blinking as he watched the moonlight move over the oily road, reflections of purple and green.

'We got our warrant. That storage facility you rented contained what we were looking for . . .'

His mind addled by tiredness, Daniel struggled to defend himself. 'That wasn't . . . I told you I—'

Lloyd's laughter was like a fistful of marbles shook. 'We got his call list from his phone provider – knew he was fixated on that storage facility. But then we tracked his movements via the phone mast and saw he was visiting that same facility. We now have Sebastian on CCTV securing the storage space with your documents. I still don't know why he went to the trouble to do that. I want to question him about it—'

'I don't know why he did that either,' Daniel said. He knew Sebastian saw himself as strangely kindred. As with so many things, the storage unit had been another way for Sebastian to link Daniel to him.

'Inside, we found a large chunk of ornamental agate encrusted with Frances Owen's blood, and fragments of her skull. He'd used latex gloves and a full forensics outfit, but it's all there, covered in blood with Sebastian's DNA on the under-surfaces.'

Daniel whistled, all the air leaving him.

'We also found a lock of Frances Owen's hair—'

Daniel remembered what Leila had said about the pathology report – a patch of hair missing.

'Several strands of hair, torn out by the roots probably just after the fatal blow.'

Daniel was stunned, a blood-deep exhaustion lulling him to the sound of the detective's voice.

'So we know Sebastian killed Frances Owen. We have proof.'

Throat dry, Daniel swallowed.

'The hair probably was some kind of trophy—' DCI Lloyd cleared his throat '—particularly as we found other hair, belonging to another woman.'

'Another woman?'

'Unfortunately, that "Daniel Hunter" storage unit has confirmed what we suspected; that Frances wasn't Sebastian's first victim—'

'He's killed before,' Daniel repeated, aware that he sounded out of breath, even though he had barely moved since he took the call. 'You might not have been aware, but we were looking again at an open case ... an ex-girlfriend of Sebastian's from Cambridge, a young woman called Sarah Doyle. She dropped out and got into drugs, had a breakdown, separated from her family. She was reported missing while she was living on the streets.'

'Sarah—' Daniel said. He was literally so tired he thought he might collapse.

'Her body was found in the Regent's Canal just under a year ago. She's been dead for over two years. There was a murder enquiry but no leads. It took a while just to identify her body.'

'So Sebastian killed Sarah Doyle?'

'It would seem so. We will argue so. She was also beaten to

death, her face was smashed in. Sebastian had kept a few strands of her hair, torn from the roots, confirming that it was taken just after her death.'

'Just like Frances Owen.'

'And we both know that Sarah wasn't Sebastian's first victim,' DCI Lloyd said.

Even in his shock-addled state, Daniel knew that DCI Lloyd was referring to Ben.

Just as he was unable to tell DCI Lloyd that Sebastian had confessed to murdering Frances weeks before, he was also unable to say that all those years ago, after the not-guilty verdict, he had also confessed to killing Ben.

'But I'm glad I caught him now,' DCI Lloyd continued. 'He's killed both of these women he's been associated with, covered it up with great success, kept their hair—'

'Why do you think he did that?'

'When people do things like that, methodical, taking an interest, taking a keepsake, it means that they intend to continue ... killing. I'm glad I caught him now.'

Daniel felt the throb of his arm.

'Thank you for everything, Detective Chief Inspector,' Daniel said.

'There was one other link that fell into place with you ... you're like the Geordie piece of the jigsaw ...'

'What?'

'One of the Met teams that were protecting Sebastian managed to arrest the man – a campaigner who'd thrown a brick through the Crolls' window.'

'Of course.'

'He was known to the police. One of those floater campaigners who seems to go where the trouble is rather than where their morals lie—'

'Right.' Daniel felt his upper body wavering, as if he might pass out.

'That same man who threw a brick through Sebastian's window also mugged you off Liverpool Street. There was a match with CCTV but he confessed anyway. Since he confessed, it'll go straight to sentencing. You might not even be called, but just thought you might like to know.'

'Thank you,' Daniel said again.

'No need to thank me. Just doing my job. I'm glad it's ended as it has; you and your family were put in danger.'

Daniel was about to turn back to the house, then thought of something.

'One thing ... what you said about him keeping the hair ...' Daniel's head hurt. 'Hair from Frances and Sarah ... we had a break-in here a few days ago, after I finished representing Sebastian. Nothing was taken, but we found a hair brooch shortly afterwards—'

'Hair brooch?'

'One of those Victorian mourning brooches. Not ours, no idea where it came from. Do you think ... Sebastian could have left it, that he could've been in here, before?'

Lloyd's face was grave. 'Like a calling card. Maybe. I'll send a uniform to collect it.'

Daniel nodded, light encroaching on his eyes.

'Sebastian tried to kill me,' he whispered, almost to himself.

'You get some rest, lad,' Detective Chief Inspector Lloyd said.

Lad. Daniel heaved a sigh.

Back inside with Rene, Daniel took two ibuprofen, and then they went upstairs again to check on Billy.

Rene leaned her head against the bedroom wall. 'He's just fallen asleep. The shock had him tired out but he was fighting it; he was so worried about you. Kept telling me to get you to come inside.'

Daniel hooked his good arm around Rene's neck and pulled her into him. She pressed her face into his neck. They stayed like that for a few moments, taking comfort.

'Cambridgeshire Police have found the forensic evidence they need to link Sebastian to the Frances Owen murder. As soon as he's cleared to be discharged from hospital, he'll be charged and remanded in custody. It's the best result.' He could still feel her trembling. 'Are you okay?'

'I had to do something. I heard him hit you; I just knew I had to try,' she said, breathless. 'It was the only thing I could think of . . . I had no idea it was so heavy – it was hard to get it over my head but then he just collapsed. I kept waiting for him to get up and . . .' She pulled away from him just enough to look up into his face. 'What if I've killed him?'

He kissed her forehead. '*You saved me.*'

She tried a smile but it quivered on her face. 'Vases aren't faring well in this house of late.'

Daniel was also too exhausted to laugh. 'You did well getting Billy to sleep. It's the best thing for him.'

'What about us? Will we be able to sleep?'

The thought of snuggling up to her, sleep or no sleep, broken
arm included, filled him with beatific warmth.

'You need to get that arm seen to – I could call you a taxi to
get you to A&E. I don't want to wake him up now, otherwise
I'd drive you—'

'I'm not leaving you. I'm just not. I'll go in the morning.'

In the kitchen, with the empty pane of glass still reminding
them of their earlier horror, Rene took a bottle of whisky from
the cabinet and poured an inch into two tumblers.

'Will do us good—' Rene said, shrugging.

Daniel swirled the amber liquid in the glass and smelled
it – smoke and burnt sugar. They clinked glasses then Daniel
downed his in one, wincing at the burn in his throat when he
swallowed.

Rene's sip made her eyes water. 'I still feel on edge, as if
something else is going to happen.' Her voice was still tremu-
lous, breathy. 'Like it's one of those films . . . you know what I
mean . . . what if Sebastian's already ripped off that oxygen mask
in the ambulance and is now coming back to find us.'

He ran a hand through her hair and pulled her towards him
gently. 'It's over,' he whispered. 'Everything's okay. We're all
okay.' As he said, *we're all okay,* he thought of Frances Owen
and Sarah Doyle and Ben, and Michele and Jackson Atkinson.
'Listening to DCI Lloyd talk about what he'd found in that

lock-up, it made me think about that day I went to Cambridge to meet Sebastian again. On the train, I felt ...' He looked down into his drink. 'I mean we'd just separated so I felt like shit anyway, but I had this sense of not wanting to see Sebastian again. In my gut I didn't want anything to do with him, but there he was all grown up and together. I was completely taken in by that for a while, that he'd grown up to be alright, even after everything. I think I wanted to believe that. I wanted to know that was possible. I knew he had killed Ben, but he had been a boy and it was, or I believed it was ... a result of his upbringing—' Nausea rocked through him; he wasn't sure if it was the pain or the whisky, or the shock itself. He put a hand to his mouth.

'Try not to think too much about it tonight. It's so much to take in ...'

'He's killed two women, three people. DCI Lloyd said he's sure that Sebastian meant to continue. He could've killed us. I just keep thinking about that day when I went to meet him in Cambridge—'

'Stop,' she said. 'Don't do this to yourself.'

Rene's hand shook as she took a sip of her drink. 'My teeth are chattering.'

Daniel poured another inch of whisky into his glass and hers. It wasn't numbing the pain in his arm yet, but it was helping somehow.

'Thanks for staying,' she said. 'I don't want you to leave.'

Daniel looked at her, saw the sparkle in her green eyes. He wondered if she meant *for now* – until they were sure

Sebastian was in custody – or if she was talking about *them* and their future.

'I never wanted to leave in the first place,' he said, reaching out to put a hand on her neck. He loved how delicate her bones were where her collarbone met her throat, so exquisite and refined.

She took another sip of her drink and her eyes filled with tears, so he wasn't sure if it was the whisky making her eyes water. 'I don't want to split us up.' She found his hand on the counter and placed her own on top of it.

He kissed her, tasted the whisky from her lips. 'I miss you so much. I'm not right without you.'

'We miss you too.' She put down her drink and then hugged him, spontaneously, tightly.

Pain shot through him and he had to pull away from her to stop himself screaming and waking Billy. 'Jesus – that really fucking hurts.' He wrenched away finally, gripping his shoulder.

'Oh my God, your arm. I forgot. I was just so happy. We should ice it or something if you're not going to the hospital. I think we've got some arnica—'

'Liar, you did that deliberately.' He tried to laugh, gently touching his elbow in an attempt to stem the throb of shrill nerves around the bone. 'You wanted to get me back.'

'Not true,' she said, giggling.

The fingers of her left hand were resting gently on his arm as if to soothe it. Immediately he noticed, with a flare of something like joy, that she was wearing her wedding ring. It was very definitely back on her finger.

Even though he was in pain, it was such a long time since he'd felt so unequivocally happy. His arm would heal, but the fact *they* were healing seemed so much more important.

EPILOGUE

Sebastian had left numerous messages with Daniel's assistant at the firm. All of the calls had come from inside Pentonville Prison where Sebastian was now on remand for the murder of Frances Owen, awaiting trial sometime next year. He would be charged with the murder of Sarah Doyle but that case was still pending.

Daniel had not accepted any of his calls and *would not*, although he and Rene had talked about whether they would go and watch his trial when it was finally scheduled. They were undecided. Daniel was wary of being spotted in the gallery – by both Sebastian and the press. A good reason *not* to attend was that Daniel was sure it would please Sebastian to see him there.

The forensic evidence against Sebastian was comprehensive and the police and the Crown Prosecution Service were confident of conviction this time. There were prints and DNA on the protective equipment that Sebastian had used to clean up the crime scene. It was as if every fibre he had meticulously removed from Frances's office had been preserved in the lock-up to be revealed months later. Keeping the hair made sense in a macabre way, but storing the other detritus had given the police pause. Had it been another way of covering his tracks – making sure the soiled protective equipment wouldn't be discovered, or had he somehow wanted to keep this too, as a reminder? Daniel wasn't sure how much Sebastian would reveal on interview. Even as a child he had seemed to get the better of the detectives.

If convicted of Frances Owen's murder, Daniel was sure Sebastian would remain in prison until his mid-thirties, but if Sarah Doyle's death was linked to him, as the Crown intended, he would be inside for a very long time.

Quietly, with as little interaction with the media as possible, Kenneth Croll had resigned from his job in the Cabinet. Daniel hadn't spoken to him, and probably would not, ever again. Daniel still wondered if Sebastian's father really had killed his mother. Had that been the act that had really warped Sebastian once and for all?

It had been Sebastian's love for his mother, his wish to protect her, that had first caused Daniel to identify with the little boy on trial.

Right now, none of them were thinking about Sebastian, even though he had played a part in bringing them back together again as a family.

Daniel parked the car; Rene got out and stretched as Billy unleashed himself from his seatbelt and jumped out of the backseat. Daniel leaned gently on the roof as he looked at the farmhouse, its roof and windows dilapidated but still seeming like a familiar friendly face. The plaster cast had been removed from his arm only a week before

After Sebastian's attack, when Daniel had finally made it to the hospital, he'd discovered that his arm was actually broken in three places: two fractures in the ulna and one in the radius of his right arm. It had been a complex fracture that had required surgery to secure the breaks with plates and screws. It was healed now but his right forearm still ached occasionally. He was wearing a polo shirt and jeans; looking down at his bare arms resting on the roof of the car, he noticed how mismatched they still looked. The arm that had been in the cast was thinner and paler: no press-ups for a while.

The air here smelled comfortingly familiar, despite his long time away: manure and the distinct scent of wet, freshly tilled soil. It smelled so different from London, more nourishing somehow. From this vantage point, the fields descended below them, overlapping, with the town of Brampton nestling at the bottom.

Filled with nervous excitement, Daniel slid his key into the lock and it opened for him straight away. Taking Billy's small hand, they stepped inside. The old place was cold and smelled of damp. There were dark clouds of black mould along the ceiling, inky blossoms in the corners and some of the wallpaper was beginning to peel. Slates had become loose in the storms over the years and the leaks had caused the dampness. He couldn't believe that he had hung onto it this long, allowing it to fall into such a state of disrepair. Finally being here, in the flesh, it was worse than he had imagined. Daniel had always felt conflicted: wanting to get rid of this place, yet somehow unable to relinquish it, as if selling the farmhouse was severing his last tie with Minnie.

There was no sign of her here any longer. No animals, the piano gone and, with it, books and piles of newspapers; no array of Wellington boots by the door that she would don to go out and feed the chickens or the goats. He had hired a firm to have the place professionally cleared not long after she died; the only things he had kept of hers had been a shoebox of items that she had personally put aside for him: a porcelain butterfly that had been a gift from her little daughter.

'It smells funny in here,' Billy said.

Daniel didn't reply but squeezed his hand twice before letting it go. Rene was shivering, hugging her arms. She threw open the thin curtains to let the light in and an insect fluttered into the kitchen, stumbling from the windowsill to settle on the bare floorboards.

'Is it a little moth?' she said, startled.

'It's a butterfly,' said Billy.

Daniel saw that he was right – a 'small white'. 'We should take it outside. It won't survive in here long.'

'I want to do it,' Billy said, as Daniel squatted and cupped his hands around the butterfly.

'My hands are bigger. Gives her more room. We have to be quick.'

Daniel indicated the back door and Rene unbolted it, opening out onto the yard where the chickens and the goats had lived. As he opened his hands, the butterfly took flight.

'How did it get in?' Rene mused.

'There's a small broken pane in the kitchen window. Maybe that,' Daniel said.

Inside, they went into the living room as Billy ran upstairs. The sun spilled through the bay window, illuminating dust particles in a golden shaft of light. The cable for the TV aerial was lying on the floor and Daniel remembered Minnie's old box telly.

Rene put her arms around his waist and he drew her into him, resting his chin on the top of her head.

'Thanks for bringing us here.'

'Are you being sarcastic?' He pulled away from her to see her face, but her expression was genuine.

'No, it's nice to see where you grew up.'

'Not quite Barnes, is it?' he said, mimicking a posh accent.

'It's more. I've always wanted to know more about your family. It always seems like such a sore spot. I want to know more, but I'm afraid to ask—'

Daniel blinked. He had shown her the letter confirming who his father was. Her reaction had bolstered him.

'I love you,' she'd said, 'I love *you*, the good man that you are. You are not your father. I know you, and I love who you are.'

Now, Daniel sank his face into her neck. He didn't know how he would ever be able to tell her how humbled he felt by her. He didn't know how he could have jeopardised this love.

Unlike Leila, Daniel hadn't gone to meet Steven Salter who had half of his DNA inside him, and who would be in jail until he was an old man. Daniel knew he never would. The paternity results only underlined for Daniel how important this life was – the life he wanted to live with his family: Rene and Billy. How much he wanted to be who they needed him to be. He didn't doubt that there were aspects of his make-up that made him difficult to live with, but, if this year had taught him anything, it was that he still had the potential to change and to grow. Like father like son, but Daniel didn't want Billy to be held to Daniel's failings any more than he wanted to acknowledge that there was a code for violence inside him: a synaptic Braille that meant he was bound to become what had gone before.

'Is this yours?' Billy's footsteps thumped into the room. All the floorboards were bare and every move each of them made was advertised. 'Come upstairs and see—'

They followed Billy to the bedroom upstairs. It had been Delia's bedroom – Minnie's daughter – and then the bedroom for the children she fostered, of which Daniel had been the last.

Even on his previous visits – during Sebastian's trial, or to meet the engineer – Daniel hadn't stepped into this room. He might not have entered this room since the last time he slept here, which would have been the Christmas before their argument. The damp was bad up here – the ceiling and the corners of the room blackened – but it was the memories rather than the mould that unsettled him.

'Wait and see this,' Billy said, squatting over one of the exposed floorboards. As they stood and watched, Billy traced his forefinger around the outline of the board, slipped a finger underneath, so it lifted like a lid.

On all fours, Billy reached inside. Daniel was about to stop him, thinking about mice or electrical cables and all sorts of reasons why it wasn't good to be reaching down there with seven-year-old fingers.

Suddenly, Billy spun around from the hole in the floor. There was a glint of metal in his hand and Daniel didn't realise it was a knife until Billy flicked it open. 'Look what I found—'

Swooping in before Daniel even had time to react, Rene snatched the knife from Billy's hands. 'That's not for little boys.'

Shocked, trembling, Daniel watched as Rene carried it out of the room. Immediately he knew it had been *his knife*. He had forgotten hiding it there. He wouldn't tell Rene and certainly not Billy, but he wanted to take it home with him now it had been found.

Deprived of the knife, Billy began to pout. 'I found it.'

'So you did. But knives are dangerous.' Daniel lifted him into his arms, carried him to the window. 'Mum'll put it somewhere safe. Well done you for finding it . . . You know, when I was your age, this was my bedroom, and I used to look out of this window and watch the birds and the fields—'

'It's nice,' Billy said, not impatient to be let down, resting his head against Daniel.

From here, Daniel could see some slates loose on the roof below. There was so much work to be done to the house. This visit wasn't just a family trip. He was going to speak to local contractors to get work underway.

'We should go,' Daniel said, putting Billy down.

Returning – eyes rolling comedically to communicate her horror at the knife-find, Rene slipped one hand into the back pocket of Daniel's jeans.

All three of them stood looking out of the window at the view that had been Daniel's when he was a child.

'I feel close to her here. It makes me not want to sell. I suppose that's why I've dragged my feet over the years.'

'Take all the time you need. I know how hard this is for you. You forgave her, but now you need to forgive yourself.'

Daniel half-smiled. *Forgiveness.* He didn't feel confident he would achieve that in his lifetime, but so long as she and Billy were by his side, he was able to keep working towards it.

'Let's get dinner and call the builder,' he said.

Hand in hand they walked out into the Brampton sunshine. It was autumn now, cylinders of hay dotting the landscape below them. Daniel felt strange in his skin, as if it wasn't his own, or as if he had grown another when he was in London. Still there was something beneath the surface that belonged here and always would.

He thought about all the cases he had handled where DNA, biology, had proved the turning point for justice. DNA was irrefutable as proof, as it was sure to be in Sebastian's upcoming trial.

Daniel now knew that he came to this farmhouse as an eleven-year-old boy, the son of a murderer and a drug addict. The code in his blood had foretold another story than the one he lived out.

Almost despite his DNA, Minnie had been his mother: every shred of her, every whiff, every strand of her grey curly hair. As he put the key into the ignition and reversed out of the driveway, headed to Brampton for a dinner of fish and chips, he felt filled with a courage and confidence that Minnie had given him. His troubled Newcastle blood pulsed with not a speck of her gin-pickled Cork DNA, yet she was his mother, his *real* mother. She had given him himself.

Daniel rolled the windows down so that they could smell the Cumbria farmland air as they rushed down the hill, the car almost taking flight on one or two of the dips in the Carlisle road. He looked in the mirror, delighted to see Billy's face pink with laughter. They were together again and they were going to be alright.

ACKNOWLEDGEMENTS

As a story, *The Innocent One* has been developing in my mind for some years now, but I would not have been able to make it a reality without the help of several people to whom I owe a debt of gratitude.

Firstly, enormous thanks to Gerry Considine for his patience with me and my stream of legal questions, and for his careful and intelligent responses. At a time when you had so many more important things to think about, I really appreciated how you shared your vast knowledge of the legal system with me and helped apply it to my story. Great thanks are also due to Eileen Leyden for her invaluable assistance on police procedural matters. Thank you to Liz Paterson, Carol McDonald and Heather Greenwood for answering my questions about social work and children in the school and care system.

I am indebted to Emma Beswetherick and Hannah Wann for their extraordinary skill and patience in editing this book. Thank you to Sophie Lambert and Katie Greenstreet at Conville & Walsh for their time and advice as the story began to develop and for letting me know I was headed in the right direction.

Lisa Ballantyne

Special thanks to Morag Lightning for her help with my research, and support for my writing over the years. Thanks are also due to my family and friends who continue to encourage me and receive each new novel with enthusiasm. And thank you Crawford, for your love, creativity and inspiration.